A Dance of Storm and Starlight

and Starlight

DREAMBORN, BOOK I

K.A. Vanderhoef

Printed in the United States of America

ISBN : 978-1-7363101-0-6

Design by Waheduzzaman Manik, Savage Edits

Author website: kavanderhoef.com

For my nephews, and for all the young

hearts who dream of a brighter world.

PART I

"It is during our darkest moments that we must focus to see the light."

-Aristotle

CHAPTER

L ike a drowning soul from the River Styx, Layna claws her way back to her body to avoid being torn away by the undercurrent. Life comes thundering back into focus with the familiar feeling of waking from a dream she can't remember into a life she wants to forget. She stands in a dreary hallway beneath the crushing weight of some fifty pairs of condemnatory eyes. The muted glow of fluorescent lights helps cast the shadows from her mind, and the stale scent of bargain-brand antibacterial cleaner prickles her nostrils. And as a bell chimes overhead, Layna realizes with horrifying clarity where she is.

Oh god, no…I'm at school. It happened at school.

Her psychiatrist calls them fugue states. Layna calls them the end of life as she knows it. And she isn't safe from them even here. Right in the middle of Caledon High's junior hallway, surrounded by her friends and classmates, she can still lose her mind. Literally lose it, as it goes wandering off somewhere without her body in tow. She has no idea what she is capable of doing during one of her episodes. To the rest of the world, she carries on as normal, but she has no memory of her actions once her fractured awareness becomes whole again.

"Um...Layna?"

She narrows her focus to Kathleen and Suzanne standing in front of her. Her solace and her lifeblood. They gape at her in disbelief, and she realizes she is standing in protest against them, hands raised in defense. She peers over her shoulder at the boy standing behind her, his eyes transfixed on the floor and his belongings scattered about him. And she remembers. The ineloquent tirade Suzanne was unleashing on their sophomore prey. The jeering from the growing crowd of onlookers hungry for entertainment. She can't recall what exactly Suzanne was yelling at this kid about. The memory of it burned up in the firestorm that erupted inside her as she watched Suzanne rip the pages out of his notebook. As she watched him silently wait for it to end. As she struggled against the compulsion to go to his defense, knowing the weakness it would signal to the vultures she gets to call classmates.

At the time, she convinced herself it was just her wayward conscience returning from its extended hiatus, and she attempted to squelch it. Whatever it was, apparently it squelched her instead. Because now here she stands on the brink of committing reputational suicide for the sake of this short, quiet kid with the overflowing backpack and the ink-stained fingernails.

Layna senses the blood blossoming in her cheeks. It's the one stubborn reflex she's yet to tamp down in her efforts to bury herself beneath layers of meticulously constructed chillness. A task that has become ever more challenging since the Delaware incident in November turned her relatively normal teenage life upside down.

Since then, it's been her lonely crusade to prevent any gossip about what happened in Delaware from seeping into the rumor mill of the school. Though it has been a big help that her best friends basically run the mill at Caledon High. It may be this, more than the fact that Suzanne's last name is Miller, which has earned their little squad the title of *The Millers*, iterated with either animosity or reverence depending on the speaker. Layna and Kat have no problem with the association—the three have thought themselves sisters since the fourth grade. Besides, Suzanne is a queen out of time, and to stand close to her is to be eclipsed in her shadow. In truth, Layna has little hand in the mill. But like many things in her life, she's accepted her involvement as a necessary evil. Even more so now. Now, when she can't even trust her own brain and body to stay on the same damn page one hundred percent of the time.

A toxic chorus of hushed murmuring grows around them as the throng of students continue to gawk with greedy, eager faces. Thumbs hover over record buttons as they wait for the fallout of Layna's inexplicable mutiny. For a moment, Layna wants to give up. Let them see the real her, let them pass their judgments. Maybe this is an opportunity for her to politely bow out of the limelight. Maybe she could simply fade into the periphery, like so many of her classmates choose to do.

But she sees the gleam in Suzanne's sea-glass eyes as she scans the growing crowd, reacquiring her sophomore target behind Layna.

3

So, if only to stop Suzanne from unleashing any more of her scorched-earth drama on the school for the day, Layna casts her defeatist thoughts aside for the moment. She can still salvage this. And besides, as exhausting as it can be, she's not ready to give up her hard-earned place at Caledon High.

She heaves a sigh, feigning boredom, and relaxes her stance. "Remind me why we are wasting time on *him*," she drawls loudly, thumbing over her shoulder toward the sophomore. "We were *trying* to cut out early to head to Izzy's. Hunter and Cameron are probably already there."

As she expected, the steely glint in Suzanne's eyes shifts to something both softer and darker when she hears Hunter's name. Nothing trumps Suzanne's need for attention like her need for attention from a particular boy.

"He'll wait for me," Suzanne replies, her voice equal parts pleading and certainty. "Come on, Kat," she says, as she flips her auburn hair at the boy and turns on her heel toward the exit.

It's an abrupt end to the promising scene of high school theatrics, and disappointed groans accompany the crowd as they disperse.

Layna releases a breath as the clenched fist of apprehension subsides. As she turns to follow her friends, she steals a final glance at the boy she'd defended, who has bent down to pick up the scattered papers that once occupied his sketchbook. Though she can't get a good look at his face through the copious waves of black hair, he isn't at all familiar.

He doesn't look up from his task, his shoulders hunched in defeated misery. Guilt gnaws at Layna's insides as her eyes fall on some of the displaced pages being trampled by the departing students. Sketches of crowded classrooms, fancy cars, lonely roads, a gnarled oak tree. The last one, in particular, catches her eye when she notices a girl hidden behind the leaves of the tree, her face twisted with fear. It gives Layna the creeps, but before she can linger any longer, she feels a tug on the crook of her arm. Kat gently steers her away, down the hallway, out onto the streets of Caledon, and into the sticky heat of early summer in South Jersey.

The waitress unceremoniously plops their smoothies down without a word before moving on to the raucous group of seniors at the next table. Izzy's Parlor is bustling, as it always is in the waning school hours of a Friday afternoon. Even more so today on this last Friday of the school year. Most of its customers are kids from Caledon High, as the spot is just two blocks from the school.

After the rundown diner was flipped into a vintage ice-cream parlor last year, it became a magnet for class-cutters, hooky-players, and less than virtuous after-school activities. So, like her fellow mutineers, Layna is here with her friends instead of in her mind-numbing social studies class. The newest in a long history of traditions for their inseparable squad of three. They always get the same orders, and always try to snag the same booth closest to the door because it's "better for people-watching," Suzanne once insisted.

To Layna, this place is an escape. An echo of a bygone era of comforting simplicity with its checkerboard floor, marble bar top, and retro-red booths. Old black-and-white photos adorn the interior walls, depicting the quaintness of their downtown square in days past. And the entirety of one wall is devoted to headshots of celebrities who hail from New Jersey—Bud Abbott and Lou Costello, Whitney Houston, Frank Sinatra, Joe Pesci, Buzz Aldrin, David Copperfield, Shaquille O'Neal, James Gandolfini, and many others. Golden oldies, interspersed with modern pop, gently serenade customers as they dine on organic smoothies and juices, sweet teas, lattés, and a rotating selection of baked goods—blackberry muffins, chocolate and currant croissants, lemon pastries, and avocado toast with pine nuts and goat cheese. The servers buzz about in their vintage, white waist aprons trimmed in red, and traditional soda jerk paper hats.

It is a space untethered from time, free of the clock and the calendar, the rules and anxieties of her seriously abnormal teenage life. It's all illusory, of course. Life was never simple, not for anyone at any point in the history of the world. There was always conflict, between and within. Seen and unseen. Probably in a hundred years, people will look back through their rose-colored glasses on the era in which she is stuck to observe how easy they had it.

Layna picks idly at her peeling, blue nail polish as she tries to imagine how she would capture the feel and timelessness of Izzy's in her daydream career as a branding consultant. She begins conceptualizing the graphics on Izzy's website and merchandise that do not yet exist. Design is often where her mind wanders in its quiet moments when it needs a break from life. It is safe, and stable, and nourishing.

As her mind wanders across the space around her, she notices a little girl at the counter swiveling on a red-cushioned bar stool between her parents. Magenta cat ears adorn the girl's tight, black curls, and glittering, silver shoes with little unicorn faces smile up from her swinging feet. Paired with her multi-colored jumpsuit, it's quite the eccentric outfit, and a wistful smile plays at the corners of Layna's mouth. There was a time she would have dressed like that. Now there are rules. Rules for fashion, rules for association, behavior, *everything*. Sometimes her life doesn't even feel like her own anymore. Her mother always called her an old soul, and maybe she is. Maybe it's she who is untethered from time.

Cat-ears plucks the cherry off the top of her sundae and offers it to her father. He obliges, popping it into his mouth as they share a thousand-word smile. As Layna tries to ignore the part of her imagination that wonders what that must be like, she senses in her peripheral vision a small, black object stealthily approaching her head. With an aggravated grunt, she dodges the oncoming mascara brush and shoots Suzanne a contemptuous look.

"Come *on*, Layna. It'll totally bring some much needed depth to your face," Suzanne says, as she flashes a pearly-white smirk and continues her assault.

Suzanne has a passion for makeup and has earned herself some clout on her YouTube channel. She is constantly pushing Layna to make a guest appearance in service to the wonder that is mascara. Suzanne is adamant that just a touch of it will play up the golden flecks

7

that sprinkle Layna's hazel eyes, and this apparently would be a prime example for her fandom.

"I'm perfectly fine with my shallow face," Layna mutters, swatting Suzanne's obstinate hand away.

"Stop being so salty and let me makeup you!" Suzanne laughs.

Layna glances at Kat over her smoothie with a silent plea for help. But Kat continues to rant right through their mascara battle about how unfair the voting scheme is on some reality competition show. Something about starting a Twitter campaign to bring back a guy named Hugo Cruz. Layna can tell she means it by the intensity in her molten, amber eyes, and from the way she slips seamlessly between Spanish and English, a happenstance of only her most impassioned appeals to justice. Her corkscrew curls form a quivering halo of agitation as she assaults the table with clenched fists to emphasize points that are, in all likelihood, totally legit.

Layna is barely listening, but she observes her friend with quiet bemusement. One day, Kathleen is going to be one of those fiery activists who gets pepper-sprayed by the cops and taken proudly to jail. She loves a good cause to fight for. That is, she loves a good cause so long as it takes place outside the confines of Caledon High, where ruthlessness gets you farther than compassion any day of the week. Layna can often sense her friend's internal struggle in the moments of hesitation before throwing shade, in the way she averts her eyes in the face of Suzanne's fury. At this point, they've all learned the masks required of them in front of anyone but each other.

"It's not funny, Layna!" Kat cries, as she observes the upturned corners of Layna's mouth. "I'm serious. It's totally unfair!" On cue, she pounds the table on the final word, and Suzanne's smoothie takes a perilous dive straight toward her favorite, stark-white summer skirt. Suzanne yelps in alarm, but before the strawberry-mango monstrosity can wreak havoc on her expensive wardrobe, Layna's reality is upended for the second time that day.

Everything slows down, like the world itself is holding its breath. Like the Earth has stopped turning. The room dims as though it's been dipped in murky shadow, and a silence falls, so deep that Layna can hear the beat of her heart speeding up, out of time with the rest of corporeality.

Her initial thought is that she must be passing out. Then when that doesn't happen, perhaps a stroke. But the moment passes, and the world remains in trippy slo-mo.

Her friends sit as still as effigies, their mouths fixed in little O's of alarm. Their waitress is half-turned toward them, exasperation frozen in her life-worn features as she no doubt anticipates the mess she will have to mop up. Cat-ears holds her spoon in front of her mouth as an errant dollop of melted, vanilla ice cream hangs beneath it.

Suzanne's smoothie hovers in the air next to Layna, and she numbly reaches for the cup. Layna's fingers curl around the plastic. And just like that, time speeds up again and the parlor explodes with sound.

The world having righted itself, Layna blinks slowly at the cup in her hand. Not a drop of its contents has spilled. Kat has been stunned into silence, which is broken only by Suzanne's exaggerated sigh of relief.

"Um…wow. Killin' it with those reflexes, Layna," she says with an uneasy chuckle and a fleeting glance at Kat. She finally caps her unwelcome makeup and shoves it into her bag. "And honestly, Kat. It's just a show," Suzanne rebukes, changing the subject. "Don't be so extra." She straightens out her unmaimed skirt as she settles into position ogling the boys in the corner booth.

"*I'm* extra?" Kat protests. She opens her mouth to argue further but realizes it's useless, as Suzanne's attention has already moved onto the next worthy subject.

What the—? It wasn't real. I am still in control of my own brain. I am still in control of my own brain.

She silently repeats the mantra and forces herself to look at Kat and nod like she's there in the conversation. But she can't shake the sense of doom that has now cloaked itself around her. First the fugue state earlier and now…what? A horrifyingly realistic hallucination? It wouldn't be the first time this year, but this wasn't like the others. The disturbing visions and the nightmares. This one was new, and new is *not* good. It's getting worse. Coming to the tipping point.

"Hey, you, can you go be obnoxiously tall somewhere else?" Suzanne snaps at a girl who just moved into her line of sight of the boys' table.

"Suzanne," Kat chides.

"What? She is. You are," she adds, as the girl looks up blearily from her manic texting. She gives Suzanne a one-finger salute before moving toward the bar top to place her order.

"Girl, bye," Suzanne mutters, as she now pretends to be not interested whatsoever in the table of boys.

Hunter is at the center of the bunch, lounging idly among his entourage, a six-foot-two blond-haired, blue-eyed emperor. Much to Suzanne's disappointment, by the time they got to Izzy's, Hunter's table was full of the whole senior squad, leaving no room for Suzanne to make her move up close and personal. It's where she does her best work. And, of course, Layna noticed as soon as they walked in that Cameron—always the more responsible of the two—wasn't in his usual spot next to Hunter. Layna always notices his presence, or lack thereof, even though they haven't been a thing since early in the school year, before Layna's life imploded. But he has one of those magnetic kind of personalities that make you look up and take notice. And admire. Plus, Cam's honestly a good guy, a rarity in a school full of wannabe bad boys.

There wasn't so much an ending to them as there was a gradual decline in snaps and texts. He didn't hang with her as much at Izzy's, and the rumor mill has it that Cam and Natalie—another junior in their extended squad—may now be a thing. And as into him as Layna had been, beyond a fleeting sense of wistfulness, the news didn't bother her all that much. She considers that maybe she just doesn't have the emotional capacity to deal with anything outside her own brain at the moment. Not even her heart.

Hunter sniggers at something one of the other boys says. He flicks the pocketknife attached to his keys open and closed—his habitual flex to all that, *hey, I'm super chill, but don't mess with me. And also, I own a Camaro, bitches.* Layna watches him, irritated at his existence in the world, when he abruptly looks up and catches her eye, giving her a sly wink.

Layna fights the inclination to stick her finger down her throat to gesture her disgust, as Suzanne gasps with glee. "He winked at me!" she whispers feverishly. "Did you see that? I think I just died."

Layna gives her a weak smile and hopes the wink was, in fact, meant for Suzanne and not for her, as she thought. She regards the drab remnants of her blueberry-banana smoothie and fights the urge to head home. It's not that she wants to leave her friends and the comforting hum of organized chaos that defines Izzy's, but the dread inside her is growing, driving her out of the parlor as though directing her to where she ought to be. Really, she *ought* to be in school. But she no longer tries to fight this restless force of nature in her head. She stands up to leave as she formulates an excuse for bouncing so suddenly.

"Layna, wait," Suzanne says, grabbing her arm. Speaking softly out of the side of her mouth, she mutters, "They're paying the tab. Move slowly. If we time it right, maybe Hunter will offer us a ride home again."

Layna sighs and stalls, though she's itching to escape. Sure enough, moments later, the four of them are piled into Hunter's ugly, green Camaro as he peels out of Izzy's parking lot and toward their neighborhood.

"Don't forget to be at my house by six so we can get ready for the party together!" Suzanne yells out the open window.

Layna waves an acknowledgment as she watches the Camaro speed away down her quiet street toward Suzanne's house. Its final stop.

Layna hopes that the stupid, green atrocity will stay parked in Suzanne's driveway this time. Just a little longer than the five seconds it takes Suzanne to get out of the car. Just long enough for a quick make-out, maybe. Or maybe he'll go inside. Maybe he'll profess his undying love and bring an end to this endless game of cat and mouse. Honestly, though Layna isn't a fan, she just wants to ship them so she and Kat can talk to Suzanne about something else for a change. Even if that something is every detail of their newfound romance, it will be better than the incessant pining. And—added bonus—once she has him, Suzanne will get sick of him before Layna and Kat can even get used to his increased, irritating presence.

It's the end of the girls' junior year, whereas Hunter is a senior about to graduate, and still *nothing*. It took about half the year for him to even start noticing Suzanne, another quarter for them to exchange snap IDs, and now he will occasionally give the three of them rides home, the last five minutes of which being the only alone time Suzanne has with him. It's been like bingeing one of those frustrating Netflix shows where you know two of the characters are going to end up together but they drag it out for five seasons and by the time they actually get together you're all, *I just don't care anymore!*

Layna feels a twinge of guilt for being so dismissive of Suzanne's potential happiness. It may be selfish, but she longs for the days when the three of them had other things to talk about—when she and Suzanne would make Kat pee her pants from laughing so hard. Or when they were satisfied with discussing the latest *Supernatural* episodes while helping Kat's mom bake experimental desserts for her popular Dominican bakery downtown. But lately it's like they are all developing sharp edges to their personalities that once fit together like pieces to a puzzle. Layna hoped it was all just hormones and whatnot, but she is starting to accept the fact that this might just be the new normal.

She sighs and leans back against her front steps to soak in the afternoon sun, hoping to get a bit of color before summer is in full swing. A nostalgic *Fall Out Boy* jam blares through her earbuds, and she tries to clear her mind and let Patrick Stump serenade her about dreams of tearing her apart. She studies the cookie-cutter modern colonials lining her block, each surrounded by a flawlessly manicured lawn. Like overpriced delicacies presented upon sterling silver serving trays. The sprinklers go off right on cue, and for just a moment, she returns to the summer days of childhood, running through the sprinkler in her backyard with the carefree spirit of a girl who did not yet know the world.

She has to get back to that girl. At least she has to seem like it by the time her mom gets home. If her mom knew even half of what Layna's been experiencing lately, she'd run straight to Dr. Nettles, and it would be the end of Layna's life as she knows it. Dr. Nettles is Layna's well-meaning but horribly unpleasant psychiatrist, who has that kind of *Downton Abbey* British accent that always makes Layna feel belittled.

After having effectively lied her ass off for the better part of the year, Layna was released from Dr. Nettles' care about three months ago to return on an as-needed basis. Or, as Layna sees it, never-the-f-again. If she gave it a little more thought—which she makes a habit of not doing—she would probably admit this isn't the best tactic to maintain her sanity. But that's future-Layna's problem. Right now, she just needs to deal with today.

It's days like this when she really wishes she could tell her mom everything. Until so recently, she did. For a good portion of Layna's life, she and her mom were all each other had. It was not long after her parents bought this house—then a fixer-upper in an up-and-coming neighborhood—that Layna's father decided to ghost his family.

One of Layna's first memories is walking into the kitchen to find a sweaty, pudgy man sitting at the table with her mom. The man wore a suit and her mom wore an expression that shaped the future of her and Layna's relationship. Though Layna was too young to understand at the time, her mom had just been told she had to declare bankruptcy, and the look was one of a woman utterly defeated by life. And by love. After that, her mom's façade of stability was always so fragile that Layna worried a single wrong word could make it shatter. Not that her mom ever did. Shatter, that is. Turns out Layna is the one who can't hack life.

But during that delicate period, at least, Layna became her mother's protector. She did everything she could to be good and obedient. It was not out of fear, but out of the hope that she would never have to see that expression on her mother's face again.

And she never did. Because Julianne Emery has more pride and determination in her middle finger than everyone else Layna knows combined. And for a while, that defiant finger was the only thing holding up their world. So, they survived, and three part-time jobs, plus evening classes at community college, eventually whittled down to one full-time, lucrative accounting career. Because her mom is kickass at everything. And though she and Layna remained an indivisible pair throughout it all, it always seemed like her mom was waiting for something. Her husband to come back, her daughter to leave her, her life to start, the world to end. Layna doesn't know which it is. But it's always been there—that waiting, dreading undercurrent to their relationship.

The Delaware incident nearly cost them that relationship. It almost reverted her mother back to that woman at the kitchen table. *Almost.* But now everything is eggshells again. Her mom must maintain the belief that Layna is doing better, and that means that Layna must maintain that lie, however painful and lonely it is to do so.

She only gets through three songs on her *Weekend Jams* playlist before the humidity gets the best of her, making her whole life just unbearably sticky. She sits forward, her feet slipping in her signature purple Keds, as she lifts her thick, golden waves of hair to wipe the back of her neck in disgust. It isn't even officially summer yet and already she's wishing she could just chop this long, wool blanket off her head. If only she could pull off Kat's curly pixie cut. Kat's always complaining about her family's 'Curse of the Caribbean Curls', but honestly, she rocks it, and at least she doesn't have to deal with a gross, sweaty neck in the summer.

Layna folds her hair into a messy bun atop her head and stands to go inside. Her pre-summer base tan will have to wait for a more clement day. She relishes the blast of chilled air that washes over her as she thrusts open the front door, her skin breaking out in grateful goosebumps. Moxie, the world's chubbiest tabby cat, is snoozing lazily on the bottom step of the wooden staircase but is startled awake by Layna's entry. She stretches and trots across the vinyl floorboards to weave between Layna's legs, purring with appreciation at her favorite human's unexpectedly early return. Layna sheds her backpack and sneakers by the door, tenderly scooping up her cat as she heads through the foyer to the kitchen at the back of the house.

She winces as she turns the corner, still not entirely accustomed to the canary yellow of their kitchen walls that seem to capture and reflect the intensity of the afternoon sun. Her mother decided to spruce up the house earlier in the year to make it 'more cheery'. It was after things between her mom and Jim started getting really serious, so she was all smitten and giddy, which was weird but cool.

Layna and her mom painted the kitchen and living room themselves. That evening, they ordered a feast of Chinese take-out and sat on the plastic laid out over the living room floor. Both of them caked head-to-toe in dried yellow and cerulean paint, they stuffed their faces and watched *The Matrix*, her mom's favorite. For some reason, that day was perfection. Like everything in the world was going to be okay. Layna has held tightly to that memory—that brief moment of bliss— during all the difficult days that followed.

"Don't tell Mom, little one," Layna whispers, as she puts Moxie down to pour a little extra food into her dish. Her cat meows in conspiratorial reply and begins gobbling up her snack.

Layna trundles back to her backpack by the front door and rummages around in it, pulling out the plastic, orange bottle marked

LAYNA EMERY. She carries it into the powder room on the left side of the front hall, where she stares at her face in the mirror and contemplates a nap. Her sleepless nights have long since caught up with her, the shadows beneath her eyes a permanent stain on a heart-shaped face otherwise rich with youth. Rose-kissed cheeks and cupid's bow lips, milky skin not yet reflecting the hardships of her life. After dumping one of the pasty, pink pills into her hand, she stares at it with profound loathing for everything it represents.

Pink, of all colors. Like fear and dread and the end of life as you know it all wrapped up in a pretty, little package and tied with a bow. The end of friends and fun and a future you were never going to have. Swallow it down like a good girl.

"I hate you, pill," she whispers, throwing it to the back of her throat. As she takes a gulp of water from the sink to drown the dreadful thing, a loud knock at the front door startles her, and water floods into her windpipe.

She clamps a hand over her mouth to muffle the sounds of her choking to death. She's still supposed to be at school, and whoever is coming to call could potentially blow her cover.

Throat aflame and eyes watering, Layna peeks around the bathroom doorway to see if she can tell who it is through the frosted glass windows that flank the solid oak of the front door. The shadowed figure of a man looms on her front porch.

Probably another Jehovah's Witness—these people are relentless.

She pulls her head back inside and waits for him to leave. But without so much as a creak of the door or breath of hot air from outside, she hears the unmistakable whisper of footfalls heading across the foyer and into the study on the left.

Layna grips the sink as her whole body tingles with fear. How could he get in? Her front door locks automatically, and only she and her mom have—

Jim! It's not a rogue Jehovah's Witness, it's Jim, who has earned his own key to the house.

Jeez, my mom is dating a freaking ninja.

The bubbling relief in her gut is fleeting. She and Jim may be buddies, but he doesn't keep secrets from Julianne. If he finds out Layna left school early, he would be obliged on his honor to tell on her. Maybe he's just here to pick something up and then he'll leave. She prays to God he's not here for some clandestine afternoon tryst with her mom.

Layna peers cautiously around the doorway again. She can hear him quietly rummaging around in the study. She needs to get up to her room where she can hide properly. He'd never go in there uninvited.

She forces herself to move, creeping toward the staircase as her heart threatens to leap from her throat and abandon her. She is immensely grateful that they replaced those old, creaky, wooden floorboards with the vinyl ones a few years ago, otherwise she'd not stand a chance. She reaches the stairs and tiptoes up, alighting from the top step as Jim re-emerges from the study and walks across the foyer toward the living room.

Layna stands frozen on the top step, horror blossoming inside of her as she watches the top of his head disappear around the corner. Jim's hair is a neatly-trimmed brown with a small balding spot at the crown. This man's hair is a thick, dark blond, falling almost to his shoulders.

The man in her house is not Jim.

Layna launches herself toward her bedroom door, pulling it open soundlessly and slipping inside. Her brain seems to have stopped communicating with her fingers, and she fumbles with the lock. She thinks of her cell phone, in her backpack by the door. Her only means of getting help is impossibly out of reach. Why did people ever get rid of landlines?

Scenes from old slasher movies her mom is always telling her not to watch blaze through her mind. The ones where the idiot girl traps herself in a room with no escape so the killer can easily stab her to death. She always made fun of those girls.

Not today, Satan! I refuse to die as a horror movie bimbo.

She hears steady footsteps on the stairs. He's not in a rush, so he must not have heard her yet. Except...of course, that's exactly what happens in the movies. No matter how fast the girl runs and hides and tries to escape, some psychopath taking his sweet-ass time always manages to catch up and kill her.

Spinning wildly, she searches for a sufficient hiding place and her eyes fall on her bedroom window. The two-foot overhang above the front porch. A little slip of roof between the first and second floor accessible through her window. It's steep, but it should be wide enough for her to shuffle along and get out of view. *Please let it be wide enough.*

She crosses to the window and slides the rusted latch over, lifting the window as quietly as possible.

Scuffling in the hallway outside her bedroom.

She spins toward the door, eyes wide and muscles frozen like an animal in a trap. And then it happens for the second time that day—what Layna can only describe as a time-lag. Everything moves in slo-mo again. The whirling of the pedestal fan in the corner, the streaming of the sprinklers outside, the ticking of the clock on the wall. All nearly grinding to a halt. And though the sky outside remains cloudless, the room dims as if night has come early. The only sound is her own terrified panting amplified as though she has cotton in her ears. She shakes her head to try to clear it of this falsehood, all her senses amok.

This isn't happening. It's all in my head. Focus on the real threat.

Trying her best to ignore the hallucination, she sticks one leg out to get her footing on the overhang before ducking under the frame and popping back up outside. As she glides the window closed, whatever little piece of her brain keeps glitching corrects itself, and the world erupts in noise and light and movement around her.

She stifles a cry and starts inching a safe distance away from the window. That's when she makes the mistake of looking down.

The ground seems so very far away. If the slasher decides not to stab her to death, she could still lose her life to gravity today. Her bare feet scrape against the rough shingles as she moves sideways along the small slip of roof hanging over the porch below. She prays that the locked door to her bedroom will be enough to deter him. But not a moment later, she hears him shutting the drawers to her dresser.

He's picked the lock. He is in her room. All he needs to do is look out the window and she's as good as dead. Time drags as she stands there motionless, getting twisted and tangled with her fear. Was there ever a time when she wasn't standing barefoot on this bit of roof waiting to be killed? Will there ever be anything else?

A lot of inconsequential thoughts go through Layna's mind in those endless minutes. She remembers that her grandma's jewelry is sitting on top of the dresser right out in the open. Her mom is always nagging her to lock it up. She tries to remember the last time she cleaned her room. She worries that if she dies, her mother will find the journal that she keeps hidden in her third drawer and will know she's been lying to her. She promises herself she will destroy it if she gets out of this. She wonders why her cat has not scratched this man's eyes out yet. She decides she should get a guard dog if she lives. She also wonders if Suzanne will ever get to make out with Hunter and feels a sense of loss at possibly never knowing how that story will end. She thinks about how she may never know what it feels like to fall in love, get married, go to college, get her first job, travel, have babies. And as her mind flashes across her last twenty-four hours or so, it snags on something. Something that, for some reason, in that moment, needs her attention.

An image—a sketch. Of a girl behind a tree. Her back pressed against a shingled wall and her face contorted with fear.

Layna's breath hitches and stalls. She tries to get it back, but all she can do is stare. Stare, breathless, at the gnarled oak tree in front of her house.

"Oh...my...god," she croaks.

It was me. I was the girl behind the tree.

Her mind tentatively offers up the conclusion that must logically follow. That boy drew this. He drew it…before it happened.

No. She shakes her head in defiance of the suggestion. This is real life, and people cannot see the future in real life. She's misremembering. It will all be clear later—if she's lucky enough to have a later—when she's not at death's door.

The sound of footsteps below startles her and almost makes her lose her balance on the steep incline. The slasher is walking down her front steps. He's leaving.

She remains motionless, just another fixture upon the house, hoping the oak tree provides enough cover should he happen to look up. Her bright, green shorts aren't helping the situation, practically shouting, "Look up here, it's me, your conveniently trapped victim!"

Layna watches the man crouch down next to her bike that leans against the front porch. She squints, trying to focus on what nefarious deed he could possibly be undertaking against her bike, of all things. He places his hands on the handles and she is certain he is about to ride it right out of her life. But he just sits there crouched next to it, eyes closed as though in prayer. Maybe he is a rogue Jehovah's Witness after all. They're always preaching about God's judgment and the end being near. Maybe this guy just decided to end people for a living instead of waiting for God to do it. Stranger things have happened *today*.

Apparently done with his praying, he stands and walks, not down the walkway, but across their property toward the edge where the lawn meets the woods. There, he pauses, head inclined ever so slightly back toward the house. He peers around him, behind him, as though scouting for onlookers. Layna stops breathing as she looks down onto his face through the thick branches of the oak tree.

The slasher doesn't really look much like a slasher. He is in his late twenties most likely, the start of a beard growing on the lower half of his face, which is pretty average looking from what she can see. She's not sure what, exactly, she was expecting. Maybe a horrific gash down his cheek or a missing eye or something sinister like that. But he just looks sort of...mild.

She clings tighter to the side paneling as a gust of wind shakes the branches in front of her, obscuring her view of the man for only a moment. But a moment is all it takes.

The man is gone.

Layna's heart takes a dive to the ground below as she blinks and looks around, scanning the edges of her property, the woods, the street. She's sure it is just a trick of the eye. But the man is nowhere. He was standing there one second and gone the next, as if he was never even there at all.

She wills her feet to start moving back toward safety. They finally oblige, inching their way toward the window. She heaves it open and falls into a heap on the bedroom floor where she promptly bursts into hysterics.

After allowing herself a minute of ugly-crying, she glances through the curtain of hair sticking to her tear-soaked face to assess the damage to her room.

It is not at all what she was expecting.

Her bedroom looks absolutely untouched, as though some creepy dude had not just been rummaging through all of her worldly possessions. She stands and examines the top of her dresser. Everything is in place, including all her grandma's jewelry. She snatches it up and lays it in her jewelry box, locking it with the key. Then she opens each of her dresser drawers with increasing urgency before moving onto the drawers of her desk. Not a thing disturbed or out of place.

But he was in here. He *was*.

She closes her eyes and pictures the man. His blond hair, his mild face. The white t-shirt and khaki shorts he wore. His footfalls on the stairs, the sound of the dresser drawers slamming. It was real, it had to be. She can almost still feel him in here.

She needs to get out of this room.

Jumping up, she crosses to the door and yanks at the cold, metal knob. But the door doesn't open. She slowly removes her hand to look.

It's still locked.

She stands there, thunderstruck. The door only locks from the inside. It wouldn't shut if he had tried to lock it on his way out, which could only mean it was never unlocked in the first place.

Layna heads downstairs in a stupor. She investigates the study, the living room, the kitchen. Completely normal. Everything as it should be.

She grabs her cell phone from her backpack and runs to the powder room, shutting and locking the door behind her. She slams the lid to the toilet down and perches on top of it, phone in hand. Her eyes blur as they remain locked on the screen, at the three numbers she's entered to call for help, at her trembling thumb hovering over the call button. She stares until the screen goes black.

25

There would be so many questions, and she would have to give a report. What would she tell them? That a man somehow broke into her house just to take a leisurely stroll through all the rooms? That nothing at all was taken or misplaced? That there was no evidence of a break-in and the man just vanished into thin air before her eyes? What about the world standing still while she escaped out of her window? What about the prophetic sketch of the whole thing drawn by a complete stranger with whom she just happened to entangle on the same day this all happened?

Could it be possible that she imagined...*all* of it? Maybe it's the medication. It makes her feel drowsy. Maybe it's making her see things too.

It's not the medication. It's what the medication is supposed to be treating.

She presses the palms of her hands hard against her eyes with a groan, but it doesn't stop the flood of memories that she knew would come. The blue-and-white, striped cot at Mount Hope. The smell of ammonia and soiled linens. The little paper cup holding one green-speckled pill and one white, and the thick lock on the metal door. Keeping her in. Trapped and helpless.

I will not go back to that place.

Her mind shifts to the black duffel bag she keeps in her closet. The one with a stash of money, protein bars, some spare clothes, and a few mementos from happier times. Her hand is a death-grip on the phone, but her feet are itching to run. Run upstairs to retrieve her bag. Run away from this house and this life and this inescapable future.

Layna slams the phone onto the sink and weaves her hands into her hair, breathing deeply, steadying herself. Reassuring her itching feet that it isn't time yet. She pushes the memories of Mount Hope back into the dark corner of her mind as she tucks her knees under her chin, cradling herself. She closes her eyes and rocks her body back and forth like her mom used to do for her when she was little. She's not sure which idea scares her more—that the last twenty minutes actually happened or that they didn't. Either way, she thinks she should probably convince her mom to get an alarm system or a guard dog or something.

As though in protest, Moxie meows loudly from the hallway. Layna unravels herself from the top of the toilet and reaches over to open the bathroom door. Moxie sidles in and jumps up on Layna's lap. With one paw on Layna's chest, she reaches up to place the other paw gently against Layna's nose as if to comfort. Layna gives her cat a weak smile and scratches between her ears.

"You saw him too, didn't you, Moxie girl?" she asks, as she lifts the cat from beneath her front legs so their faces are even with each other. "And a lot of good you were. A regular attack-cat. Maybe we should teach you some fighting skills," she suggests.

Moxie mews softly in reply. Layna chuckles and releases her cat, who jumps onto the tile floor and immediately begins licking her fur back into place. Layna rubs her hands along her thighs to wipe off her sweaty palms, then turns on the sink and tosses cold water on her face, washing away the evidence of the whole traumatizing experience before her mom comes home. Just a few more hours, and then her mom will bring her to Suzanne's. They'll get ready for what promises to be

27

the most epic party of the year, and she will try to just forget today ever existed.

CHAPTER

L ayna sits on the edge of Suzanne's bed watching shirts flying out from the walk-in closet in front of her. She can hear Suzanne in there cursing her wardrobe and groaning with exasperation. A sizable, colorful pile of clothing already lies in a heap in the center of the floor where the shirts are now landing.

Layna arrived over an hour ago, and she and Kat have seen at least thirty combinations of outfits for the seniors' end-of-year party. It harkens back to the hurried costume changes they would undertake with giddy enthusiasm in between scenes of the plays they'd put on for Suzanne's parents. It was Suzanne's favorite pastime, and she even started writing screenplays for them as they got older. All of that ended with the start of high school. Though they still have recordings of their more elaborate productions, which they watch occasionally on uneventful weekend nights in Suzanne's finished basement with popcorn, blankets, and pillows.

For Suzanne's current costume, they finally settled on a royal blue, chiffon skirt about twenty minutes ago, but no such luck with a shirt. Layna doesn't mind the menial process. It helps her to focus on the moment rather than all the unpleasant things vying for her attention. On the bed next to her, Kat lies on her stomach propped up on her elbows, her face melting into boredom against her hands. She is a creature of sweats, t-shirts, and her field hockey uniform, and she can only be a good sport about fashion choices for so long. Judging by the glaze over her eyes, that time came to an end some time ago.

Suzanne emerges from the closet pairing her blue skirt with open-toed wedge heels and a white and yellow crop-top that shows off her voluptuous figure.

With just a twinge of envy, Layna looks down piteously at her own curves, or lack thereof. *Late bloomer, my ass. My non-existent ass.*

"What about this one?" Suzanne asks as she steps in front of the mirror.

"That's totally cute!" Layna says. "It's casual but hot at the same time."

"Yeah, that's fire," Kat grumbles.

"Hmm…but is it *too* casual?" Suzanne turns to investigate her reflection from various angles. "This is going to be the most lit party of the year, and I don't want to show up looking like I'm ready for a pool party."

"No one would wear a chiffon skirt to a pool party, Suzanne," Kat argues.

"I'm not concerned about the skirt, Kat. But I don't think this shirt is going to work. Too beachy, it's canceled."

Kat groans and face-plants into the bed, burying a stream of aggravated Spanish into the comforter. Layna knows they're entering dangerous territory. Once Kat's temper flares, there's a good chance she and Suzanne will start arguing and the promising night will go south fast. Layna is in no mood for one of their blowouts that have become increasingly common this year. She pats the top of Kat's head and quickly suggests, "What about the black tank you originally tried on with the red pants, could that work?"

Suzanne snaps her fingers and points at Layna. "You may be right!" she remarks, as she starts digging through the pile of clothes on the floor. She finds the plunging, lacy, black tank top and puts it on with black pumps. As she examines her reflection in the mirror she yells, "I think we might have a winner!"

"Dios mío, finalmente!" comes Kat's muffled shout. She looks up and adds, "Yes, that outfit is going to slay. Now, let's all finish getting ready and go get dinner. I'm *starved.*"

As Suzanne runs to the bathroom to put on her makeup, Kat and Layna change and use Suzanne's vanity for their own finishing touches. Side by side in the mirror, Layna catches Kat's hesitant glances. It's an understatement to say it's unusual for Kat to be willingly silent for more than two minutes. Especially when it's just the two of them.

Layna sighs. "Okay, what's up?"

"Oh, what? No, nothing. All good," Kat says as she lines an eye in black.

"C'mon, Kat," Layna argues, pulling the blonde locks back from around her face and into a clip.

31

"Really, it's nothing. It's just...I don't know. I'm worried about you." She turns her back on Layna, indicating toward the zipper running along her spine, but Layna still glimpses the wounded look in her pinched features.

Guilt lands like a rock in her gut as she zips up the red dress Kat borrowed from her. She hasn't confided much in her friends this year, and her inability to do so has made it harder to be herself with them. But Kat is her person, and she is Kat's, and she's certain Kat must feel her withdrawal as a personal affront. But Kat has enough on her plate as it is. With her father stationed for combat overseas, her older brother having just joined the military, and her mom working to keep business thriving at the bakery, Kat has basically become her little sister's primary caregiver. Layna can see how it weighs on her, while trying to balance it all with classes, field hockey, and track.

"I'm sorry, Kat. I'm okay. It's just the meds, I guess." It's the easy way out. Kat and Suzanne know she's on medication—a mood stabilizer, she told them. Normal enough, and who really wants to ask follow-up questions about that?

"Yeah. So, about that." Kat turns to face Layna again. "No offense, but you seem to be getting sort of...worse. I mean, you hardly come out anymore and it seems like you always bounce early when you do. You don't always answer my texts or snaps anymore, and, I don't know, it's like you're barely...*here*. Like your shell is, but not you. Not all of you anyway—not *my* Layna," she says, trailing off. Then, more playfully, "I mean, I would think maybe you're just over us, but we are way too awesome for that to be true. You don't have to tell me if you don't want to, but I was just thinking maybe something else is going on that you want to talk about," she finishes with an apathetic shrug.

Layna offers a tepid smile, her mind racing across all the other somethings going on, none of which she is prepared to talk about with anyone, not even Kat. But this little primer is Kat-speak for 'spill the tea right now or I'm just going to keep guessing until I get it right or you break down and tell me anyway'.

"Okay, so you don't have to say anything, but I think I know what's going on," Kat declares, throwing an uneasy glance toward the bedroom door. Layna anticipates a whole host of false conclusions to which Kat's sleuthing mind may have led her, but the whispered declaration leaves her staggered. "You like Hunter, don't you?" She says it as fact she's already accepted as truth.

"What the—*no*! No, Hunter sucks, I do *not* like Hunter. Are you confusing me with Suzanne?" Layna balls her hand into a fist and raps her knuckles lightly on Kat's forehead. "I'm Layna, remember?"

Kat swats at her hand and scowls. Layna knows that look. Being wrong is not something that Kat can come to terms with easily, and she is going to go down swinging. Layna looks mournfully at the door, hoping Suzanne will come and rescue her from having to take part in this futile debate.

"No, but it makes all the sense!" Kat blurts in a barely contained whisper.

Here we go.

"Suzanne's thirsty for him like day one of junior year, when you get with Cameron, right? But then, come winter, you and Cam are over for like no reason. Meanwhile, Hunter was always looking at *you* all thirsty when you were with Cam, and maybe you feel the same, but you don't say anything, because Suzanne. And, you know, we love her but also watch out for that shade. Then you have to go through the whole year listening to how much she loves Hunter, and how Hunter said hi to her this day, and waved at her that day, and winked at her today. But, hello, I know he was winking at you today and not her. And then the thing with the sophomore? I mean, *big* yikes, Layna. But I was thinking more about it and maybe it all was just too much with how long you've kept your mouth shut about Hunter, and you were just done when Suzanne was yelling at that kid. Anyway, it makes sense."

Layna gapes at her friend. Apparently, this is something she's been holding back for a while, and for Kat, that is a nearly insurmountable feat. If only it were all true, and it was just jealousy at the heart of her insanity. But unfortunately, the real explanation is not that simple, and she is not in love with Hunter. She never even spends time thinking about him outside of his potential future escapades with Suzanne or how his face annoys her.

Kat is staring at her, waiting for a response. Her amber eyes blaze with victory as she watches Layna struggle to formulate a response.

"Ha!" she yells, a wide smile spreading across her face. "Admit it. I'm right."

"No, Kat. As much as it may seem like you've figured me out, I have never even given Hunter the time of—"

"Liar! I totally saw you checking him out at Izzy's today. You couldn't keep your eyes off him. You were barely listening to anything I was saying to you."

"That's not fair," Layna argues. "*No one* could keep their eyes off that table. They were laughing like crazed hyenas!"

"Yeah, but you had googly-eyes."

"I did *not* have googly-eyes!"

"Yes, you did!"

"No, I did not. Those are just my eyes. I think I know what I do with my own eyes more than you do."

"How can you? I'm the one who can see your eyes. You can't see your eyes with your own eyes, and I'm telling you—googly-eyes."

They begin to laugh despite themselves, and then the door bursts open.

"What are you two idiots giggling about?" Suzanne demands. Her smile is casual, but there is a familiar ache in her eyes.

Layna mentally kicks herself for sometimes forgetting that beneath that bearing of self-confidence and autonomy, Suzanne is still soft and delicate at the core. And one of her most irrational fears is being discarded by Layna and Kat like an outgrown pair of shoes. As strong as she may seem now, she's still the same little girl who ran away to Layna's house after her mom died and clung to Layna as if she was the only thing keeping her from drowning.

"Oh, um, just Layna's eyes," Kat chokes out, stifling her laughter.

"Makes sense. They are pretty funny looking," Suzanne agrees with a solemn nod. "Maybe if you let me add some mascar-a-a-a," she sings, whipping out the concealed makeup from behind her back and waving it in her hand.

"No! Leave me alone!" Layna laughs.

35

Suzanne grins as she charges at Layna with the force of a Spartan warrior. Layna leaps onto the bed as Suzanne elicits Kat's assistance.

"Come here," Suzanne coos, as she and Kat corner Layna on the bed. They pounce on Layna together amid a fit of twittering laughter and pin her arms above her head.

"Let me cake your face, damnit! It's my only skill!"

"Fine!" Layna yells in breathless mirth as she relents, allowing her friend to maul her face with the sticky blackness. They let her up to fix herself in the mirror as Suzanne awaits her reaction.

"Hideous," Layna jokes, earning a playful smack from Suzanne before she runs down the hall to rouse her older brother for a ride. Layna inspects her reflection and can't help but admit, only to herself of course, that Suzanne was right. The mascara does accentuate the curious golden hue in her eyes and makes her look somewhat fierce.

Suzanne's brother, Nick, drives them to Portobello, the Italian restaurant conveniently located a few blocks down from the house party. Suzanne tells him they're meeting up with their senior friends and will get a ride back with them, which may be the truth if the night goes as planned. Her brother just nods in response. She probably could have told him they were all going to sell themselves on the street corner and he wouldn't have even blinked. Layna can never be sure whether it's because he's stoned or just doesn't give a crap. Both are always valid guesses. Nick is a bit lacking in the personality and integrity departments, following in his father's footsteps in more ways than one. But an accessible twenty-four-year-old without much of a moral compass can serve a valuable purpose. So, they keep up the rapport.

After wolfing down the family style lasagna and Italian salad at Portobello, they make the fifteen-minute walk out of the downtown square and toward the party. While the humidity has abated and allowed the night to grow crisp at the edges, Suzanne's excitement has only escalated. She is a chatterbox, becoming more animated with each step, and they can barely get a word in edgewise. Tonight, it's finally going to happen with Hunter, she tells them. She could tell by the way he said he would see her later when he dropped her off. The way he looked at her when she got out of the car. From Kat's muted response, Layna can see she did not succeed in convincing her that she is not some resentful, lovesick Juliet. She tamps down the bubbling of frustration, reminding herself that tonight is about letting go and having fun.

It's easy to give herself over to the contagious thrill of anticipation as they make their way up the lighted walkway to the enormous Tudor-style home of Brandon Bardot. His is the kind of house where you might say, "Oh, that's over in the east wing." Brandon's family owns some successful five-star hotel chain in France, and his parents probably spend half their time over there without much regard for their son's habitual debauchery. He's easily the wealthiest kid in their school. At least for one more week, then he'll be off to Dartmouth to study business, where he'll surely be just another boujee bitch among the rest.

The bass coming from inside is a living thing, an intrepid heartbeat fueling the energy of the party and filling the partygoers with reckless abandon. Layna's own heart begins to beat in time with its thunderous pace.

Out of polite habit, Layna rings the doorbell, but any sound it triggers is swallowed up inside the house. Suzanne shoots her a pitying look and shoves the front door open, and the full blare of the music hits them like a nuclear shockwave. It's a good thing they're on a big plot of land. If this were Layna's neighborhood, her neighbors would definitely call the cops before the night is through. But also, Brandon somehow lobbied his neighbors early in his high school years to make sure that never happens. It would be zero surprise to Layna if there was blackmail involved. Current sleaze and future politician, for sure.

They walk into a massive hall with a grand staircase and ceilings that must be at least twenty feet high. There is already a big turnout even though it's still early in the night, with many attendees gathered in this front hall where the DJ is set up and pumping out the EDM. Suzanne scans the crowd. A frenzied wave of her hand toward what appears to be a sitting room off the front hall tells Layna she's located the squad.

They make their way to where the twins, Emma and Chloe, have snagged a corner, along with their boyfriends, Dylan and Sean. No sign of Hunter yet, but Cameron is there with Natalie, hand in hand. Natalie stares intently at the pattern in the rug under her feet as Layna approaches, and Cam offers Layna an uneasy grin. Layna allows herself a moment of pitiful regret as she remembers the way he used to smile at her before. How his deep, russet eyes would sparkle and the dimple in his left cheek would appear. She remembers tracing the black tribal tattoo imprinted on the chestnut skin around his left bicep, and the sweet way he used to kiss her. She exhales heavily, purging the memories along with her breath, and returns a genuine smile that she hopes conveys her assent. Natalie seems to catch Layna's intention and reaches over to greet her with a hug and kiss on the cheek, and everyone breaks out into grateful chatter.

Other than Natalie and Dylan, who are in Layna's year, the rest of the group are seniors, and the shouted discussion mostly revolves around wistful reminiscing and college preparations. Over the blaring music, Emma and Chloe babble in tandem about the respective majors they are electing at Rutgers. Cam gushes about the football team at UPenn, at which he's earned himself a scholarship, and Sean boasts about all the partying he's going to do in New York City once he starts at John Jay's.

Before long, Layna mentally excuses herself from the conversation and focuses on disentangling the tendrils of dread that have returned to coil their way around her heart. There was a time not long ago when she thought she had her whole bright future planned out too. She would be a much sought-after branding consultant or graphic designer in New York City. She would travel for at least a year, marry in her early thirties, and have no more than two babies. Now, her future is an impenetrable mist of chaos. Thankfully, Suzanne interrupts the banter and announces, "Hey, I'm thirsty! Let's see what they've got going on out on the deck!"

Layna and Kat leave the others and follow Suzanne through the crowd toward the back deck that appears to be serving as the keg depository and beer pong station. Suzanne slides up in line behind two others in front of a keg as a pair of boys at one end of the beer pong table erupt in shouts of triumph and do a victory lap around the deck.

Well, great, Layna thinks. She for sure can't mix alcohol with the meds she's on. Plus she's agreed to random urine testing by her psychiatrist, and she will *not* risk a return to Mount Hope for one lousy beer. But she also doesn't want to seem like the only lame one at the party.

Kat catches her eye and gives her a familiar look that says, *I got you, boo.*

As the senior working the keg helps Suzanne, Kat surreptitiously reaches around her and grabs two solo cups, handing one to Layna. She pulls a Diet Coke out of her bag and cracks it open, pouring it equally between the two cups. By the time Suzanne steps aside to let them get drinks, Kat's disposed of the empty can and announces to the senior, "No worries, we brought our own harder stuff."

The senior gives her a sultry smile in reply, and they move out of the way of the growing line and toward the edge of the deck.

"What'd you do that for?" Suzanne questions, sniffing at their drinks to detect the lie.

Layna cups her hands around her mouth and words silently, "Medication."

"Oh," she replies, despondent. "What about you?" she says, turning to Kat.

"Don't feel like it," Kat says with a shrug.

"You guys suck!" Suzanne shouts, as she looks at them pointedly and takes several sizeable gulps of beer.

"Live your best life, sis," Kat laughs.

"Come on, let's go dance," Layna suggests as she gives Kat's hand a grateful squeeze. She pushes her way back inside to the growing sea of undulating bodies in the front hall and feels a spirited tug on her arm.

"Look who finally showed up," Suzanne shouts in her ear.

Suzanne has spotted Hunter in the sitting room. He is reclining against the couch, surrounded by his following. He is apparently telling some enthralling story, which is accompanied by the ritualistic flicking of his pocketknife. His face is comically animated, and Layna can tell he is about to deliver a punchline. Everyone around him leans forward like kids at a magic show, waiting for the big reveal.

He too leans in, pausing for dramatic effect before throwing his hands in the air and exclaiming some inaudible clincher. They all erupt in hysterical laughter. He returns to his reclined position, wearing a satisfied smirk as he resumes the annoying flicking of the knife, open and closed, open and closed.

Kat was right. Layna does have feelings for him. Very strong feelings deep in the pit of her stomach. Looking at his face now, she knows for certain that she completely, utterly despises him.

Hunter stands and leads the others toward the makeshift dance floor. Suzanne downs the remaining contents of her cup and shoves it at Kat's chest, and she steers through the crowd toward her quarry. After some brief flirtation, he grabs her waist and they begin to dance. Despite his being a full foot taller than Suzanne, they move together fluidly, bodies pressed close. As they turn in time to the beat, Suzanne exchanges a spirited look with Kat and Layna.

"Hey, let's dance," Kat shouts at Layna, grabbing her by the arm and turning her away from Suzanne and Hunter.

Layna stifles an eye-roll at the obvious and unnecessary diversion. But as she starts dancing with Kat by her side, she finally does start to feel herself relax. Her mind clears as she loses herself in the music, and she remembers what it's like to just *be* Layna. The night turns into a rhythmic blur of sweaty, dancing partyers, increasingly inebriated conversations shouted over increasingly deafening music, flirtations and rejections and some juicy hookups.

When Kat finally breaks Layna's trance to tell her she's going to grab another soda, Layna scans the room for Hunter and Suzanne. Layna knows Suzanne can take care of herself, but she can't help feeling uneasy.

She checks the sitting room, the patio, and the kitchen with no luck. She begins to feel slightly panicked until she catches a glimpse of Suzanne's auburn hair in the doorway of the laundry room on the other end of the kitchen. Suzanne is leaning back against the door frame with Hunter standing intimately close. Her green eyes are effervescent, and she wears her seductive smile that she reserves only for the likes of him.

Relieved, Layna starts to turn back toward the front hall, but she stops as she notices Hunter lift a small bottle from his pocket. He pours some of its contents into Suzanne's cup, and then his, and they both take a swig. Layna looks more closely at her friend and realizes the sparkling of her eyes may not only be lovesickness.

She weaves her way through the kitchen and walks right up to them. "Hi," she growls at Hunter before turning to Suzanne. "How's it going, Suze? Everything okay over here?" Layna hopes her friend is sober enough to recognize the true meaning of her words as, 'Hi, Suzanne, what the hell are you doing with that bottle of liquor?'

Suzanne replies with a forced laugh and yells, "Yeah, obviously, this party is lit!" Her true meaning of course being, 'Hop off, you're ruining the moment'.

Ugh, I totally am.

Layna feels stuck. She doesn't want to ruin Suzanne's chances with her year-long crush. But is she just supposed to let this play out? She doesn't trust him. Not one bit. Not with Suzanne.

She walks out of Hunter's line of sight and mimes the act of drinking and throwing up a few times so Suzanne can get the picture. Then she remembers that she is in a room full of people and looks around to find several of her peers watching her insane pantomime. *Cool, cool. Way to be totally cool, Layna*, she thinks as the heat rises in her cheeks.

Suzanne stifles a laugh, but beyond that, Layna's warning is ignored. She gives up and decides to go find Kat for reinforcement. She's always been better at talking sense into Suzanne, and Layna too, for that matter.

When she returns to the front hall, Layna realizes she's lost Kat to the senior who was working the keg, the two of them now wrapped around each other on the dancefloor. She glances around for the rest of the squad, but she honestly has no more energy to play the socialite right now. Feeling lost, she sneaks off to the bathroom upstairs, shutting the door on the bumping bass and chorus of voices below.

She grips the sink and stares at herself in the mirror, willing the knots in her stomach to unwind. If she can't learn to let go and act herself again, she's going to lose her friends. That thought scares her more than she's willing to admit. She's been finding it more and more difficult to connect with people—certainly not anyone new. Always somewhat out of place in her own skin. Without Kat and Suze there to fill in the gaps of her life, she will have to address that nagging disquiet that has been ever-present, floating beneath the surface of her mind. For now, she'll just go find the squad and keep her eye on Suzanne until Kat is free and they can figure out what to do.

Layna takes a deep breath and walks back out into the unlit hallway. Someone is stumbling down the hall toward her. As he snickers idiotically, she realizes it's Hunter, who's clearly wasted. He looks at her with unfocused eyes and says, "Ohhey! Enjoying thapary?"

"Sorry, what? Didn't quite catch that," Layna snaps, as she moves to sidestep him.

Hunter stares at her for an uncomfortable moment and then takes her by the shoulders and pushes her back against the wall, pinning her with his body. "I said...you enjoying...this party?" He takes great effort to form the words in his half-functioning mouth.

His face is an inch from hers, and Layna can smell the alcohol, strong on his breath and clothes. Stunned by his sudden aggressiveness, she tries to release herself. He holds fast, keeping her in place and sliding a hand down the side of her arm.

"You're awhole meal, y'know," he whispers into her hair. "These *lips*..." he murmurs, as he lifts his hand to run his finger roughly over her mouth.

"Get off of me *right now*," Layna snarls with as much venom as she can muster. He doesn't remove himself but instead presses his mouth against hers as he holds her arms against her sides in a vice grip. Her body screams in protest as she tries in vain to turn her head away and get leverage to push him off. Her muffled cry for help cannot compete with the pitch of the music below, and she realizes no one is going to save her. She needs to fight now.

As she gathers herself for the struggle, Hunter pulls his head back. But to Layna's horror, it is no longer Hunter in front of her, holding her down.

Hunter's once vibrant, blue eyes are now hollow, black pits, his ivory skin now the greyish color of a decaying corpse. And a dense, nebulous shadow shrouds his entire body, an incarnate vapor, foul and turbulent, that clings to him like a parasite sapping him of life.

A scream gets snagged in Layna's throat, drowned in a river of fear. This is the image that haunts the darkest corners of her nightmares. The very thing she has spent the year convincing herself wasn't real. That none of it happened. And now it's right here in front of her, and this time it wants to hurt *her*.

Not again. It's not happening. It doesn't exist.

Through the ringing in her ears, she hears someone coming up the stairs. And just like that, in a blink, the shadow around Hunter is gone and he is himself again. She stares at him wide-eyed, her mind a fistful of thunder. Somewhere amidst the inner storm is the recollection that Hunter is still a threat, and help is nearby. She looks toward the staircase to call for help. But her words fail her as she realizes who is standing at the end of the hallway staring at them in dismay.

Suzanne.

She imagines what Suzanne must see through her eyes. Layna and Hunter entwined in a quiet, unlit hallway, away from the crowds. Caught in the act.

"Suzanne, wait!" she cries, but her friend is already moving back down the stairs.

Hunter also stares after Suzanne in a bewildered stupor. Layna takes advantage of the distraction to wrench herself sideways, allowing just enough leverage to thrust her right knee straight up into Hunter's groin. He cries out and goes stumbling backward into the opposite wall, both hands clutched between his legs. His face is blank with shock for only a moment before he lurches forward and vomits all over the floor where Layna was just standing. But she is already on the move, leaping toward the staircase on quaking legs. She runs down after Suzanne, continuing to shout her name.

Suzanne has nearly reached the patio doors when Layna jumps the last two steps. A number of people are staring at them already but right now she doesn't care. She just needs to get to her friend and explain.

"Suzanne, stop! That was *not* what you think!" she yells, as she catches up with her.

Suzanne whirls around, eyes furious and feet unsteady. "What the hell's the matter with you?" she screams. Her voice is slurred like Hunter's, and Layna could swear that her eyes too flash to black.

Mind reeling, Layna sputters, "Wait—no, I don't know...I thought I saw..."

Hunter then stumbles down the stairs behind them looking ill. The DJ lowers the music as someone calls out to Hunter to ask if he's okay. The crowd of people begin to back up, forming a circle around them. Layna sees Kat trying to shove her way through toward her friends' voices.

"No, Layna, I don't care what is *wrong* with you! I meant how could you *do* this to me?"

"Suzanne, no," Layna pleads, regaining her awareness of the situation. "I promise, it's not what it looked like. I would never hurt you—"

"Oh, shut up! It's exactly what it looked like—you stabbing me in the back!"

The music shuts off altogether and the room becomes a vacuum of silence, broken only by the shattering of an eleven-year friendship.

"You couldn't just let me have this *one* thing? Just one thing that didn't have to be all about you and how crazy you are! I am so *done* with your mysterious, messed-up girl routine. Just get over yourself already or go ask your psychiatrist to up your meds or something. I don't care anymore!"

Layna's jaw falls slack. This has to be a nightmare. There is no way those horrible things just came out of Suzanne's mouth. No way that one of her best friends just roasted her in front of half the school.

But she did. And now everyone knows. Layna's shock surrenders to a wave of fury as it rolls over her. In this moment, she wants nothing more than to tear a chunk of that lovely, auburn hair from Suzanne's head. She takes a threatening step toward her friend, but then, a scrambling of her senses and a disorienting shift in perspective. She is now standing next to Suzanne looking at...herself. Her *self*—her body, still standing where she was a moment ago, now shrouded in the same menacing shadow that had a hold of Hunter upstairs, eyes hollow and skin ashen. No one else seems to see it. No one knows it's not her anymore.

It has her body. It has control.

Layna watches helplessly as she takes another step toward Suzanne, and Suzanne takes an unsteady step backward.

Screw this! I am not helpless. Just as her psychiatrist taught her, she channels all of her awareness and will toward a single thought, and then she screams it inside her head. *GET OUT OF MY BODY!*

Layna feels a lurch and she is back in place. Possessed of her own self again. The second she is, the disturbing out-of-body experience fades like a dream. In the periphery, Layna sees Kat reach out a pleading hand to her feuding friends, and Layna advances no further.

"What, you want to hit me?" Suzanne taunts. "Go ahead and do it. Prove me right, psycho."

"Suzanne!" Kat yells, the hurt in her voice palpable. Suzanne gazes in Kat's direction, her eyes heavy and unfocused, and then she seems to gain awareness of the throng of people gathered around them. Layna can see the mortified recognition of Suzanne's betrayal start to take form on her face, but it's too late to take it all back.

Layna is trembling, her hands curled into fists as unforgivable words slip forward on her tongue, threatening to escape her lips, never to be undone. Instead, she turns on her heel and speeds for the front door as all eyes watch her go. She hears Kat shout her name as she breaks into a run, out beneath the moonlit sky and down the walkway leading from the house. She takes off her heels and continues barefoot, tears streaming down her face as she tries to outrun the emotions that chase her, the truth that bites at her heels.

Her psychiatrist was right, and she was wrong. What happened in Delaware, what's been happening since then, is that she is losing touch with reality.

Because she is a schizophrenic.

And this is the beginning of her end.

Her phone vibrates in her bag over and over, but she doesn't stop to answer it. She keeps running until she reaches home. She enters her house as quietly as possible and heads up to her bedroom. She will worry about explaining her presence to her mom in the morning. For now, she just wants to fall into bed and cry herself to sleep. So she does just that.

CHAPTER

T he grass beneath her bare feet is wet with dew. The edges of the night sky are just beginning to brighten with the approaching dawn as the birds above her chatter in anticipation. Layna is anticipating something too, but hers takes form only as an amorphous sense of doom.

She is standing on the brink of an open field. To the left, there is a playground, and to the right, a baseball diamond. To her back, woods. She knows the place. It's Trent Park, near Suzanne's old house in the Ironbound neighborhood.

Voices, carried on a breeze from the outfield to her right. *Someone is coming.*

With the distinct instinct that she should hide, Layna bounds toward the tree line and leaps behind the nearest tree just as she detects the obscure outline of three people heading her way. She can't hear what they're saying, but their tone is strained. She peers around her tree as three boys walk into the clearing between the diamond and the playground. They pass right by, unaware of her presence, and she recognizes two of the boys as Jay-One and Jay-Two. Sophomores at Caledon High. Not their real names, obviously. They both have generic J-names she's always mixing up. Jack and John? John and Joe? Neither of them holds a very positive reputation at school. When they're actually at school. They're both supposed to be in her year but have been left back—always getting in fights and getting thrown in detention or getting suspended. Almost always together, hence her confusion.

"Man, I swear if he don't show again, I'll kill him. *And* you," barks the unfamiliar third boy.

"Chill, bro. He's going to show," says Jay-One.

Layna hears the creaking of metal coming from the playground to her left. Two more guys emerge from the shadows, ambling between the swings and toward the three boys. The Jays and their companion stand in tense silence and await the others to reach them. Layna shuffles around the tree to shield herself from the view of both groups.

The newcomers look to be a little older, a little rougher. One chubby and one lanky. Neither of them familiar. Probably graduates who haven't and never will leave the boundaries of Caledon. Layna then notices a third newcomer who remains in the shadows by the swings, surveying the meeting from a distance, his hood pulled over his head. The older boys stop a few feet from the younger ones.

"He couldn't come himself?" Jay-Two snaps.

Lanky nods in the direction of the swings where a spark of light flares from a cigarette lighter, illuminating the surveyor's face for only a moment. He's too far for Layna to distinguish his features, but something about him seems familiar. Jay-Two aims a derogatory comment in his general direction.

"Okay, so what'd ya got for us?" Jay-One asks, returning the focus to the task at hand.

Chubby pulls off his backpack and unzips it, throwing it on the ground between them. Layna is observing so intently that she doesn't hear the approach of another party until a twig breaks right behind her.

Her knees almost buckle as she spins around to face whatever fate awaits her.

But whatever fate this is, at least it is stunningly beautiful. Or maybe not so much an *it* as it is a...*who*.

It's a boy, sort of. Very much unlike a boy, this one is *glowing*. An unearthly shimmer surrounds him, one that is somehow both light and dark. A brightness that glistens blue-black at the edges like the halo of light around a full moon. The most remarkable thing, though, is his eyes—an iridescent, sapphire blue, shining brighter than the rest of him.

"L-Layna?"

Layna startles at the sound of his voice. It's so human compared to the rest of him. "Um, yes. Do I...know you?" she whispers.

"Oh, I'm Blake. We, uh, sort of met yesterday?"

Well damn. I do know him.

It's the boy with the picture. The boy who drew her on the roof. Or at least...some hella blinged-out version of him. "Oh. Yes. Sure, we did. And why are you, um, glowing?"

53

"Why am *I* glowing?" He looks at her and then down at himself in confusion. Like her, he is barefoot. But while she is dressed in cotton shorts and a t-shirt, he is wearing only a pair of boxers. He seems to notice it then too, clearing his throat as he slowly crosses his arms.

Behind Layna, the confrontation seems to have devolved into a shouting match. Blake puts his finger to his lips and peers around the tree. Layna tears her gaze away from his midnight glow and follows his lead.

To her dismay, Lanky has pulled a gun on the group of younger boys. But it's not that alone that causes her guttural reaction to the scene playing out before her eyes. Lanky not only has a gun in his hand, but a caliginous shadow surrounds his body—a body that is now sallow and grey. Bottomless darkness where his eyes once were. The shadow around him looks almost alive itself, and it tickles at a memory...something terrible and formless.

The corpse-like version of Lanky is now screaming commands at the younger boys. They toss their bags on the ground and back up, hands raised in front of them in surrender. The surveyor has disappeared, apparently having made a run for it when shit got real.

Layna looks sideways at Blake, whose sapphire eyes are wide in helpless dismay, his mouth agape. But as Lanky takes another step toward the boys' backpacks, Layna is overcome with an inexplicable certainty that she is meant to stop this. That she is *capable* of stopping this.

Without another thought, she steps around the side of the tree.

Blake grabs her by the arm. "What the hell are you doing?" he hisses.

"I can help," is all she can offer in reply.

"What are you, nuts? You're going to get us both killed!"

"Do not call me that. Let me go," she says calmly. And she *feels* calm. That ever-present, restless energy is quiet for the first time in her life, as though it's been waiting for this moment.

She turns back toward the field, but Blake doesn't release his hold on her. As she tries to wrench her arm free, she keeps her eyes on the boys. She senses it just before it happens, but it is over before she can react.

The Jays' unfamiliar companion draws his own gun from the front pocket of his hoodie, and the sound of a discharge pierces through the early morning stillness and shatters Layna's fleeting sense of composure.

It was Lanky's gun that fired. The shadow around him dissipates, and his chest heaves as he stares at the singular curl of white smoke rising from the barrel of the gun.

All the boys scatter. Save for one.

Jay-One stands there motionless, staring down at his white shirt, where a crimson stain has already begun to spread across his chest. He drops to his knees and topples sideways.

"No!" Layna shrieks, running out toward him.

None of the fleeing boys even turn at the sound of her scream. She lands in the grass next to Jay-One.

No. He's not Jay-One. The least you can do is remember his goddamn name, Layna.

She squeezes her eyes shut in search of a memory. An announcement over the loudspeaker, and him rising from his chair in the auditorium as students jeered and heckled. *Joe*…his name is Joe.

"J-Joe?" she stammers through chattering teeth.

He coughs. A drop of blood rolls down his chin from his mouth, etching through the humble beginnings of facial hair. Joe stares at the sky, eyelids fluttering, unaware of her presence. Layna lays a hand on one of his as she watches the life ebb from his eyes. A moment passes, and Layna realizes it was his last. Joe is gone. She tastes bile in the back of her throat, and she claps a hand over her mouth to keep from throwing up or screaming, or both.

I didn't stop it. I was supposed to stop it.

The distant wail of a siren tears through the silence. Layna looks back over her shoulder for Blake, but he isn't where she left him at the edge of the woods. He's nowhere. The world around her starts to whirl, images and colors seeping together like a watercolor painting. She jumps to her feet and yells for Blake, but he is gone, and she is alone. Did Lanky and the others come back for them? No loose ends?

She turns back around to find empty grass at her feet. Joe's body is gone.

"What the…" Layna buries her hands in her hair as she spins wildly. The ballfield and playground have also disappeared. The woods close in on her, the branches of the trees reaching for her like the grasping claws of something wicked. And with euphoric clarity, she realizes what's going on.

I'm dreaming, she thinks. *This is just a nightmare, and I need to wake up.* The woods become shadows, encircling her, pouring toward her and down her throat. Choking her. The sensation of drowning on darkness is real enough itself, and she gasps for air, wishing that Blake would come back and save her from the darkness.

She wakes with his name on her lips.

Her heart thumps madly as she sits up in bed and emerges from dream to reality. She begins to identify her surroundings in time and place—her bedroom, Saturday morning, last night's party. Suzanne and Hunter, the picture, the break-in, her obvious mental deterioration. With all of that on her mind when she went to bed, it's no wonder she was having such a horrible nightmare. Nightmares are certainly not unfamiliar to her this year. Though now that she's awake, she's not quite sure which is the true nightmare, the dream or her reality. If you can call it that, considering she has no idea what is even real anymore.

Last night, Layna felt certain that her brain had reached the tipping point and dove straight over the edge of sanity into the early-onset schizophrenia diagnosis that her psychiatrist had so mercilessly lain at her feet. If it's true, it's time to collect her bag from the closet. She can sense it in there, only feet away, pulling on her like the gravity of a black hole. She wants to resist, to hang onto the shadow of her life for as long as she can.

So maybe it's not true. Her psychiatrist upped her meds at the beginning of the month. Maybe that's the reason things have escalated. It's her last shred of hope and she clings to it. She drops her head in her hands as it begins to ache, and she realizes she's drenched in sweat.

"Gross," she mutters. She reluctantly gets out of bed to shower, ripping the equally sodden sheets off her mattress. The clock on her nightstand reads only six twenty-five a.m., and she wishes her troubled mind had let her sleep a little bit longer on a Saturday. But summer is around the corner. Maybe she'll sleep then.

She plods down the hall and into the bathroom and examines the bottle of pills sitting on the vanity. "You did this to me, didn't you? You little, pink atrocities."

Surprisingly, reprimanding an inanimate object doesn't make her feel any better. But she doesn't take her morning dose, tossing the bottle into a drawer and slamming it shut. She'll call her therapist and just tell her the higher dosage is making her puke or something. Dr. Nettles will drop it back down and everything will go back to semi-normal.

After a long, hot shower, she steps out of the bathroom to the smell of pancakes coming from downstairs. It brightens her mood momentarily before she remembers she isn't supposed to be home from Suzanne's until this afternoon. She has to come up with an excuse for why she came home in the middle of the night, and her mom will be waiting for it.

Fighting the overwhelming urge to crawl back into bed and avoid the world, she dries her hair as best she can with her towel and throws on a pair of jean shorts and a plain, white t-shirt. She vows to brave the day, whatever it may bring. After all, it honestly can't be worse than the last twenty-four hours.

Layna shoves an enormous forkful of pancake into her mouth to avoid answering her mother. This tactic is not going to work forever. As she attempts not to choke on the syrupy mush, her brain tries to come up with a mom-friendly version of last night's events.

Her mom looms over her, all five-foot four of her slender figure about as threatening as a papercut. Her soft, toffee eyes are narrowed at her daughter, but Layna can tell that her anger is only skin deep. She need only come up with a simple, rational excuse so her mom can carry on with her worry-free day.

Layna holds up a finger to request more time in the battle to swallow her food. Her mom begins impatiently tapping her foot on the floor as she glances at the watch on her wrist. She's dressed in her workout clothes, dark blonde hair pulled into a ponytail. Likely she was preparing to go for a run but was waiting to see if Layna wanted to join her. Saturday runs on the trail around the reservoir have become their favorite pastime, though Layna hasn't had quite as much energy to do it regularly this spring.

As she finally forces the lump of food down her throat, Layna glimpses the image on the TV mounted on the wall behind her mother's head. Whatever half-truth had formed on her lips evaporates, and her fork clatters onto her plate. She springs to her feet, sending her chair toppling over behind her.

"Layna! What is it? Are you choking?" her mom cries, grabbing her by the shoulders.

Her mother's pleas barely register in her brain, which is too consumed with the words that have appeared beneath the image on the screen. The image of a park. Her mom is forcing her mouth open, checking her airway. Layna's gaze doesn't waver, and neither does the headline.

It can't be real. Another hallucination, Layna concludes. But then—

"Oh my god, how awful! Honey, did you know him?" she hears her mom ask, her voice far away. She is referring to the picture of the boy that just popped up on the screen. The picture now displayed above the headline that reads:

17 Y.O. BOY FOUND SHOT TO DEATH IN TRENT PARK

The picture of Joe.

It really happened. He's really dead.

She digs her fingernails sharply into the skin of her palms and feels a stinging pain.

Not still dreaming.

Her mother starts shaking her lightly by the shoulders, and Layna realizes she's been yelling her name.

"I'm okay, Mom," Layna finally murmurs.

The tension on her mother's face eases only slightly. "You don't look okay, Layna. Why don't you sit back down a minute?"

Her mom rights the chair Layna knocked over, and Layna lowers herself back into it. Her mom sits across from her and grabs her hands.

"I'm so sorry, honey. You knew him?"

Layna sucks in a steadying breath. "Not well. He is—was—in the grade below me at school. I just can't believe he was actually....*murdered.*"

The word sounds foreign on her tongue. Murder is something that happens far away from her world. In movies, television, books, maybe state or national news. Or in nightmares. But not in her hometown. Not to someone she knows. Someone who passed her in school hallways, who played a practical joke at the last pep rally, who she has seen laughing and fighting, kissing girls, skipping class. That person was alive, and now he isn't. And she...*dreamt* that? His end? It felt so real at the time, but she woke up in her bed. And it faded, as dreams do, into the obscurity of abstraction.

"Do you want to talk about it?" her mom asks, as she strokes the hair from Layna's face and tucks it behind her ear.

Layna shakes her head. She knows her mom is trying to be supportive, but there is only one person she can talk to right now.

"Thanks, Mom. I...I just need some fresh air. I think maybe I'll go for a quick bike ride downtown."

"Oh, that's a good idea. Do you want me to take my bike out and go with you?"

"No, don't worry about it. Thanks, though. I think I just need to be alone for a little while. You go get in a good run for the both of us, 'kay?"

Her mom hesitates. "Alright, well...make sure you have your phone on you. Try to be back in a couple of hours, okay?"

"I will," Layna promises, plastering her well-rehearsed everything-is-totally-fine smile on her face. She grabs her cell phone from the kitchen table and shoves it in the back pocket of her shorts. "See you in a bit," she announces, planting a kiss on her mom's cheek for good measure before speeding for the front door. She slips into her purple sneakers and leaps down her front steps. Her bike is still propped up against the front porch where she saw the slasher manhandle it yesterday. She takes hold of it as she tries to dismiss the false memory. She doesn't know exactly where she is headed. She just knows who she needs to find.

Half an hour later, Layna finds herself standing in front of a line of yellow police tape. She watches the cops beyond it as they roam about the ballfield and playground of Trent Park. Joe's body has been moved, and there are small, orange markers scattered about the area where she watched him die.

But not really, of course. Because what she saw was only a dream. A disturbingly accurate dream. The news broadcast said it happened early this morning, the police suspecting a drug deal gone wrong. It was too precise.

"Okay, Dr. Nettles, maybe a little Occam's razor—what's the simplest explanation?" she mumbles to herself.

She could have been sleepwalking. But, no, Trent Park is miles from her house. There's no way she walked all the way there and all the way back without being noticed or stopped. And why weren't her feet covered in dirt from the woods and the field? Not simple enough.

Maybe the TV in her room was somehow on in the early morning and she incorporated the news broadcast into her dream? It's slightly more likely, but her TV wasn't on when she woke up, and the remote was over on her desk. Maybe there's such a thing as sleep-watching?

That doesn't fit in Occam's stupid razor either. The simplest answer, of course, is that she dreamed about something that really happened. But that's impossible.

All she knows for certain is that she needs to find Blake. He was the anomaly. He didn't follow the rules of the dream, and he didn't fade into obscurity with the rest of it. She can still picture him with vivid accuracy, as though he's standing right in front of her. She just needs to question him. If he has no idea what she's talking about, then great. Unexplainable freak dream it is. At least it narrows down the weird.

And if he does…

A cop walks by on the other side of yellow tape and Layna has to fight the urge to flag him down and tell him everything she saw. Because of course she would sound like a complete lunatic if she tried to explain that she suspects she saw the whole thing while sleepwalking or dreaming or hallucinating or whatever.

She sighs in exasperation and walks across the street to plop onto a dilapidated, wooden bench. Her phone starts vibrating in her pocket and she pulls it out to see that it's Kat trying to FaceTime again. Her calls and texts have been coming non-stop for the past few hours, and all have gone unanswered.

Ugh. Why can't I just deal with one effing problem at a time, world?

Layna shoves her phone back into her pocket with a mixture of annoyance and guilt. But she thinks about the awful things that Suzanne said and she doesn't know how they will get past this one. Not that Suzanne is probably super eager to get past it anyway, given what she thinks she saw. Layna wishes she could just rewind the video of her life to last night before everything went wrong. When they were leaving Suzanne's house, all excitement, clambering into the car with—

Oh. Her mind snags on an image from the dream. The surveyor at the swings who seemed so familiar. She only saw a glimpse of his face from too far away, but it was the way he held himself that she recognized. It was *Nick.* Suzanne's older brother. Could he have been involved in this too?

No, idiot. Your version was a dream.

She groans and drops her head in her hands as her eyes start to burn, still raw from last night's tears and fighting hard against their return. Nick and Blake and even the creepy shadow were all only in the dream because of everything that happened yesterday. Talking to Blake, talking to Nick, none of it is going to explain how she had a dream about someone dying then woke up to find him dead in real life.

She has never felt so confused and alone in all her life. But she's not going to get any less confused or alone by sitting on this rotting bench for another second.

She pops up off the bench, eyes cast downward, and walks straight into something unexpectedly solid. She staggers backward as her heel catches on the broken pavement, but before she can topple over, an arm reaches out and deftly snags her elbow.

"Oh my god," she says, shoving the curtain of hair out of her face. "I'm sorry for walking into y—" Her words catch in her throat as she realizes who she's speaking to.

"Hey," Blake says impassively, putting his hands in his pockets as he glances at the developments across the street.

Without the spectral dream-bling, he once again looks like the boy Suzanne was bullying yesterday, and Layna feels her cheeks flush with shame. She thinks of the way Suzanne spun him around after he'd bumped into her, accusing him of doing it intentionally to touch her boobs. Layna knew he hadn't, but she just stood there and watched. At least until her brain glitched, that is. It's different now without her friends next to her. Without the crowd around her. Without other people to blame for her own part in it all. Now it's just him and her. She wishes she could disappear or sink into a hole in the ground or something.

Blake sort of looks like he would like to do the same. Behind his black-rimmed glasses, his eyes still refuse to meet hers. She takes the opportunity to quietly examine this odd dream-fellow of hers. Toasted, copper skin and oval face, punctuated by a slightly crooked Grecian nose and framed with soft waves of raven-black hair. He wears a decrepit, black t-shirt embossed with some band logo, and massive, red headphones that are currently wrapped around his neck. Everything about him, from his averted eyes, to his baggy clothes, to his hunched posture, makes it seem like he's trying to make himself appear as small as possible. And he's already on the short side, coming up just above Layna's own five-foot-five-inch height. Mostly, he just seems to want nothing to do with her, and for some reason, that bothers her.

"Why are you here?" she asks, not trying to hide the irritation in her voice.

He finally turns to face her. As their eyes lock, Layna feels something else locking into place deep in her gut. Something that causes an intense jolt of energy to surge through her as though someone has just plugged her into a socket. They both spring back in surprise.

Layna scans her surroundings for some source of the charge, but she finds her gaze drawn back to his eyes, which haven't wavered from hers. No longer shimmering, but still sapphire blue, they are nearly as spectacular in real life as they were in her dream.

"D-did you know him?" she asks more evenly, trying to focus on the issue at hand.

Blake shakes his head.

"Then…why are you here? Morbid curiosity?"

In his eyes, she can see the same internal battle as the one raging in her own head. So unless the universe is playing some cosmic coincidental trick, he knows *something* about this.

"You…um…" She wavers, unsure whether she really wants to ask this aloud. "Did you happen to have a dream—"

"Yes." He sighs, visibly relieved that she brought it up first.

"About this?" she asks, pointing across the street.

"Yeah. I did. And uh…you were in it."

Well, damn. It just got one hundred percent weirder.

"You for real? Because I did too, and you were in mine. How did we both dream about this? Why were we in each other's dream? How…how did we know Joe was going to die?"

He only shrugs in response.

"Then tell me what you *do* know, Blake, because I'm freaking out and you seem pretty calm about all this."

"Well, for starters…" He hesitates, his eyes unsettled. "How'd you know my name?"

Layna raises an incredulous eyebrow. "Because you told…" She stops. He never told her his name yesterday—they didn't even speak. He told her in her dream.

He watches her, his lips pursed expectantly.

"I just…I must have seen your name somewhere. Like it was in my subconscious or whatever. Maybe I read it on one of your sketches."

He gives a slow shake of his head. "I don't sign *those* drawings. And even if I had, my signature is J.B. Knox. James Blakely Knox. How would you know I go by Blake unless I told you?"

"Um…" Occam's stupid razor continues to fail her. "You look like a Blake?"

Blake examines his hands as he and Layna lapse into an uneasy silence. He seems to struggle with something he wants to say. She waits, letting him work it out, hoping that the next thing out of his mouth gives her some answers rather than creating more questions.

"Layna, don't freak out, but…did something happen to you yesterday? Something, um, bad?"

Her jaw falls open in stunned reply and the world takes a nauseating dip sideways. "You *did* draw that sketch of me. It was real?"

"Wait, you saw the sketch?"

"Yesterday. On the floor of the hallway. How the *hell* did you know what was going to happen to me?"

He drops his gaze again. "I didn't know. Not exactly. But…yes, I did draw the picture of you. And it wasn't the first time."

"What?" she demands. "Explain."

"Uh, it would be easier if I showed you. My house is just a few blocks away."

Layna narrows her eyes at him as though it will help her focus in on his true intentions. But, as usual, her curiosity is drowning out the clanging bells of warning in her head. *Wouldn't Mom be proud?*

"Okay, fine. But you better tell me what the hell you know and how any of this has to do with what happened here," she says, nodding toward the park.

Layna grabs her bike, glancing around for anyone she might know. All she needs is someone from school seeing her hanging around with this kid. That'd be the nail in the coffin of her reputation, which is already struggling on life support after last night's party. Blake picks up his skateboard, and they walk down the street away from the park in hastened silence.

CHAPTER

Blake's is the last house on a quiet, dead-end street in the Ironbound section of town. No one has bothered to cut the grass, put a name on the mailbox, or repair the splintering shingles of the single-story ranch. Layna wonders whether it was intentionally painted that dull, grey color or if that was the handiwork of wear and weather.

The squeaky storm door slams shut behind Layna as she follows Blake into an enclosed porch abutting the front of the house. Rather than furniture, the porch is filled with a multitude of overflowing brown cardboard boxes in varying shapes and sizes. Some are scrawled with black marker designating a room destination, but obviously none made it past the threshold.

Blake unlocks the front door and leads Layna inside to a small living area that blends from living room to dining to kitchen. A badly stained beige rug runs from the entrance to the kitchen, where it changes over to pink, laminate flooring. The inside is considerably tidier than the porch, but it fills Layna with increasing apprehension. As she looks around, she realizes why. There is no *life* inside the house. Besides your basic necessities like a kitchen table, microwave, and living room furniture—still partially covered in shrink wrap—there is nothing. No pictures, decorations, books, movies, photo albums, or the like. It seems the house's occupants left all life in boxes at their doorstep.

"Just move in?" she asks, trying to keep her voice light.

"Not really," Blake mumbles. "My parents are out." He strides ahead of her down the hallway toward the right side of the house. Layna pauses at the edge of the hallway as Blake disappears into a bedroom. Presumably, his bedroom.

Way to go, genius. This is how you die.

Here she is, alone in a strange kid's home who just yesterday she helped humiliate in front of half the junior class. And now he's admitted to drawing a creepy picture of her and knowing something bad happened to her. What part of this seemed like a good idea fifteen minutes ago?

She starts to turn back when Blake reappears in his bedroom doorway. "Coming?" His blue eyes are earnest and beckoning. Layna walks into his room without another thought.

She is instantly hit with the undeniable scent of teenage boy. A stuffy mixture of lazy weekends and rushed weekdays, textbooks, dirty laundry, and some cheap, heady cologne or aftershave, or something meant to be enticing. For her, it just entices a brief sneezing fit.

His bedroom feels nearly as empty as the rest of the house, but somehow still manages to be a total mess. A few posters are taped to the walls sporting angry looking bands with mononymous names like *Warbringer* and *Obscura*. On one wall, there is a bookshelf filled haphazardly with piles of tattered sketchbooks. Blake throws the bedspread over the mess of clothes on his mattress and tries shoving some dirty socks into the corner with his foot.

"Okay, just hold on two seconds. I need to find the right one," he says, as he leaps up and over his bed to the bookshelf on the other side of the small room. He crouches in front of it and runs a finger along the spines of the sketchbooks on the lowest shelf, each of which are designated with a date range.

With no other seating options, Layna lowers herself cautiously onto the corner of the bed closest to the door. She glances at the mess on the floor next to her and identifies a few recognizable textbooks mostly buried beneath a pile of countless crinkled drawings. Oddly, these drawings are all of the same thing, over and over. Images of some boujee sports car, each drawn from the same perspective. Some are indistinct, as if done in halfhearted habit, and others in such intense detail that the paper is pitted and pocked from the force with which they were sketched. Layna raises a judgmental eyebrow at them. *Boys and their dumb sports cars.*

"Here we go," Blake murmurs. He pulls a sketchbook from the bunch and plops onto the opposite corner of his bed. He flips through the pages for an eternity, and then freezes. His eyes meet Layna's, apprehension and eagerness warring within them.

"Whatever it is, just show me already," she pleads, her impatience mounting.

"Don't freak out," he says again.

She replies with an exasperated eye-roll as she grabs the open sketchpad from him. It's another picture of her. Close-up this time, the surroundings are less clear. She is in her winter coat, staring out a large window at what appears to be a blur of trees. Her brows are knitted, and her eyes look troubled—distracted. She marvels at the skill and level of detail as she makes out more heads of people in rows behind her and realizes what is depicted in this sketch. It is a picture of her on a train. The one and only time in her recent history that Layna has been on a train. The Delaware incident.

There is a date on the bottom right hand of the drawing. Bewildered, she looks up at Blake.

He has been watching her closely. "You recognize it, yeah? And you're wondering about the date. So…here's the thing. I can't tell you anything about what's happening in this picture, but I can tell you that whatever this is, it happened six days *after* the date that's written on it."

Layna thinks for a second and then her mouth goes dry. She swallows thickly. "It was exactly six days later. How…?"

"I don't know how it happens, but, well, I kind of…dream the future."

There it is. The answer Layna was both waiting for and dreading to hear. He drew the picture of the break-in before it happened. He saw the future. It sounds even more ridiculous out loud than it did in her head. Could he be messing with her?

She tries replaying their conversation outside the park. Tries to pinpoint any moment he could have tricked her, used her confusion and played on her fear to get her to admit more than she was willing to say. This whole thing could be some elaborate, manufactured prank. She glances around the room, looking for a hidden webcam somewhere.

"Hey, listen, I know how it sounds," Blake confesses. "It's taken me a long time to accept that this is for real, but I'm positive it is. And I'm even more positive after last night that you are a part of it, and I know you know it. I mean, you seriously think I would say something this insane to a girl like you if I thought there was a chance of you leaving here and destroying my life?"

"Uh, we'll get back to whatever it is you're implying with that 'girl like you' bit later, but what makes you so sure I'm not going to do that?" Layna asks.

"Because, I don't know how or why, but about seven or eight months ago, you kind of just started appearing in my flashes, and then, last night—"

"In your flashes?" Layna interrupts. "Maybe you should start from the beginning."

"Oh, right. Sorry. This is obviously the first time I've ever tried explaining any of this to someone." He offers her a fleeting grin and Layna realizes it's the first one she's seen on him. It suits him much better than the apathy he'd worn like armor until only moments ago. "When I was younger, I started getting these night terrors. You know what those are?" he asks.

Layna shakes her head.

73

"I guess it's sort of like…a really intense nightmare, except that you seem like you're awake when you're not, and you have no memory of it after."

"Then how do you know it happens?"

"My parents. Apparently, I'd start screaming bloody murder in the middle of the night, and they had a really hard time waking me up. When I was twelve, they took me to a clinic, found out it was night terrors. They said it was why I was, um, afraid all the time. They gave me some meds to help me sleep, but I stopped taking them a while ago because, well, something else started happening. Whenever I'd forget to take the meds, the last thing I'd remember right before waking up were these crazy, vivid flashes of some random image. Kind of like the way an image stays on the back of your eyelids after a camera flash, you know? Except way more detailed." He closes his eyes and continues more softly. "They stay with me for hours, days even. Whenever I close my eyes, I can see…"

He falls silent, and Layna watches as his eyeballs dart beneath his lids, studying a memory. He sucks in a breath and his eyes burst open, refocusing on Layna as if he's returning from some distant place.

"Sorry. Anyway, I started drawing every flash I saw at the end of my dreams, but they were so random, they meant nothing. They just, I don't know, *felt* important. Eventually I just stopped taking the meds altogether to see what would happen, and now I get the flashes *all* the time, with or without the terrors. It was when I came to Jersey with my parents to look at this house for the first time that I realized what was going on. It was the first time I'd ever left Philly, but I swear I had already seen this house. And not just the house, but the same exact

74

moment. The cloudy day, the realtor lady's clothes and the lipstick on her teeth, my dad at the door, and my mom on the sidewalk looking back at me. Like some kind of crazy-ass déjà vu."

Layna listens intently as his words spill out over each other, his mouth barely managing to keep up. It's as though he has been waiting his whole life to speak his truth, to unburden himself of the weight of such a credence. And in his doing so, Layna feels the burden of her own truth itching to be free, to be shared.

"So, after that, I started dating the sketches and experimenting with it. I don't always recognize it. I mean, some of those images could really be anything. But when I do, it always happens six days from the flash. I'm dreaming stuff *six days* before it happens." He stops, taking a deep breath as he waits for her response.

She's certain that at least *he* believes what he's saying is true. And how else could she explain the sketch on the train and the sketch of her behind the tree? There could be a rational explanation, but her brain is struggling to come up with any alternatives. And if he is telling the truth about his sketches, then maybe, just maybe, everything she's been experiencing—the time-lags, the out-of-body episodes…the Delaware incident—hasn't all been in her head. If he's crazy, then so is she, and if he's not, then…maybe she isn't either. And so, she decides in that moment to believe him.

She glances back down at the sketch of her on the train and notices an inconsistency. "Wait, if you've been drawing images of your *own* future, why was I in it for months before you ever met me?"

"Yeah, good question. No clue. Like I said, around seven months ago, I started seeing you in my flashes. This was the first one," he says, pointing to the picture open on Layna's lap. "Then maybe once or twice a month after that. I'd look for you each time at the six-day mark, and I'd see you in every girl that looked at all like the drawings. But it was never you. The six days would come and go, and you'd never show up. So I convinced myself you didn't really exist and that the visions of you weren't flashes of the future like the others. I stopped looking for you. And then, go figure, turns out we've been going to the same school for a couple months now. I had no idea—been sticking pretty much to the freshman-sophomore building—until I saw you walking through the juniors' hallway yesterday. It was trippy, like seeing a ghost or something. That's why I bumped into your friend."

What a great first impression. He sees her in his dreams for months and she turns out to be a total nightmare in person.

"So, you just started witnessing moments of *my* life through your dreams, through these flashes, and you have no idea why?"

"No idea."

"So what about Trent Park? We didn't dream that six days before it happened. You think for some reason we both just dreamt about it *right before* it happened?"

"No…that was definitely different. It wasn't just that we both had a dream about it."

"How do you mean?"

"Think about it for a sec. You knew my name earlier. Because in your dream, I told you my name, right?"

Layna hesitates and then nods.

"In my dream, after I told you my name, you asked me why I was glowing, even though you were the one glowing. Like this bright, golden light, even your eyes. Sound familiar?"

"Wait...so...we actually had that conversation somehow?" Layna replies, her mind racing.

Blake watches her for a moment, then lifts his hands to his head and gestures his brain exploding.

"What else happened in your dream?" she asks.

"Well, it started with you hiding behind a tree. There were boys out in the field and one of them pulled a gun on the other ones. Three guys against two. Only, the guy holding the gun didn't look normal, he—"

"Had a creepy shadow around him and looked like a corpse?" Layna finishes, her voice tight.

Blake nods slowly, his eyes wide.

"And then I tried to walk out there and you—"

"I tried to stop you," Blake whispers. "The gun went off, that guy fell, and I woke up."

"And that's when you disappeared from my dream." Layna lets out an uneasy laugh and puts her hands to her cheeks. "Okay, Blake. We didn't just have similar dreams about that murder before it happened. We were...*in the same* dream, interacting with each other, like telepathy or something. And what we dreamt, I think we were really seeing it, together, real time. I think we somehow witnessed a murder last night."

Blake squeezes his eyes shut and shakes his head as though trying to clear it of the memory.

"I mean, we couldn't have been like sleepwalking...right?" Layna asks.

Blake drops his gaze and Layna can almost feel him pulling back. "Both of us sleepwalking at the exact same time to the same exact spot for no apparent reason? Even if that wasn't like a trillion-to-one odds, no. I had issues with sleepwalking when I was younger. This wasn't the same."

"How do you know, though?"

"I just do," he replies tersely.

They sit in silence as Layna holds tightly to one single fact in all of this. The fact that Blake saw them too. He saw the shadows. The shadows that haunt her nightmares. The shadows that fuel her worst fear. While she's horrified at the idea that those things could exist outside the darkest parts of her own mind, this changes everything.

"I thought maybe there would be something in the sketchbooks that could give me a clue about what this dream meant, but I looked through just about all of them. I'm stumped," Blake says.

"There was nothing from six days ago that could be even a starting point?" Layna asks.

"I checked." He reaches over and grabs the sketchbook sitting on top of the bookshelf and hands it to her. She begins flipping through the pages. A lot of the pictures are vague, but some she recognizes from school—Mrs. Bachman, the tenth-grade biology teacher, in front of the class, a hallway of lockers, the photography lab. She turns to the picture of herself on the roof. Though it's from a distance, he got every detail— her hair, her eyes, her lips. The terror drawn in her features is a reminder of how scared she'd truly been, and the fluttering remnants of fear rematerialize in her belly.

Blake reaches over and gently turns the page to a more innocuous image.

"You really are talented, you know," Layna murmurs. "It's amazing you were able to draw me with that much detail when you had never even seen me in person."

"Yeah, well, I did see you a bunch in my flashes, so I guess I sort of...memorized you."

Layna glances up at him but he doesn't meet her eyes. His modesty throws her off-guard. She finds it refreshing to have a genuine—albeit super effing weird—conversation with a guy, rather than constantly fielding lame pick-up lines and pretending to laugh at dirty jokes. Maybe in another life they could have truly been friends.

She returns her focus to the sketchbook and continues scouring the pages, but there is nothing from the dream. She reaches the last sketch, and after that are only blank pages awaiting the life that Blake will eventually give to them. She closes the book in defeat, but then her brain actually registers the last image she saw. She flips the book back open to the last picture.

"What is it?" Blake asks. "Did you recognize something?"

"Yes," she chokes out, "but not something from the dream." She turns the sketchbook around to show him, but he just looks at it blankly, unaware of its significance to her.

"This is a picture of my house," she begins.

"Oh, okay."

"And this man standing here…that's the guy who broke in yesterday. He was real…"

"Oh damn, someone broke into your house? That's what my sketch was?" Blake asks, wincing at the thought. Layna nods as Blake leans forward to inspect the date on the picture. "But that can't be the guy because I only drew this yesterday morning when I woke up."

Layna frowns and flips the book back around and looks more closely at the picture. It's a view of her house from the front. The image is shaded, giving the impression of nighttime. Halfway between the sidewalk and the house, the man stands on the lawn, looking back over his shoulder so only half his face shows. He seems to wear the same mild expression she saw when she looked at him from her roof, and he has a light beard with hair that hangs to his shoulders. She's sure it's got to be the same man.

"Was it nighttime? In your flash?"

Blake shuts his eyes and responds, "Yeah, it was dark, like middle of the night dark."

"So he's coming back to my house sometime between Wednesday night and early Thursday morning. And I guess I'm going to be there."

She should be more afraid of the idea. But all she feels is resolve. He's a part of all this too, and if they can't come up with the answers themselves, maybe this guy will have some for them.

"Not you. Me," Blake affirms, "It'll be me. Remember, in all the flashes I see of your future, you're always the subject. So, it's either my future, or now I'm seeing *this* guy's future, which would be a new level of weird."

Layna shakes her head. "It doesn't matter whose future it's meant to be. It's both of ours now. I have a feeling that, whoever he is, he has answers we need. And now that we know he's coming, we should be ready when he does."

Layna drops her bike on the lawn and trots up the steps to her front door. She barely makes it through the doorway before her mom appears in the foyer looking furious. Moxie follows at her heels, looking up at Layna in a way that seems to say *you're going to get it*.

"What did I tell you before you left this house, Layna?" her mom demands.

Layna glances at the clock on the wall and realizes it's already past noon. *Whoops.* She is usually careful to check-in when her mom asks her too—she knows how her anxiety can snowball when Layna disappears for longer than expected. Particularly this last year. Layna didn't realize how much time had passed while she was at Blake's. They worked out a plan to deal with their mystery man, which was rewarding in itself. One step forward. But she now has to wait until Wednesday to actually act on the plan, and she's already crawling out of her skin with impatience. Answers, right there at her fingertips.

"Uh…to be careful?" Layna responds with a hopeful grin.

"No. I told you to call me if you were going to be out this long. I must have called you ten times. Layna, you know…" The anger melts from her face, and her eyebrows knit into the well-worn stitch of distress that has become so characteristic of her still-youthful skin. "I just don't know what I'm going to do with you."

"I'm sorry, Mom, my phone died," she says, pulling the phone out of her pocket. It did, in fact, die.

Her mom pinches the bridge of her nose with her fingertips, a familiar signal to tread lightly. "Yeah, the last couple times I called, it went straight to voicemail. Layna, what is the point of you having a cell phone if you aren't even going to keep it *charged*?"

"It won't happen again, I promise. I'm sorry," Layna blurts, ready for this confrontation to be over.

"Make sure it doesn't. Now...you have visitors," she says, gesturing toward the back of the house.

Layna frowns and follows her mom into the kitchen. Suzanne and Kat sit at the kitchen table with cans of Diet Coke in front of them. They both look up at Layna when she walks in. Suzanne rests her forehead against the palms of her hands, looking somewhat like a survivor of the Black Death. Her face is ashen, smudged eye makeup from the previous night blending into the shadows beneath her eyes. Her hair is pulled back in a sloppy ponytail with some rebellious frizz escaping its confines to form a halo around her head. She would never let anyone else see her in such a state.

"I'll let you girls chat, but not for too long because you all have studying to do for the rest of your finals this week," Layna's mom says with a knowing look. "Anything else you need, just let me know. I'll be upstairs." Layna is sure her mom can feel the tension in the room. She wonders what the girls would have told her, if anything.

"Thanks, Ms. Emery," Suzanne and Kat say together.

Layna sits down at the table. No one speaks for a solid minute, and Layna fights the urge to get up and just leave them there. Naturally, Kat is the one to break the ice.

"We've been trying to call you all day, Layna. We were worried."

Layna notes Kat's tactful use of the word "we" but she is well aware she didn't have any missed calls from Suzanne, nor does Suzanne look particularly worried. She's now sat back in her seat, arms folded across her chest as she gazes out the window at nothing. It infuriates Layna all over again to see her performance of indifference. Or maybe it isn't a performance at all. Maybe Suzanne really doesn't care about her anymore. Maybe she doesn't feel the least bit guilty about the things she said last night.

"What could you possibly have been worried about? That I was going to have some breakdown and land in a mental institution?" Layna snaps. "If I remember right, that's what Suzanne wants. Sorry to disappoint you, but I'm not going anywhere."

Kat sighs, a pained expression on her face. "You know that's not what I meant. You know we love you and would never want that to happen." She glances at Suzanne, waiting for a concurrence. "Right, Suze?" she presses.

Suzanne turns to look at Layna but purses her lips together and doesn't answer. Layna is about to explode at her when she notices Suzanne's lower lip is quivering. She realizes that Suzanne is doing everything in her power to maintain her composure. Layna melts with relief just as Suzanne bursts into tears and buries her head in her arms on the table.

Through muffled sobs, Suzanne chokes out, "Layna, I'm really sorry. I can't believe I said all that stuff. I just felt so hurt and angry. But I didn't mean any of it! The whole thing is just a big mortifying blur. I feel so bad, and I feel so sick, and I just want to *die!*"

Before Layna can react, Suzanne bolts back up in her chair and clamps a hand over her mouth. She leaps up and runs for the bathroom. Layna stares after her, dismayed, and gets up to follow, but Kat grabs her by the arm.

"Don't worry, she's just throwing up," she says casually. "She's been doing that all morning. Let me tell you, watching that girl puke her guts out for the last seven hours has sworn me to a life of sobriety. Hella gross. She'll be fine. Anyway, it's her own fault."

Layna sits back down and feels the tension melting from her muscles. She needed this. She needs *them*. As messed up as last night was, she just wants to move on and have them all go back to normal.

When Suzanne returns from the bathroom, she resumes her defeated position at the table, head buried in her arms. Layna sighs and reaches across the table to give Suzanne a cautious pat on her head. "Um, sorry you feel sick. I'm trying really hard not to tell you I told you so on that one…or, at least, mimed it to you."

Suzanne snorts with laughter at the memory.

"Suze, I promise you that I did not want anything to do with Hunter last night. He was just drunk and came on super strong. I was trying to get him off me when you came upstairs. He probably didn't even know it was me, seriously."

"I believe you," she mumbles into her arms. "He was coming on pretty strong with me too, right before."

84

"I'll only say this once, Suze," Layna adds. "He's not good enough for you. He is a d-bag and you deserve better. There, I said it."

Kat sits still as stone, her eyes darting between her friends.

Suzanne lifts her tear-stained face and shakes her head as delicately as possible. "I love you, Layna. But I know him, and he's not a d-bag. He was just having an off night is all."

Layna sighs. "Okay...well, I hope you're right. But either way, can you just try to do some damage control this week at school?"

Suzanne nods and replies, "I don't think it'll be a problem. Have you seen Facebook? Joe Draper got shot in Trent Park this morning. Right near my old house. *So* crazy."

The sound of the gunshot blazes through Layna's mind as she watches the life leave Joe's eyes again. Shuddering, she replies, "Yeah, I saw the news. It's so awful."

"I can't believe he's dead," Kat murmurs. "He seemed like a nice guy. Little messed up, but nice. I wonder who would have done that. Last I checked they're saying the police don't have any suspects."

"Yeah," Layna says, clearing her throat. She can't just ignore the fact that she saw Suzanne's brother at the park in her dream. She has no idea what that means or if it even means anything. But what if he was really there? What if he really knows who killed Joe? If Layna did witness the truth of what happened in that park, she at least owes Joe some justice for it. "Suze, have you, um, talked to Nick at all?"

Suzanne narrows her eyes at Layna, ever over-protective of her older brother's shady reputation. "Why are you asking that?"

"It's just…they are saying it was drug related and, I don't know, I thought maybe he might have heard something or knows something that could help. He could do like an anonymous tip or something."

"You serious?" Suzanne asks, eyebrows arcing toward the sky in protest. "First you call the guy I love a d-bag, and now you're calling my brother a murderer?"

"Oh my god, no! Of course I'm not saying that. But let's not pretend we all don't know he's heavily involved in dealing. I'm just saying he might *know* something—he could help solve a murder, give Joe's family some peace, that's all."

"I just don't understand why you'd immediately assume my brother is involved. I don't get it, Layna. I said I was sorry and that I believe you about last night, even though Kat told me how you really feel about Hunter. And now it's like you're *trying* to pick a fight again or something, and—"

"Wait, *what?*" Layna yells, her head snapping toward Kat.

Kat stares at the table, eyes wide and lips pressed in a thin line, as though she can suppress the incrimination that's already been exposed.

"For the last time," Layna hisses through gritted teeth, "I do *not* like Hunter! Never did. Never will."

Neither one of her friends respond, nor do they look convinced, and she can feel the anger swelling in her gut at their obstinacy. The idea that she could like *Hunter,* especially after what he did. Could they actually think she was enjoying herself? She closes her eyes and breathes deeply through her nose the way she was instructed. But the scene from last night begins to replay in her mind, the feeling of helplessness and panic as he trapped her against the wall. His lips crushing hers and making it difficult to catch a breath. She *hates* him, and she hates that her two best friends can't see the truth of it. They can't understand it, just like they can't understand her anymore. No one can. The fury and loneliness and fear swirling inside of her explode, and she hears herself yell, "Just forget it! Believe what you want and leave me alone!"

She regrets it as soon as it escapes her lips and she sees the looks of shock on their faces. She doesn't want them to leave her alone. She *wants* them to understand, to know who she is and what she's going through. But how could she explain to them what she herself doesn't even understand?

She clears her throat and says, as calmly as possible, "I'm sorry. I just…really can't deal with this right now."

"Fine," Suzanne grumbles, as she rises from her seat. "Let's go, Kat."

But Kat doesn't move. She scrutinizes Layna for a moment then asks gently, "What's really the matter?"

"I don't know, Kat," Layna huffs, throwing her hands up. "You tell me. You seem to have all the answers."

Kat's face falls and she stands up to leave with a defeated sigh. She and Suzanne walk to the front door without another word. Layna doesn't move until she hears it shut behind them. Then she runs up to her room and jumps into her bed, pulling the covers over her head to block out the world.

She stays there for hours, pillow soaked with tears and her mind drifting in and out of an uneasy, dreamless sleep. Her mom comes in to check on her, but she pretends to be asleep. Moxie also comes in for a visit, pawing at the covers over Layna's head, until she gives up and settles in at the foot of the bed.

Around dinner time, her mom opens her door again, and Layna can smell the bowl of New England clam chowder in her hands. Her favorite comfort food. Her mom sets the bowl and a packet of saltines down on the nightstand and sits on the edge of Layna's bed, lightly patting Layna's shoulder.

Layna reluctantly emerges from beneath her covers. The sky outside her window is giving way to dusk, stretching shadows across her room.

"You hungry, baby?" her mom asks softly.

"Not really," Layna responds.

"Well, you should try to eat something if you can. How are you feeling? Do you want to talk?"

"I'm okay, Mom, just tired. But thanks for the soup," she says, sitting up in bed and picking up the bowl. As she crumbles some saltines into the soup, her mom presses the back of her hand to Layna's forehead, and Layna gets a whiff of the subtle, flowery perfume she wears. She hears Moxie purring at the foot of the bed and feels the steam from the soup drift up toward her face as the bowl warms her hands. The familiarity of it all comforts her, and she settles into the moment, seizing it with all of her senses and committing it to memory.

"I'm sorry you girls are fighting," her mom says. "You've had kind of a rough day today, huh?"

If she only knew the half of it. But Layna just shrugs and answers, "It wasn't the best."

"Well," her mom says, patting the covers over Layna's knee, "you get a pass today, but tomorrow you need to get back to studying, okay? And in the meantime, I'm here if you want to talk. I know things have been rough for you lately, but it will get better, I promise. You're a strong girl, stronger than you realize. You just keep your head up, okay?"

Layna's troubles are far past the reach of her mother's well-meaning reassurances, but she gives her a feeble smile of thanks anyway.

"And don't forget, Jim and I leave for the cruise on Wednesday so I'm going to drop you off at Kat's on our way to Bayonne. I spoke to Mrs. Taveras this morning and she's very excited to have you for the week." She sighs and adds, "I still wish you were coming with us, baby. It won't be the same without you."

It was meant to be a family trip, but after Layna left Mount Hope, Dr. Nettles advised against it. Her mom tried canceling, but Layna and Jim conspired to turn it into a romantic getaway for the two of them. Their lighthearted scheming is actually what made Layna finally decide he's a keeper. Plus he's been great about the whole insanity thing. Mostly because he knows how to keep things light—the kind of guy who can fill a room with his positive vibe and contagious laughter. But Jim owes her a favor for all that co-scheming, and now she has one to ask of him. Because now it's vital that she be here on Wednesday night and not at Kat's. So she'll cash in her favor and persuade (blackmail) Jim to persuade her mom to let her stay home alone one night and have Mrs. Taveras come pick her up on Thursday morning instead.

As her mom shuts the door behind her, Layna turns on the television, trying not to think about the studying she needs to do tomorrow. She has her three main finals starting on Monday and she's barely started reviewing all her material. Concerns over school seem so far away, but there is nothing she can do about the more important stuff until Wednesday. Wednesday, when she and Blake will try to carry out their half-hatched and potentially moronic plan. Whatever happens after that is out of her hands.

CHAPTER

5

The next three days drag by in an agonizingly slow haze. Layna spends most of the time with her nose in her books, pulling off some superhero level concentration, or otherwise taking finals. Their elective courses are over, and those periods have been replaced with study hall so students can have extra time to prepare for their exams. The unusual schedule makes it easier for Layna to avoid Suzanne and Kat and unwelcome conversations, but their absence gnaws at her with each passing day.

She gets her share of sideways glances and backhanded whispers about what happened at the party. But it isn't as bad as she feared, likely, as Suzanne had predicted, because of everyone's somewhat morbid obsession over Joe's death. They had a moment of silence at school on Monday and a vigil was held in the park on Monday night. There's been a lot of speculation and rumors and dramatization of what might have happened that night. Layna makes sure to avoid most of it.

She's been having nightmares about it enough as it is—though nothing like the original dream itself. And no more shared dreams with Blake, anyway.

She sees Blake only once in passing as she leaves school on Monday. Their eyes meet from across the hall and he gives her a nearly imperceptible nod, but they don't speak to each other. She's simultaneously grateful to him and ashamed of herself for this unspoken acknowledgement of the way things have to be within these walls. In that moment, everything about being in school feels fake and trivial and wrong. Like he's out of place here—like they both are. He now occupies a space in a stranger, more complex part of her world. A part she is anxious to return to, no matter how much it may scare her. That's where the answers are, and she doesn't know how much longer she can bear to be kept in the dark.

When Wednesday finally does arrive, Layna can hardly contain herself long enough to make it through her last exam. Not even the tidal wave of summer euphoria from the departing students is enough to distract her from what she and Blake have planned for the night.

When she bursts through her front door that afternoon, she hears Jim's booming voice coming from the kitchen and sees suitcases lined up in the foyer. Jim and her mom leave in an hour for the cruise. Her mom has been an absolute bundle of nerves since Sunday, trying to make sure she has thought of everything and is leaving Layna safe in their absence. Jim did his job and used his wily charms to convince her mom to let Layna stay home alone the first night. Layna is honestly surprised he pulled it off, but only Jim could have such sway over a woman as stubborn as Julianne. Of course, it's on the condition that her annoying neighbor, Ms. Fitzsimmons, would be able to come check on her before nightfall.

Ms. Fitsimmons is fifty-three, single, and has two passions in life—reality television and talking about reality television. She will talk you to death if you are unfortunate enough to cross paths with her. Literally, one time a guy had a heart attack and died in her driveway right in the middle of her monologue about the latest on some show about immigrant fiancés. At least that's what Layna heard, and it didn't surprise her in the least. Even her mom, who would be willing to talk to a tree just so as not to offend it, won't leave for work in the morning until the coast is clear. But death by gossip is a risk Layna is going to have to take tonight for the greater good.

She hears her mother's laugh echo from the kitchen and feels a wave of gratitude for Jim's ability to effortlessly dispel her anxieties. Layna walks into the kitchen, where they lean toward each other across the corner of the island, their hands clasped and their heads inches apart. Her mother is beaming in a way that makes her look ten years younger, and she wears a colorful summer dress that brightens the whole room. Jim wears a customary plaid shirt, paired with uncustomary cargo shorts and boat shoes.

As Jim notices Layna, he shouts, "Hey, look who it is, the high school senior! How does it feel to be three quarters of the way through high school, Colonel?" She smiles at the nickname he gave her the very first time they met. He told her later it was because she had a very 'commanding' presence that inspired confidence, and it gives her a little boost of assurance now in anticipation of what this night may bring.

"It feels great," she says, grinning broadly as she goes to greet him. He wraps her in a bear hug, and it makes her feel so safe that part of her wants to abandon the entire plan and just make them stay here with her.

"Oh, don't remind me, my baby is growing up so fast!" her mom says, as she takes her turn hugging Layna.

"Now, now, Julianne," Jim teases, "don't you go feeling old on me. We've got to play the part. We're young, we're carefree, we're going cruising! And you're already doing so well *looking* the part," he says, as he grabs her by the hand and spins her. She laughs as he dips her and plants a kiss on her lips.

Layna sits in the kitchen chatting with them until the car comes to take them to the cruise port. Jim helps the driver load up the car as Layna's mom turns toward her and takes her by the shoulders. "You're sure you're okay with this?" she asks again.

Layna rolls her eyes in lighthearted exasperation. They've been through this twenty times. "Mom, I'm fine, I promise. We're going to check in every day through email. Ms. Fitzsimmons is going to be checking in on me tonight, and Mrs. Taveras is coming to pick me up before noon tomorrow. You told Officer Clarke that you were going to be away, so now the entire block and the police department all know you don't trust me, which is super embarrassing, by the way. And I have the emergency cash you gave me, and I'm seventeen. Please stop worrying."

Layna's mom winces at the litany of her anxious tendencies. "Well, it's precisely *because* you're seventeen that I'm worried," she replies, as she tucks a lock of Layna's golden hair behind her ear. Her brows knit in their telltale stitch as she asks, "You promise you've been feeling okay? No...episodes or anything lately?"

Layna nods, trying to keep the guilt off her face. "I promise."

"And promise me you won't do anything reckless, and you'll be safe, and if anything comes up and you need us to come back, just tell me and we'll get off at the next port and take a plane home, okay?"

"Promise again," she replies, giving her mom a long hug.

"And don't forget to take your medication," her mom adds, as Jim runs back over to give Layna a hug goodbye and shuffle Julianne toward the car. He salutes her as he climbs into the car, and Layna continues to wave as it disappears down the street. The second it turns the corner out of sight, she runs inside and pulls her cell phone out of her bag to call Blake.

For the last hour, Layna has been frantically pacing the foyer. The sinking, orange glow winks through the trees that line the western side of her property. Moments of daylight left, and Blake still hasn't arrived. She starts to wonder if maybe he's abandoned her and she will have to face the intruder on her own tonight. There is no way of knowing exactly what time the man will show up—once darkness falls, it's fair game.

Ms. Fitzsimmons has already blown through—a cyclone of musky perfume, red lip liner, leopard print, and hairspray. Of course she made herself at home for well over an hour, explaining to Layna in excruciating detail all about the latest season of *The Bachelor*. She finally got sick of the one-sided conversation and retreated back to her vodka and her lounge chair and her shows.

As soon as she was gone, Layna ran upstairs to change. She pulled on a black pair of yoga pants and a black, zip-up hoodie. It was still warm out, but the temperature was dropping, and she knew it would be an unusually cool summer night. She replaced her favorite purple sneakers with her black Nikes. Tying her hair up into a messy bun, she assessed herself in the mirror. The only thing missing was some black war paint on her face. She was as ready as she was going to be.

Layna stops her pacing to look out the window and watch as the last light of day dissolves behind the trees. Her heart darkens with the sky.

She is alone. Again.

But as she starts to turn away from the window, she sees him gliding up the street on his skateboard. As swift and smooth as a bird in flight. She feels everything leaping inside of her at once—relief and fear and hope and dread. She yanks open the door as Blake jumps from the skateboard and ditches it on the lawn. He leaps up the first two steps and pauses when he sees her waiting at the door. "Anxious much?"

"*Late* much? What took you so long?" she demands.

"Sorry, my parents made me eat dinner with them," he says, rolling his eyes. "They dropped me down the street at Todd's. I told them I was sleeping over."

"Alright, well, come in then." She steps aside so he can walk past, scanning her street before shutting the door to be sure no one is watching. She isn't sure whether the effort comes more from fear of her mother finding out or the students of Caledon High finding out.

"Nice place," Blake announces, as he glances around.

"Oh—uh, thanks," Layna murmurs, suddenly hyper-aware that she is alone in the house with a boy at night. She's fantasized about a variety of such scenarios over the past couple of years, but this to-catch-a-killer situation definitely did not make the cut.

"Well, I guess we should get started," Blake says, as he peers out the window at the darkening sky. He is wearing a weathered, black t-shirt—this one without any band logo—a pair of dark, baggy jeans, and his black Vans. She has the feeling everything he owns is just some variation of this outfit.

He puts his backpack on the ground and unzips it, revealing a pile of webcams that would each fit in the palm of a hand. On the side of each device, there is a label indicating:

PROPERTY OF CHS

"How many of these things did you take?" Layna asks, as she looks into the bag over his shoulder.

"You told me to get as many as I could take."

"Without them *noticing*. There are like ten cameras in there. You don't think the school will notice they're missing?"

He scrunches up his nose as he ponders this, and then shrugs. "It's the summer, who cares? We'll return them when school starts back up and no one will ever know they were gone." He carefully takes the little video cameras out of the bag along with a tablet designated with the same label as the cameras. He flicks a switch on each camera as he watches a growing number of images popping up on the screen of the tablet.

"So far, so good. Why don't you go start putting these around the house," Blake says, handing her a camera. "Make sure they're hidden but can still get a good angle."

"I'll do my best," Layna says, gently scooping the rest of the tech into her arms. As she turns and walks toward the study to find places for them, one of the cameras comes loose from her grip.

She curses as it falls from her arms, anticipating the crash and likely the few hundred dollars they will have to pay to replace it. But there is no noise. She looks down and Blake is on his knees next to her, holding it in his hand. He was several feet away when she dropped it, fiddling with his monitor.

"How did you just catch that?" she presses, already knowing what his answer will be.

Blake assesses the camera in his hand as if surprised as to how it got there. "I'm...not really sure. It's happened before, actually. It's like—"

"Time slows down?" Layna finishes.

Blake looks up at her in surprise. "It happens to you too?"

Layna just returns his gaze and sighs. "We better get some damn answers tonight."

Blake gently places the camera back in her arms, and she disperses them throughout the house. He shouts directions to her from the foyer on which way to position them based on the image coming through on the monitor.

Layna turns off all the lights in the house and reconvenes with Blake in the foyer. They head outside with the remaining three cameras. Blake places one of the cameras among the shrubbery lining her front porch, then runs around to the back of the house to place another. The last one he puts in his pocket as she follows him back inside to enter the garage.

"Have you done this before?" Layna asks, as Blake lifts the garage door as slowly and quietly as possible.

"What, opened a garage door?" he quips.

Layna puts her hands on her hips and glowers at him. "No, this, all of this with the cameras and stakeout and stuff."

Blake finally gets the garage door up and looks back at her with an impish grin.

There are stories inside his smile. Secrets and questions and answers that suddenly have Layna on an irresistible hook. How easy it'd be to get lost in that smile and everything it might hold. But instead, she reigns herself in. She is used to feigning disinterest in others, and it comes easily enough.

"You know what? Maybe I don't want to know what you do in your spare time."

"Maybe you don't. Let's just say in the few months I've been here I've already spent enough time in the video production room at school that they sort of let me do whatever I want with their stuff," he boasts.

Layna rolls her eyes. "Okay, show-off, so have you ever backed a car out of a garage?"

"Well, no. But how hard can it be?"

Layna groans as Blake opens the car door and places the last camera on the dashboard, facing out, then he holds his hand out to Layna expectantly.

She stares at it, fearful for a moment that he has wildly misinterpreted the situation. *Does he seriously expect me to hold his hand right now?*

"Keys, please," he chirps.

"Oh, right, sure," Layna replies, deflating with relief or embarrassment or something. "Maybe I should back the car out. You told me you've driven your dad's car before, but if you haven't, then I might as well do this." Layna never got her permit like Kat and Suzanne did in the fall. Her psychiatrist had advised heavily against it. And if she was being honest, Layna wanted no part of trying to control a deadly machine when she couldn't even control her own brain.

"I *have* driven my dad's car, just not out of a garage. Pretty sure the same rules apply."

Layna scrutinizes him. "You seem entirely too chipper for the occasion."

"I like a little adventure from time to time, don't you?" he says with a shrug.

Layna can certainly empathize with that. Adventure is something she has craved from a young age. But the unsettling thought of their mystery man snooping around her bedroom is too fresh in her memory, and her apprehension outweighs any sense of true adventure.

As if reading her thoughts, the smile vanishes from Blake's face and his ears flush red. "Wow, I'm sorry, I'm...I'm being a total jerk," he splutters. "That guy broke into your house and I'm over here making this into some stupid game."

"No, no, it's fine," Layna says. "It's easier to think of it that way now that I have company." She offers a smile, but he doesn't return it, clearly ashamed by his tactlessness.

She fishes her mom's car keys out of her pocket and drops them into his hand, then heads out the garage door to help guide the car out. Over at Ms. Fitzsimmons' house, the multicolored, flashing lights shining through her curtains indicate that her television is on. She is probably already on her third or fourth martini and hopefully won't notice the covert activity occurring next door.

With Layna's direction, Blake slowly inches the car out of the garage with the lights off. It's a tight squeeze, but luckily there's not much maneuvering involved to get it to the bottom of the driveway. Blake spins the wheel to back it up beneath the tree across the street. Though he goes up on the curb at one point, the car escapes the experience unscathed. Hidden in the shadow of the tree, they now have a good vantage point of the front of the house from the street.

Layna opens the back door and slides into the backseat as Blake turns the car off. He opens his backpack again and pulls out the monitor and two small, cylinder-shaped objects. He checks the monitor to make sure the night vision is working properly and twists to face Layna in the backseat.

"This is pepper spray," he says, handing one of the cylinders to her. "Be really careful with it, and make sure the nozzle is pointed away from your face if you're going to spray it, otherwise you'll wish you were dead. Trust me. And there's a little safety button—here—that you have to slide over before you use it, otherwise it won't work. Got it?"

"Uh...maybe you should handle the scary death-spray," she says, gingerly handing it back to him. "I have my own weapon of choice, one I will not accidentally shoot myself in the face with."

Blake takes the spray back with a shake of his head. "And what's that, your good looks?"

"Ha ha, very funny." She gives him a mischievous grin as she reaches under the front passenger seat, pulling out a wooden baseball bat.

"You're kidding? What are you going to do with that, bash his head in?"

"Or his knees," Layna replies with a shrug.

"Yikes. I think I might be kind of scared of you."

"As you should be," she replies, smacking the bat into her palm for effect. It's heavier than she expected and hits harder than intended. She wrings the sting out of her hand as Blake throws his head back with unabashed laughter. Not the reaction she was going for. But the sound of his laughter opens something up inside of her, and when it dissolves into the night, she feels somehow empty, wishing for it back.

They take up their stakeout positions, leaning back against the driver side doors to watch the perimeter of her house through the passenger side windows. They play Twenty Questions to pass the time, which Blake is delightfully terrible at, and before long, the night presses in on them as the moon melts into the clouds. The only streetlamp is down at the other end of the block, and Layna's eyes strain to search for movement.

"No night vision goggles in your bag of tricks?" she goads.

"Caledon was fresh out of those, I'm afraid. Maybe if I were still in Philly." He says it with a touch of darkness, and Layna isn't sure if it's directed toward Philly, or toward Caledon for not being Philly.

She looks at him around the side of the driver's seat and realizes that, while she may know Blake's deepest secret, she knows almost nothing else about him. Except that he likes angry bands, angry t-shirts, and skateboards, which he'd also probably like to be angry if they had emotional options.

"So, you're from Philly, huh?" she probes.

"Yeah. Lived there my whole life. Until we moved here end of March." He casts narrowed eyes at her and asks, "Why? What, are you a Mets fan or something?"

Layna scoffs at the idea. "Um, *no.* Just curious. I could care less about baseball."

"Uh, careful there, champ. You're currently holding a baseball bat in your hand that you intend to use as a weapon. Don't want any bad baseball juju."

"Ha, this bat has *all* the good juju, just like its owner."

"Whose is it?"

"Jim's, my mom's boyfriend and one of the nicest humans on the planet."

"Oh, your mom has a boyfriend? What about your dad?"

Layna glances at him, astonished at his brazenness. Coming from anyone else, she might have been offended. But on Blake, it's somehow endearing. Someone who she instantly labeled as a total introvert turns out to lack any kind of standard social filter once he opens up a bit.

With convincing sincerity, she replies, "Oh, my dad's fine with it. He's fine with all of her boyfriends."

Blake quickly looks away, nodding politely in response. He adjusts his glasses with obvious discomfort as he turns his attention back toward the monitor in his hands.

"Well, you know, they're swingers, so it's no big deal. My mom is fine with his girlfriends too," Layna adds for good measure.

He snaps his head back to look at her, his jaw slack. She can't help but burst into laughter at his reaction.

"I'm totally kidding, you idiot. My mom isn't married. My father left before I was born."

"Oh." Blake breathes a sigh of relief. "Thank God. I mean—no, not thank God that your dad left. Damn, that came out wrong. I meant...you know, I just didn't know how to react to...You know what? I'm going to shut up now."

Layna snorts with laughter as Blake's ears deepen to a violent shade of magenta. "I knew what you meant," she offers with a smile.

Layna pulls out her phone and puts on low volume the *Stakeout* playlist she created for the night. Though it pained her to do so, she included a couple of singles from *Warbringer* and *Obscura*. Blake rewards her with a delighted grin as he rocks out to a particularly creepy song called *Hunter-Seeker*. Other than an Eminem lyric battle, they sit in relative silence for a long time, listening to the tunes and searching the deepening night and the monitor for any sign of activity.

After a while, Layna pulls out her backpack, unzipping it to reveal its contents.

Blake hears the rustling and looks over the seat. "What have you got in there?" he asks buoyantly.

"See, without me, you would have forgotten the most vital supply of this stakeout," she replies, pulling out two wrapped deli sandwiches, a couple of bags of chips, and cans of Diet Coke.

"Genius move!" he exclaims.

Blake unwraps his sandwich as he asks Layna, "So…you never knew your dad?"

Layna pops a chip into her mouth and shakes her head. "From what I can remember, it's always just been me and my mom. And my grandparents for a little while when I was younger, and then a few years ago, Jim."

"Does it bother you?"

"I mean, I guess I'm sort of curious about who he was and stuff. And I feel bad for my mom because it's been really hard on her, raising me alone. But we make it work. And having Jim around has been so great."

"So do you know what your dad looks like? What if this mystery man is your dad, like, coming to check up on you?"

Layna chokes on a gulp of soda and barely manages to keep from spitting it all over herself. She turns to look at Blake, who is watching her with an amused smirk.

"The guy is like late twenties, tops! Didn't you see him in your flash?"

"Maybe he's like Benjamin Button or something and he's aging backward. Would have made for a good story, don't you think?"

Layna laughs and rolls her eyes. "Oh yeah, great story. 'Hey, Dad, nice to meet you, thanks for repetitively burglarizing my home. Sorry for crippling you with my bad-juju baseball bat and blinding you with pepper spray. Want to go share a sundae?'"

Blake's smile widens. "That's Hallmark material right there."

Layna shakes her head in mock disapproval. "Well, what about you? What's your family like?" She sees at once that it is the wrong direction to take the conversation. She can imagine an invisible wall sliding back up between them.

"Oh, just me and my parents. We're all pretty busy most of the time, especially my dad. He works really late hours most days with his new job. But we all get along alright."

It comes out like a rehearsed speech, and Layna knows she shouldn't, but she decides to try and probe a bit further. "Is that why you moved to Caledon? He got a new job?"

"Yes and no. Lots of reasons. Partly it was because of me."

"What do you mean?"

"Well...back a few years ago when my night terrors were getting pretty bad, the docs said that a suburban environment might do me good. You know, get out of the city, away from crime and pollution and all that. Mom bought it, Dad thought it was a bunch of bull, so we decided not to. Until he got laid off in January and my mom convinced him to look for jobs here. He got one pretty quick but the timing kind of sucked because I had to transfer mid-semester. Luckily, I had enough time to get caught up before finals since all of my friends are back in Philly and I've had basically no social life. It hasn't been the best year."

Layna hangs her head and examines her fingernails. "It definitely has not been," she replies with a rueful sigh.

Blake has had it even harder than she has this year, and she and her friends had to go and be jerks to him and make it even harder. If she had only known what he's going through, and the strange experiences they have in common…but that's no excuse. She wishes she could just be one of those kind, empathetic people who knows when someone is in pain and can be supportive instead of tearing them down. And what will happen when she and Blake return to school in the fall? It's day one of summer and she can already tell they are likely going to be spending a lot of time together figuring out their messed-up lives. Walking down the halls of Caledon High, will she be able to pretend once again that she doesn't know him?

A beep from the monitor disrupts her penitent reverie, and they both jump at the sound. "It's showing activity in the kitchen," Blake whispers.

Layna stares intently at the little square on the screen. She holds her breath as she waits to see the figure of a man appear. When an eye flashes across the screen, she and Blake both gasp in surprise. But then the image shifts to show whiskers and a tiny nose sniffing at the lens and Layna sighs with simultaneous relief and disappointment. "It's just Moxie," she says, as Moxie paws at the camera, knocking the image askew.

Blake chuckles. "Well, at least now we know the sensors are working." He yawns and looks at his watch. Layna does the same and notices it's already getting close to midnight.

"Blake?"

"Layna?"

"Remember the shadow that we saw surrounding the guy in the park?"

"Yeah, I remember."

"Have you ever seen it before?"

Blake studies her over the seat. "*You've* seen it before."

Layna hesitates, still unsure whether she wants to admit this out loud. Saying it out loud makes it real. "Including that guy, I've seen it three times since Friday, and once before that, back in November." She tells him about what happened at the party with Hunter, and then what happened to her afterward when she confronted Suzanne.

Blake lets out a long breath and runs a hand through his waves of black hair. "What the hell is going *on*?" he murmurs. "Also, that guy sounds like a real dick, Layna. I'm sorry that happened to you."

"He is," she says with a sigh. "And thanks. So, do you remember seeing the shadows before too?" Layna asks.

"I'm...not sure. When I saw it in the park, it seemed really familiar to me, but I couldn't place it. But there's no way I wouldn't remember seeing something like that. Not if I was awake for it anyway. I think maybe I've seen it during my terrors, and that's why part of me recognizes it."

"It's certainly scary enough to belong in a night terror," Layna mutters.

"What about November?" Blake asks. "You said you saw something once in November."

"It's kind of a long story."

"We've got time," he encourages.

She's tried so hard to keep this all a secret from everyone she knows. But ever since she met Blake, the truth has been itching to be free. And it feels right sharing it with him now.

"Okay. I've been having some…problems this year. Part of it is I have these episodes. They start with this intense feeling of restlessness, like a compulsion almost. Like I'm not where I'm supposed to be and something is pulling me away. And sometimes it's so strong that it's like I split in two—my mind goes off to wherever, and my body stays where it is—but I can't remember what happens afterwards. I've had a few of them lately, none as crazy as what happened in November. Like once at Kat's while we were watching a movie, and once while I was on a run with my mom. She said I just suddenly booked it and flew off into the woods like something was chasing me. Another time, actually, was the other day at school…when Suzanne was yelling at you. I don't know why it happened. I never do. My psychiatrist—yeah, I have a psychiatrist, whatever—calls them fugue states."

She pauses to await the typical knee-jerk judgment at the mention of a psychiatrist. But there are no looks of pity or discomfort. If anything, he just seems contemplative.

"Wow," he says, eyes trained on the roof of the car. "Kind of sounds like…day terrors. If there is such a thing." He returns his gaze to her and nods. "Go on."

"Okay...um, don't tell anyone this, okay? *Any* of this." She waits for Blake to agree before continuing. "So, back in November, I'm in the middle of a math quiz and I get one of those compulsions. So, I ignore it. They hadn't been really strong up until that point and I could usually shake it off. I try and finish my quiz, but I just start seriously zoning out for like full minutes at a time. Before I know it, I'm in the hallway and I don't remember how I got there. So I turn around and start walking back to class. Then after that, the next thing I know it's like ten hours later and I'm sitting in a Delaware police station, handcuffed to a chair, and screaming my goddamn head off."

"Woah, that is...crazy messed up," Blake whispers.

"Tell me about it. From what people helped me piece together, I left school, walked downtown, hopped on a local bus to Trenton train station, and caught a train to North Carolina. I guess I didn't have enough cash to get me to North Carolina, so my ticket only took me to Delaware. That's where the conductor tried to make me get off, and apparently, I refused. Not politely."

"*Yikes.* And you seriously remember none of it?" Blake asks.

"Not any of that, no. Usually these things, these 'fugue states' or whatever, only last a couple minutes at most. But *ten hours*? I remember when I was walking back to class, it felt wrong, like there was something really important I had to do and that I was running out of time. But there's only one thing I remember from the entire ten hours I'm missing. And that's the shadows. A bunch of them, the same as the one we saw. But just an image, and like this overwhelming feeling of dread, and that's it. My first rational thought when I came out of it was that I got abducted by aliens or something. You know, you hear those stories about people who lose time and whatever. But it was so disorienting that I started panicking and had a full-blown panic attack right there in the station. I don't remember anything clearly for days after that because I was so disoriented, and terrified, and drugged, I assume. Because I at least can remember the people from Mount Hope coming to take me away."

"What's that?" Blake asks.

"A mental health residential facility...a.k.a., loony bin, insane asylum, mental institution. Whatever you want to call it. The cops called them because of all the stuff I was saying and doing when I was out of it. I got kind of violent, I guess, hitting and kicking. The officer who arrested me put it all in his report, which they had me read over and over at Mount Hope to try and get me to remember. It said I was incoherent and screaming about how the shadow people were trying to kill us all. That they were going to murder someone, and I had to stop it otherwise we would all die. I must have been pretty desperate to fight the cops. Supposedly I even bit one of them. Took four transit police just to get me off the train. And then I slipped out of my handcuffs in the back of the cop car and made a run for it when we got to the station. Skinny wrists," she adds, holding them up.

"Yikes again," Blake gasps. "Remind me not to mess with you." He shakes his head in amazement. "I wonder what you were trying to do—who you were trying to get to."

"I wish I could remember," Layna says. "Believe me, the people at Mount Hope tried to make me. I was in that place for two weeks. Some kind of protocol or something while I was waiting for my hearing. They had to make sure I wasn't a danger to myself or others,

111

especially after I assaulted police officers and all. They barely even let my mom see me, and when she did, I was all drugged up. It was…rough. For both of us."

Layna's mind wanders back to the common area at Mount Hope. The face of the young, obese guy who always sat down across from her in the recreation room. The stubble on his chin, his unrelenting grin, and the way he stared at her. She could still smell his stench of body odor and piss. The memory of the smell still wakes her up some nights and she thinks she's back there. That he's come to her room to kill her. Or worse.

"You should have seen some of the people in there," Layna says with a shiver. "They put me in with psychopaths. They treated me like I was one…and I started to feel like one. I wasn't eating or sleeping. I could barely even remember who I was. And my psychiatrist I was assigned to after that, well, she had to diagnose me with something, I guess. Had a label for everything—fugue states, delusions, hallucinations. She says that they're early onset symptoms of…she thinks that I have…um, schizophrenia," she finishes in an almost inaudible whisper, as though keeping the word confined to a tiny space will make it somehow less true. She can't believe she just admitted it out loud. The darkest, deepest part of her. Her greatest fear and most shameful secret. One she hasn't even told her best friends. And now she's gone and said it to someone she has only known a few days.

She steals a cautious glance at Blake, who is studying her over the seat. She can't read his expression. But then in a gentle voice, he replies, "Layna, you're no more schizophrenic than I am a prophet. We both saw those shadows. We both experienced that dream. There is something happening to us. We'll figure it out. And we'll find out what happened to you on that train and where you were going. I promise."

She breathes in deeply as his words nestle gratefully into her heart, replacing just a little bit of the fear that has resided there for the better part of a year. Hearing someone else tell her she's not crazy—someone who now knows her whole messed-up story—fills her with genuine hope that her life may not be doomed before it's even taken off.

Another beep from the monitor breaks through the silence. Blake lifts the tablet closer to his face to see what's set it off. "Movement in your bedroom."

Layna leans over the seat to look. "It's probably just Moxie again," she whispers.

They both keep their eyes trained intently on the feed from her bedroom, but there is no movement. Several minutes pass and Layna gives up, sure that it was just her cat.

But then he is there. Emerging from the shadows like a ghost.

"Oh my god," she whimpers. "It's really him. He's in my bedroom again! Quick, press record!"

Blake hastily hits the record button, and somewhere hidden in her bedroom with that man, a little red dot begins blinking.

"I don't get it," Blake whispers, looking up and down the street. "How did he get past us and the rest of the cameras? And how are we supposed to get his plates if he isn't in a car?"

"I don't know," is all Layna can manage in response.

She grips the bat tightly in her hands as she watches the man move about in her room, picking up objects and putting them back down. His fingers graze the photographs stuck in her vanity mirror. He moves to her desk and starts picking up the papers and things strewn across it. He doesn't read any of the documents. He just holds them for a moment and places them back where they were. Then he opens a drawer and pulls out a small, rectangular piece of paper, and Layna can see him visibly jolt. He continues to stare at the slip, then he stuffs it in his pocket.

"What was that?" Blake asks.

"I have no idea. It looked like maybe a receipt or something. Seriously, what is he *doing*? Maybe he is some sicko who gets off by going into girls' rooms just to touch all their things," Layna says with disgust. She feels an overwhelming sense of disappointment at the possibility, and she realizes how much weight she has put into the belief that this man is somehow connected to the events of the past few days. She will be utterly lost if that turns out not to be the case.

They watch as he turns toward the door, then vanishes from the shot.

"Woah, what just happened?" Blake asks, as he messes around with the tablet. "The feed must have glitched or something."

"Just like what happened last time…there and then gone in a blink," Layna whispers. "It looked like he was just about to walk out of my bedroom, so why isn't he showing up in any of the other screens? Are the cameras still working?"

"It looks like they are."

They both stare at the screen intently, waiting for him to reappear in one of the other shots, but he doesn't. Layna doesn't wait more than a minute. She slides over to the passenger side door to get out.

"Wait!" Blake yells, as he grabs her by the shoulder. "What do you think you're doing?"

"I'm going to check it out. I can't let him get away."

"Uh, yes you can, Layna. It's not worth your life. He could seriously be a psychopath—with a gun! Let's just stick to the plan and follow him when he comes out."

Layna feels trapped between recklessness and hopelessness, panic brewing inside of her as the opportunity for answers seems to slip through her fingers. "What if he gets past us? Then what? We aren't going to get another chance at this. Please, Blake," she pleads. "I need to know what's happening to me. I *need* to."

Blake looks from her to the screen, and back again. He shakes his head, then says "Okay, you win. Let's go get some answers."

Blake grabs the pepper spray as he follows Layna quietly out of the car into the darkness. As their eyes get accustomed, they creep slowly toward the obscure outline of the house. Layna scans the shadows, clutching the bat tightly in her hands.

As they step onto her front lawn, she stops in her tracks, sensing something she can't explain.

"What is it?" Blake whispers.

"I don't really know," she answers, her voice unsteady. "I just feel like he's...here."

They both stand frozen, the only sound that of their own quickened breathing. Layna feels all the hairs on the back of her neck standing up and has to fight the urge to look back over her shoulder. Whatever she is sensing, it lies ahead, not behind.

And then, he is there in front of them. Five feet away, his back to them, occupying a space that Layna swears a moment before was only empty night. She can't quite contain her shocked gasp, and the man spins around to face them.

Blake moves quickly, shoving Layna behind him with one arm and holding the pepper spray out in front of him with the other, aiming it at the man's face.

"Woah, woah!" the man yells, as he holds up his hands in defense. "Slow down with that thing. I'm not here to hurt you." He speaks with a gruff voice that would sound more menacing if not for the brogue it carries, which somehow softens it. His shaggy, blond hair falls in his face, and the shadow of stubble that Layna observed just days ago has grown into an unfeasibly full beard. Like it's been more than mere days since he last stood before her. He looms over both of them, standing at least six feet tall with an imposing, muscular build that, again, should be more threatening under the present circumstances.

Just in case her sense of the man is dead wrong, she grips the bat more tightly in her sweaty palms, holding it high over her shoulder like she knows what she's doing.

"Oh no? What the hell were you doing snooping around in her house then?" Blake retorts.

"I wasn't snooping, I..." He sighs. "It's a really long story, but I'm just trying to help."

"We're listening," Layna snaps.

"Well, I don't have time for explaining," the man says impatiently. "Sorry for scaring you—thought you'd be away. But I've got to be on *my* way." He tries to sidestep them, but Blake lithely matches his movement, blocking his path and lifting the pepper spray higher. The man stops in his tracks.

"Not a chance, man," Blake retorts. "You really think we're going to let you just walk away? You snuck into her house. Twice. At the very least, we're calling the cops on you. Unless you give us some reason not to. Like answers, now."

Layna glances at Blake in surprise. She didn't realize he was capable of such boldness but she is immensely grateful for it at the moment, seeing as her mind has pretty much gone blank. The man silently studies the two of them, and Layna's skin starts to crawl as though she can feel him poking around inside her head like he did in her house.

"Aye, maybe I do have answers for you," he finally responds. "Maybe I know something about what you two have been going through. But right now, there is somewhere I really need to be. I can meet you somewhere first thing tomorrow morning."

Blake begins to protest, but Layna puts her hand on his arm to stop him. Without any prompting on their part, this guy just admitted he knows they're going through something. She might not trust him, but she trusts her intuition. Blake looks back at her and she gives him a slight nod, hoping to convey her confidence.

"Fine," Blake says to the man. "But you're not going anywhere until you tell us your name."

"And give us a phone number where we can reach you," Layna adds.

"Name's Desmond Hart," he says brusquely, and then he rattles off a number.

"Wait, wait," Layna urges, maintaining her grip on the bat with one hand as she reaches into her back pocket for her phone. He repeats the number for her, and she saves it as *Intruder*.

"Where would you like to meet?" Desmond asks.

"Izzy's. Downtown," Layna suggests.

"What time do they open?"

"Seven, I think."

"Be there at seven, then. I can't promise I can give you the answers you're looking for. I can promise you this, though, there is quite a bit to this world that you don't understand. But you will."

Layna and Blake glance at each other as Desmond sidesteps them and heads toward the street. Blake still holds the pepper spray out in front of him as he shifts his body to keep himself between the man and Layna. "Hey, man, if you don't show tomorrow, we're going to the police," he warns.

Desmond assesses them over his shoulder. "I don't doubt it," he replies, before continuing on into the night. Once he is out of sight, they relax, dropping their weapons to their sides.

"Well, that was...disturbing," Blake murmurs.

Layna just shakes her head in awe of the whole encounter. She is vibrating with adrenaline and a mounting euphoria as his words reverberate in her head. *There is quite a bit to this world that you don't understand. But you will.* There *is* an alternative explanation for everything, and she and Blake and this guy, they're all connected somehow.

Layna and Blake head back to the car for their things, and then Blake manages to maneuver the car back into the garage. They clean it out and collect the cameras from around the house. By the time they've finished removing all evidence of the stakeout, it is only a few hours until sunrise. They collapse onto the couches in the living room, and Layna dozes into a light sleep, with questions about what tomorrow may bring chasing her into her dreams.

CHAPTER

L ayna scowls at Blake over the rim of her Carolina sweet tea. He is tapping his spoon on the table to an irritatingly monotonous beat but pauses mid-stroke as he looks up to find her watching him. He gently places the spoon back on the table and clasps his hands together so tightly that his knuckles turn white.

It's twenty-two past seven, and Desmond still hasn't shown up to Izzy's. Layna trusted her instincts last night when he told them he would be here. Now she has no idea what possessed her to make such an idiotic decision. She has already tried calling him several times on the number he gave, but it goes straight to an indistinct voicemail.

They sit at a table near the door, jumping each time the bell above it jingles. They arrived over a half hour ago, but she and Blake have barely spoken a word since they sat down. Layna knows that if she opens her mouth, she will compulsorily speak the only thing on her mind—that Desmond isn't coming. She is not ready to admit defeat out loud just yet. So they continue to sit in silence as she drains the last of her sweet tea and Blake picks absently at his blueberry muffin.

The café section of Izzy's fills with its early morning customers all going about their completely ordinary days. Layna watches them with a swell of envy at the simplicity of their lives. She lowers her head and pinches the bridge of her nose, attempting her breathing technique to soothe her anxious mind. When she looks back up, she flinches in surprise.

Standing just behind Blake, silently observing them, is Desmond. He walks over to their table and turns one of the chairs around to sit in it backward. Layna looks across at Blake, whose blue eyes gleam with relief.

Desmond appears slightly haggard as though he hasn't slept either, his olive-green eyes bloodshot. And maybe he hasn't—he is wearing the same faded jeans and grey, cotton t-shirt as he wore last night. Layna opens her mouth to berate him for being late, but the waitress comes over and cheerily asks if he would like anything.

"A strong coffee would be great, love," he responds. Despite his worn appearance, the waitress blushes a little and offers him a warm smile. As she leaves to retrieve his coffee, he addresses Layna and Blake. "Sorry I'm late. Bloody hell of a night, er—morning. Um..." He rubs his hand over his eyes and then looks at both of them in turn, silently assessing. "Well, alright, shoot."

"Alright, Desmond. So, why were you in my house?" Layna asks.

"Please, call me Des. And as good a place to start as any, I suppose." He sighs, and it is clear he is unprepared for this conversation, despite the advanced warning. "So, I have this ability," he begins, but the waitress walks back over to deliver his coffee. She lingers there attempting to make small talk, but she must sense Layna's death stare because she gives up quickly and moves on to her other customers.

When she is out of earshot again, Des leans in and repeats more quietly, "I have this ability. I can…read people…by touching objects that belong to them. That's what I was doing in your room, I was trying to read you."

"Be serious. What do you mean you can 'read people?'" Blake retorts.

"It means…" Des pauses, seeming to struggle with how to put it into words. "It means I can understand a person—no, it's more than that. I will *become* them—their feelings, their thoughts, their memories. But only relative to that particular object. Got it?"

Layna doesn't respond, her brain too busy trying to absorb the impossibility of such a thing.

"Give us an example," Blake asks, less skeptical, it seems, due to his own unique ability.

"Alright…so a woman's necklace, let's say. If I were to do a reading on it, I would get a whole cross-section of her life—every time she's ever worn or touched it, the strongest being the first and last time. So I would experience the memory of getting the necklace, feel what she felt, think what she thought, and the same thing for every time after that. But the entire life of the thing sort of hits me all at once, within a matter of seconds."

"How about *not* a hypothetical example," Layna suggests. "Like one of my objects."

"Ah, sure. How about the plastic souvenir cup on your desk that you keep your pens in? The one you got at the beach when your mom took you, Kat, and Suzanne to Cape May last summer for the weekend. I felt the way that you changed over the last year relative to that object. From your excitement the night you got it, when the three of you snuck down to the clubhouse by yourselves, to your wistful recollection of the night, to an almost tortured longing..." He trails off as he seems to get the sense he's said too much.

Layna stares at him, her mouth agape as she tries to unclench the knots in her stomach. She didn't actually expect him to answer, and now she wishes she hadn't asked. She feels invaded, sullied, and she fights the urge to run from Izzy's to protect her mind against the intrusion. But it won't help. He's already broken into it, just as he broke into her house. So he is a burglar after all—a mind burglar. A memory thief.

"So..." Blake continues uncomfortably. "How do you not go crazy, getting people's feelings and memories like that whenever you touch stuff?"

Des snorts and shakes his head. "It isn't whenever I touch stuff. I have to concentrate really hard if I want to get more than just an errant emotion or image. I've got to put myself into a kind of trance that I've had to practice for years to perfect. Like this coffee cup I'm holding. If I wanted to, I could read it now and know what that waitress was feeling when she handed it to me."

At this, he gives Blake a roguish smile and a wink. But the gesture is lost on Blake, whose expression remains frozen in a state of contemplative disbelief.

Des clears his throat and continues, "But reading unpossessed objects like this is different. Because it doesn't actually belong to anyone, nothing would come through strong enough for me to read except the last person who touched it."

"Okay, so then why were you trying to 'read' me?" Layna asks coolly.

"Well...because that's what I was told to do."

"By who?" Layna demands.

"People who have more authority than I do, and that's all I'm going to say on that," he concludes.

"You said you would give us answers," Blake argues.

"Actually, I specifically said I may *not* give you answers, didn't I, mate? I can only tell you what I can tell you."

"Alright, fine." Layna huffs. "But at least tell me what you were trying to find."

Des hesitates and looks between Layna and Blake. "Well, I've been reading both of you, to see if you were being activated."

"Wait, you've been in my house too?" Blake cries.

"Relax, kid. It was only once and it's not like I take any—"

"You take our memories, that's even worse," Layna seethes. "And besides, you're lying. I saw you take something from my desk last night. What was it?"

That catches Des off-guard. "How do you—were you watching me?" he asks with a slight hint of amusement.

"We had cameras set up around the house recording you," Blake explains, his expression smug. "We were going to turn it over to the police if you didn't agree to help us. Which is still an option, by the way."

"Ah, that'd be blackmail," Des rebukes.

"Said the *burglar!*" Blake exclaims, gesturing to Des.

"Oy, keep it down, will you?" Des whispers, glancing around. "I told you, I didn't take anything—not anything of *value*," he adds, looking at Layna.

"What was it you took from me?" Layna demands again.

She doesn't like the intense way he studies her. She doesn't like the idea that he could be reviewing the memories he stole from her right at this very moment. A shudder runs down her spine. Des seems to sense her unease and averts his eyes. He takes a sip of his coffee and finally responds, "It was a train ticket."

It's as though he reached across the table and punched her right in the stomach. *Of course it was.* She looks at Blake, who also seems to understand what it means. It was the train ticket to Delaware. "Why…" Layna says breathlessly. "Why that train ticket?"

Des still does not meet her eyes as he answers, "It was just the best evidence that you were being activated."

His words are clipped, and Layna's instincts tell her this isn't the whole truth. But before she can question it, Blake jumps in. "Why do you keep saying that? What does that mean—we're being activated? Activated for what?"

Des drops his voice lower as he replies, "I truly am not permitted to get into the specifics right now. You are both going through a change. Blake, I know you've been having prophetic dreams, and Layna, you've been experiencing the beginnings of some bloody strong telesthesia. I know that you're struggling to understand this. But hear me now—neither of you are going crazy, alright? I know how it can feel at the beginning. But I promise you, you will understand everything soon enough."

Layna knows she should be frustrated by his cryptic responses, disturbed by his intrusion into her life, but mostly, she just feels a deep sense of hopeful gratitude. She blinks away the tears of relief that pool in her eyes as she finally allows herself the coveted internal affirmation: *I am not a schizophrenic.* If this guy is right, then Dr. Nettles was wrong, and she will never have to see her or hear that word ever again. It's something else that's happening to her. Something bigger. It has to be.

"But…no, you can't just leave it at that," Blake retorts. "What change? What will we understand?"

"Listen, I've already said too much. I must be going a bit mental for even coming here," Des argues. "I just…I felt what you were both going through and, hell, I'm not your Guide, it's not my place to tell you any of this. It's too soon yet. For now, just take each day as it comes and don't do anything daft," he grumbles, as he rises to leave.

Layna grabs him by the arm, gripping tightly. "No! Please don't leave. We have so many more questions!"

"Sorry, kid, it just…can't be my problem," he says, as he gently pulls his arm from her grip and then walks to the door.

Layna looks at Blake, who seems at a loss for what to do. After a moment of hesitation, he blurts, "No way! Come on." He pulls out his wallet and drops a few dollars on the table, then grabs Layna by the hand and they run out the door. Des turns the corner down an alley just ahead of them, but as they whirl around it after him, he is already gone.

Blake cries out in frustration and smacks the building with the side of his fist as Layna cries, "How does he keep *doing* that?"

She leans back against the wall and slides down to sit on the ground, hugging her legs and resting her head on her knees. Blake slumps down next to her.

"Now what?" he asks gloomily.

Layna watches the dark clouds rolling toward her on the horizon as she rides her bike home. She and Blake parted ways at Izzy's, where he had an Uber come to pick him up. Mrs. Taveras is due to pick Layna up in just a couple of hours too, even though her normal life seems unfathomably out of reach at the moment. She's going to have to conjure the world's best game face after that incomprehensible meeting. Words from their conversation with Des tumble around in her head. *Activated, telesthesia, prophetic dreams, guides.* She struggles to come up with some logical explanation for it all, but her mind is foggy from lack of sleep.

A foreboding rumble of thunder rolls across the sky as Layna reaches the end of her street, and the first drops of rain fall as she runs up the steps to her house. She slips off her sneakers and reads the email from her mom, who is headed to their first port and seems to already be having a wonderful time. She returns a mom-friendly response, which this time carries almost no version of the truth.

Layna plods up to her bedroom as the summer squall begins raging in earnest outside. Her room seems foreign, like it's taken on a life of its own. She gazes across the objects on her dresser and desk, trying to think of which ones she saw Des touch and what memories he would see, or feel, or whatever. Her stomach turns at the idea. She walks over to her bed and plops down into her pillow face-first. She needs to shower and pack for the week at Kat's house, which is going to be super awkward considering they haven't spoken in days. But before she can muster the willpower to get back up, her mind wanders into a dream, and she drifts off to sleep before she can even think to stop herself.

She is jolted awake by an earsplitting crack of thunder. Her eyes pop open and she looks around wildly in confusion. She is standing in a dead-end alley, becoming quickly soaked by the buckets of rain falling from a sky torn open. The raindrops feel strangely hollow on her skin, the thunder tinny in her ears.

She doesn't remember how she got here. She doesn't even know where *here* is. She scans her surroundings and finds a door—what looks to be a back door to some shady dive bar. Hoping to seek shelter inside, she slogs through at least an inch of standing water, noticing also that she is barefoot. Just as she reaches the door, it explodes open and a group of men come tumbling out into the rain.

Layna shrieks and lunges out of the way as the men stagger together toward the middle of the alley. No one seems to notice her, though she is standing only a couple of feet from them. They block the door and her path to the street, and something about the way they look at each other tells her to hide. She backs herself behind one of the dumpsters lining the wall of the building that just spat this jumble of testosterone into the street.

Through the sheets of rain, she watches as two of the people— one of whom she realizes is a rather harsh-looking woman—stand back to back at the center of four others who encircle them. They all wear the kind of patched-up leather Layna associates with motorcycles and pocketknives and bar fights.

The couple at the center drop to their knees, pleading with the others, as two of the men pull switchblades out of their pockets. Layna squeezes her eyes shut, wishing that the stereotype didn't have to be *quite* so damn accurate this time around.

There is a bright flash of light on the back of her eyelids that she attributes to the raging storm overhead. But when she opens her eyes, her gaze is drawn to the opposite end of the alley where she sees a human-shaped form radiating a glow of deep indigo.

Blake.

She remembers everything the instant she sees him. She was in her bed, and now…she's in a dream. And if it is anything like Trent Park, what she's witnessing is really happening…somewhere.

Someone else is going to die. And you're hiding behind a dumpster.

Layna attempts to get Blake's attention from her hiding place as he watches the predatory circling of the men around their victims. And then she realizes something. The boys in the park, they didn't notice her when she screamed and ran out toward Joe. The men falling out of the bar just now, they didn't see her when she was standing mere feet from them. She is witnessing these incidents through a dream, and these people...they can't see her.

She steps out into the alley. Blake's eyes shift toward her, bewildered, and she thinks of the way he sees her—a glowing, golden version of herself. But the men don't turn. She shouts over the wind and the rain, "It's a dream, Blake! We're in a dream!"

Recognition registers on Blake's face, but then it quickly shifts to dismay. She sees it too. All four of the circling men have transformed into the shadowed version of themselves—ashen skin, pitted eyes, and all.

The two unarmed men restrain their victims as the two wielding knives lift their weapons to their victims' throats. The couple has fallen silent, and it is now only their eyes that cry for mercy. Layna's feet move without volition, as though something is pulling her through the rain toward the group. This time, she is certain she is witnessing this for a reason. Just like in the park, she knows she is meant to stop it. But how is she supposed to do that when they can't even see her?

Blake appears across from her, just on the other side of the group. He raises his hands, signaling her to stop, and that's when she gets her answer.

The indigo glow around Blake's body pours toward his center and bursts from his outstretched palms, like the bolts of colored lightning that dance inside the plasma balls in the physics classroom. When Blake's light collides with the shadows around the men, the darkness flickers, and the men falter with their weapons. Blake doesn't seem to have noticed what happened. He can't see it—his own light. But he can see hers. And maybe that means...

Layna holds her hands out in front of her just as Blake did. He was trying to signal her to stop and so, channeling all her will toward the single thought of obstructing these people, she screams, "*Stop!*"

Blake's reaction is confirmation that he witnessed the same thing she just did. She indicates to him to hold up his hands again, and they both do so, this time shouting in unison. The shadows around all four men fade before their eyes. The men holding the knives step back from their victims and lean together in brief consultation before pocketing their weapons. The other two take this wordless instruction and release the couple, throwing them toward the street. They scurry away through the flooded alley on all fours, before clambering to their feet and running desperately toward their second chance at life.

Blake moves out of the way of the fleeing man and woman as Layna drops her hands to her knees and doubles over with relief. They did it. She doesn't know what they did, or how they did it, but *something* definitely just happened.

She straightens up to flash Blake a victorious smile, but it falters on her face. The shadows of two of the men didn't simply disappear like the other two. Instead, they seem to be pooling in the water around their feet, spreading outward directly toward Layna on one side and Blake on the other.

Layna is frozen, watching as the shadows seep away from the men's bodies and collect into a seething blackness that begins to rise like smoke from the water. The two amorphous clouds grow higher, seven, eight feet into the air, and begin to take on an enormous, humanoid shape. Legs, torso, shoulders, arms...

Heads. Heads that appear to be looking directly at her and Blake.

Layna stares into the empty void where the thing's face should be and gets the distinct impression that she is peering into hell. There is a sensation like falling, shrinking, becoming less...becoming nothing...

She stumbles backward as she regains control of her sensabilities. There is a dissipating coldness, like unseen tentacles retracting from her mind and back into the dark depths of its body.

Then it starts to move toward her. Slowly. It lifts its legs like it is learning how to take steps. Steps that are entirely unnecessary, as it instead seems to glide eerily over the flooded concrete. She glances past it as the four men disappear back through the door from which they came, and at the other shadow figure that glides toward Blake at the opposite end of the alley. His shining, blue eyes look past his pursuer and are locked on Layna. The look of horror on his face registers an unfortunate truth that she noticed before but had forgotten.

This alley is a dead end.

She whirls in a circle, her eyes searching for another way out. There is nothing. This nightmare thing stands between her and the only exit to the street. The only door to the building. The only means of escape. She's trapped.

No. No, this is only a dream. I will just wake up—it can't hurt me. Layna tries to convince herself it's true. But everything inside of her is screaming that this thing is a threat, dream or no dream. She can feel the death that it brings, licking hungrily at her mind, beckoning her to give up, to give in to darkness. Instead, she is overcome by a will to live. By the sudden knowledge that she is meant for something more than dying in a goddamn alley behind a bar in a dream.

She spins away from the approaching monstrosity and runs for the brick wall closing off the alley behind her. She calculates as she approaches the wall. It's too high to jump up and catch the ledge with her hands. It's too smooth to climb. She needs a boost.

Dumpster.

Veering for the dumpster that sits two feet from the wall, she tries breathlessly to scramble up onto it. But the rain makes the metal slick, and her hands and bare feet slip feebly as she tries to pull herself up.

She spins around. The creature is close to her now. Blake is at the other end of the alley, screaming her name as his assailant moves in on him, forcing him backward into the street. He can run away, but he can't get to her.

Help is not coming. Get yourself out of this.

Layna backs up, pressing herself into the space between the dumpster and the wall. She places her hands on the lid and jumps up, pressing one foot against the brick wall and the other on the dumpster, wedging herself between them.

The thing is steps from her now.

Using every ounce of her strength, she straightens her trembling legs, her body rising toward the top of the brick wall. And as she gets close enough, she lets go of the dumpster, throwing the weight of her body toward the wall. Her fingers catch onto the ledge and she pulls herself up. She can just see over the wall, can just see her freedom and her life stretching out before her. And then her feet slip out from under her and she goes tumbling to the ground.

Pushing the mop of wet hair from her face, Layna finds the creature towering over her. Cornering her. Impossibly huge, impossibly malevolent. She stares at it numbly, unable to move. Unable to save herself. It raises its arms, which begin to lengthen. Morphing, reshaping themselves into five-foot-long blades that look like death. Though its face is no less the hollow void it was when she first looked at it, she swears she can sense a sinister smile forming on non-existent lips as it prepares to strike.

I have to wake up. Wake up, Layna! Wake up!

Layna is blinded by a bright flash of light as a loud crackling sound fills her ears. She's sure the alley has just been struck by lightning, but as the brightness fails to dissipate, she squints through the light to see a radiant, golden figure standing near the doorway of the bar. He holds up both his hands as he moves toward the massive shadow figure, and powerful bolts of lightning shoot out from his palms as the air crackles around them.

She watches as the thing gets pummeled with the endless barrage of light. It raises its arm-blades in defense, and the next two bolts evaporate them into nothingness. At this, the creature spins in on itself, collapsing inward to a pinpoint, then vaporizes in a small puff of darkness.

Layna looks back at the glowing figure, and now unobstructed, she recognizes him. It's Des. Only this version of Des looks like he just walked straight down from Olympus. He glows gold, just the way Blake described her own glow.

Blake. Layna jumps to her feet and looks toward the street with dread. She doesn't see Blake or the other shadow figure anywhere.

"We need to help Blake!" she yells at Olympus-Des, and then breaks into a sprint down the alley, trusting him to follow.

The wind and rain have abated slightly, and she yells Blake's name as she reaches the street, spinning wildly to find the direction he went. As Des appears by her side, she gets an inexplicable compulsion and turns left. "He went this way, a couple blocks down!" she exclaims, as she and Des continue in an all-out run down the sodden streets.

"Here!" Layna cries, as they reach the large parking lot of a supermarket. Blake is there, darting between the cars as the creature closes in on him. She races toward him as he turns mid-stride, holding his palms out in front of him in a desperate attempt at defense. Small bursts of dim light escape from his hands, but it seems to do little damage to the creature.

Finally, having reached the metal fence of the lot, Blake can go no farther. He stops and grabs a half-crushed supermarket crate, holding it up in front of him like a shield. Des disappears from Layna's side, and with a soft pop, he reappears in between Blake and the creature. Once again, he attacks it with the unrelenting bolts of golden lightning.

Layna reaches them just as the thing collapses in on itself and evaporates. Blake, who was shielding his eyes from the sudden blinding light, lowers the crate to look at them. His eyebrows climb up his forehead as he takes in Des' presence, and then he sees Layna. Relief floods his face as he drops his makeshift shield and takes a hurried step toward her.

"Are you okay?" he sputters.

"Um, yeah." She looks down at herself to be sure. "Relatively speaking. Are you?"

Blake nods. "Layna, I'm so sorry."

"For what?"

"I just ran away and left you back there with that thing," he croaks.

"Blake," she says, shaking her head, "there was literally nothing you could do."

"I should have thought of something," he murmurs. "I couldn't think. It was like the thing was trying to get in my head, and I couldn't do anything but run. What happened back there?"

"Des," she murmurs, as she looks around for him. He is squatting against the metal fence with his head in his hands. The drenching rain has calmed to a feeble drizzle, and Layna hears the distant rumbles of dying thunder as she walks over to crouch in front of him. The golden light surrounding him is beautiful and ubiquitous, save for a scattering of scar-like, dark splotches where no light emanates. Like a dozen tiny solar eclipses.

"You saved us," she says, offering a grateful smile as he lifts his head to look at her.

"Aye," he breathes, "but from what?"

"You mean you don't know what those things were either?" Blake asks over Layna's shoulder.

"No, I know perfectly well what they are. Those were the *umbrae*. I've just never seen them do *that* before."

137

"The what? Do what?" Layna says, shaking her head in confusion.

"I've never seen an umbra detach from its human counterpart," he whispers, his brows pinched with concern. Then he looks up at Layna and Blake. "And, you two, what are you even doing here? How did you know how to...Is this the first time this has happened to you? And how are you lucid? None of this makes any bloody sense," he finishes, dropping his head back into his hands.

"It doesn't make sense to us either," Blake grumbles. "Maybe if you had given us more information before instead of just disappearing—"

"Blake," Layna reprimands, "he just saved our lives, remember?"

Blake looks slightly abashed, but he doesn't offer an apology. "Did he though? What is even happening?"

"Do you two know you're dreaming right now?" Des interrupts.

Layna doesn't quite know how to respond to that. "I mean...yes? But are we?" In the back of her mind, Layna starts to feel a tugging sensation, and the world begins to get fuzzy.

"This isn't the first time this has happened. It was a few days ago when we saw a kid get murdered in Trent Park," Blake explains. "We didn't know we were dreaming that time, but when we woke up and found out it really happened, we found each other and realized we were, like, in the dream together. Just like now, I guess. We had—have—no idea what any of this is. That's one of the things we wanted to talk to you about."

"Both of you...a few days ago...impossible," Des mumbles, staring at them in wonder. His eyes drift away, unfocused and deep in thought.

"Des?" Layna prods.

"Okay, this is what we need to do," he replies. "Once you wake up, I want you to pack a bag with some clothes and any essentials you'd need for a few days. Pack light and pack fast. I'm going to send an Uber for you as soon as I wake up. It'll get Layna first and then Blake. Got it?"

"What are you talking about? We can't just leave," Layna says. "My mom is away, and I'm supposed to be staying with my friend and her family. What am I supposed to tell them? And what is Blake supposed to tell his parents? And where are we going? For how long?"

"I'll explain on the way," Des says impatiently. "You're just going to have to trust me. And don't worry about your friends and your parents, we'll take care of them."

"What do you mean you'll take care of them?" Blake retorts. "You're not going to hurt them, are you?"

Des snorts. "Oy, kid, who do you think I am, the mafia? No we're not going to hurt them. We're just going to do a harmless little...uh...a mind trick. Not to worry."

Blake looks worried.

"Now, when I say so, I want you both to shut your eyes and count back from ten. And while you do that, I want you to think about where you fell asleep, and picture yourselves waking up there. When you reach 'one', open your eyes, and you should wake up. Got it?"

139

"Should?" they answer in unison. The tugging sensation in Layna's gut gets stronger as she pictures her bed.

"Just call each other when you get up to make sure you're both awake and get your bums ready on time. Now go." With that, he vanishes before their eyes and they are staring at an empty space.

"Well, okay then." Layna looks at Blake uneasily and then closes her eyes and does as instructed. She doesn't even get to five when the tugging sensation deepens and her eyes burst open to find herself not in bed, but in a heap of blankets on the floor of her room. Now that she is awake, the dream slips away and is replaced by a creeping doubt about the authenticity of what she just experienced.

She struggles out of her blankets into a seated position and sits there for a minute before grabbing her cell phone from the nightstand. Her thumb lingers over Blake's name.

What can it hurt to call?

Before she can make up her mind, her phone begins vibrating in her hand. An incoming call from Blake. She taps the button to answer and hears a breathless Blake on the other end.

After hesitating briefly, Layna whispers, "Hey…did that just—"

"Yes," he answers.

It's enough confirmation for Layna. "Okay, see you at your house in a bit."

"See you," he croaks.

Layna disconnects and sits there on the floor, staring at her phone. Then she gets up and grabs the packed duffel bag stored in her closet, throwing in a few additional necessities—toothbrush, hair ties, face wash—while a mess of thoughts tumble around in her brain, fighting for attention.

She still doesn't understand what any of this means. It *was* a dream. But a dream in which she could affect real life events? Where she could interact with other dreaming people who glow and can shoot lightning out of their hands? A dream in which she can be killed by terrifying shadow creatures?

Layna bounds down the stairs with her duffel bag, startling Moxie out of her cat nap. She dashes back toward the kitchen, with Moxie meowing excitedly at her heels. Layna pours a heaping bowl of cat food into Moxie's dish and fills an extra bowl to be safe. Moxie rubs against her legs gratefully as Layna tops off her water bowl.

"Don't eat all that food at once, okay, little one?" she says, bending down to scratch behind Moxie's ears. "Hopefully, I won't be gone too long. I'm going to get some answers, so wish me luck. Love you, Moxie girl." She gives her cat a kiss on the nose and then heads toward the foyer.

A car horn beeps outside as Layna grabs some extra cash and her bottle of pills from her backpack and shoves them into her duffel bag. Then she pauses, reaching in to remove the bottle. Without a moment's hesitation, she stalks toward the powder room, pops the cap off, and dumps the entire contents into the toilet bowl. With a defiant nod, she presses the handle and watches those hated pink specks disappear down the toilet and out of her life forever. Her bag feels significantly lighter without them, and she allows herself a moment of vindication.

Suck it, Dr. Nettles.

She may not understand it yet, but she's starting to accept the fact that the world is, indeed, much more complicated than she ever imagined.

PART II

"True Wisdom comes to each of us when we realize how little we understand about life, ourselves, and the world around us."

- Socrates

CHAPTER

L ayna watches her life slip slowly away as the train picks up speed. New Jersey, where she was born and has comfortably belonged for the last seventeen years of her life. Caledon, with its charming downtown square, slumber parties with her best friends, their stolen afternoons at Izzy's, her morning runs around the reservoir with her mom, the church she attended on Christmases as a child, the school system that's taught her everything she knows. It all fades from her periphery and becomes ensconced in memory.

Des assured them they would be back in a few days—a week tops. But Layna can sense that when she does return, she will be seeing everything through different eyes, in a different light. She has no idea what to expect as she closes this chapter of her life to begin anew in this unfathomable one she has involuntarily entered. But, despite her apprehension, she feels remarkably ready to face her uncertain future.

Blake finishes shoving their duffel bags into the overhead racks and plops down on the worn cushioned seat next to Layna. Des stepped away as soon as they found a spot, supposedly to attend to some 'important business'. Blake glances nervously up and down the aisle in search of him before leaning forward to bury his face in his hands.

"Are you okay?" Layna asks.

Blake's head pops back up, his eyes incredulous. "Am I *okay*? Of course I'm not okay. Are *you* okay? None of this is okay. Maybe we shouldn't be doing this. Yeah, we should probably just get off at the next stop. This is cra—"

"Alright, alright," Layna says, holding her hands up in surrender. "That was a stupid question. I know things aren't okay. I'm freaked out too. But my tele—whatever you call it—is telling me this is the right thing to do. You want to know what's happening to us, don't you? Well, this guy knows. I mean, yeah, I don't think our lives are ever going to be normal again. But is that such a bad thing? Were you satisfied with things the way they were? Because I know I wasn't. Whatever happens to us now, it is what the last insane year has been leading toward. I can feel that."

Blake stares out the grimy train windows, nodding slowly as she speaks. With a heaving sigh, his sapphire eyes find hers. "Thanks, Layna."

She notices that she likes the way he says her name. There is a fullness to it, like a thawing sip of rich hot chocolate on a bitter winter night. Her hand acts of its own volition, reaching out and finding his. It lingers only a moment before she gets a hold of herself and pulls it back. But his touch leaves behind an electric, tingling sensation that reminds her of the jolt she felt when she first looked into his eyes outside the park.

Blake looks away as the tips of his ears deepen a few shades. "I trust your instincts, so...do you really think we can trust him? I mean, he clearly wants nothing to do with us, and he didn't seem to know what was going on in that alley either."

"I don't know what he knows, but I do think we can trust him. Despite the whole memory-thieving thing. I mean, he didn't need to save us from those things. And even if he doesn't know what was going on, hopefully we are going to talk to someone who does."

Blake nods again, but he remains on edge, leaning forward as he fidgets with his glasses. "What we did with that light in the alley, if what we were seeing was real like with Trent Park, do you think we actually saved those people?"

"I think maybe we did. Do you?"

"I mean, it did *seem* like we stopped those men. It's just..."

"What is it?" she encourages.

"Well, it's just that if we did stop them by, like, channeling the power of Thor or whatever that was...well, that means we could have saved Joe too."

Layna can hear the remorse in his voice, and it resonates inside her heart. She has had the same thought tumbling around in the back of her mind since she awoke from the dream. She doesn't want to admit out loud that Joe didn't have to die. That they could have stopped it. "We don't know that for sure. Maybe we would have just made things worse. Maybe we weren't meant to stop it. We just really don't know how any of this works."

147

"You knew though," Blake counters. "In the park, you knew you were supposed to help…and I stopped you."

"You were just being rational and trying to protect us."

"I was being a coward," Blake mumbles, shaking his head.

Layna opens her mouth to protest, but Des reappears and takes a seat in the empty row across from them. He looks exhausted and more than a little aggravated. "This is madness," he mutters to himself, as he crosses his arms and stares out the window. "Absolutely off their trollies, the lot of them."

"What's the matter?" Layna asks.

"Oh, nothing," Des grumbles. "The Consulate just got it in their brilliant minds somehow that *I* should be your Guide. Makes complete sense to them, never mind the fact that I am a bloody *Scout*, and I have none of the experience or training or, frankly, the patience required to be a Guide. Never mind the fact that you two are…oh, just, never mind. Guess we're just throwing logic and reason out the window now. Fan-bloody-tastic," he finishes with a contemptuous snicker.

Layna and Blake glance sideways at each other, not sure how to respond to his incoherent tirade.

"Um…guide to what?" Blake asks cautiously.

Des makes a pitiful whimpering noise as he rubs his eyes with such force that Layna is worried he will inflict permanent damage. "Guide to *ascendance*." He drops his hands into his lap and surveys their blank faces. "I'm going to be frank. I don't think either of you are ready for this. It's all too fast. But the powers that be…" He shrugs. "Just because you had your First Walk so quickly, doesn't mean we should waste what precious little time we have on you, no offense. The time, might I add, of someone who isn't even a real Guide, who could be out there helping instead of babysitting a couple of—"

"Wow, can you just chill for a second, please?" Layna breathes. "Maybe if you're done feeling sorry for yourself, you can try to see how totally messed up this whole thing is for us right now."

As intended, her reprimand manages to melt Des' irritation, and he bows his head in repentance. She takes advantage of the opening.

"How about you just start by telling us why we can do the things we've been doing?" she asks. "Like apparently being able to interact with each other in dreams, and Blake seeing the future in his, and me with my…whatever you called it—"

"Telesthesia" Des interjects.

"Yeah, right, that."

"Alright. I'm not really sure how I'm supposed to go about all this, but since they're leaving it up to me, we'll do it my way. Without all the bull." He sighs and slumps against his seat, a white flag of surrender. "The reason you can do all of these things is because…you're *Nauts*."

"Huh?" Blake grunts.

Des purses his lips and looks at the ceiling. He leans forward, Layna and Blake mirroring his action so that all their heads are inches apart in a huddle.

"Okay, both of you, like me and like the Consulate, belong to an ancient order—the most ancient order on the planet. The Order of Oneironauts was created and given the power of dream travel to protect our world from the primordial darkness, *Erebus*. Dream traveling is what you two experienced today in the alley. Now that you have, you need to go through the process of ascendance so you can join the Order and fulfill your purpose as defenders of Earth. And it's more important now than it's ever been." Des pauses and looks at them expectantly.

Layna twists her arms into an aggravated pretzel and glares at him. She's not sure what the point is of wasting their time by spoon-feeding them literal nonsense, but Des looks genuinely surprised when Blake erupts in frenetic laughter.

"You're not serious!" Blake yells between breathless guffaws. Layna tries to quiet him as several people turn to look at what has caused the unwelcome outburst. One unpleasant looking woman with purple lipstick lifts her head over the back of her seat to shush them. Blake does not appear to notice.

"C'mon, man, this isn't *Marvel*, it's the real world. Maybe if you said we were part of some government experiment or something, but *that*?" he cries. "Layna, I think we made a mistake. This is getting…"

Blake abruptly falls silent. Layna turns to face him and recoils with alarm. He has gone completely ashen, and for a single, unsteady breath, she thinks one of the shadows have taken hold of him. But his eyes have not sunken into that depthless black. Instead, his blue irises lie beneath a swimming veil of milky-white. A mixture of emotions cross his face in rapid succession like he's watching some unseen movie on fast forward. She reaches out to try to shake him free of the trance and notices that Des has a hold of both Blake's wrists, his own eyes pinched closed in concentration.

"Stop!" she cries. "What are you doing to him?"

She claws at Des' hands, trying to peel them from Blake's arms, but they are locked on as though fastened by an electric current. How could her intuition be so wrong as to trust this man? He is clearly some sort of psycho, and now he's going to kill Blake, and she will probably be next.

Out of options, she opens her mouth to yell for help. But Des abruptly releases Blake and collapses back against his seat, beads of sweat breaking out along his brow.

Layna scrutinizes Blake as his eyes clear and the color begins to return to his cheeks. She grabs him by the shoulders and turns him to face her. "Blake," she says firmly, "talk to me."

He blinks twice and his eyes focus on hers. "I'm okay," he croaks.

"What the hell was that?" Layna demands, as she releases Blake and rounds on Des.

"I'm sorry," Des mutters, his face still pained with the effort of whatever it was he just did. "I told you I'm no good at this, and you two need a crash course if they expect you to be ready in time, which I think is ludicrous anyway. I don't have time to sit here and try to convince you that I'm telling the truth. So...I took a shortcut." He examines Blake for a moment and asks, "You alright, kid?"

Blake swallows hard and returns a wordless nod, his expression flickering between humility and awe.

"I just shared some of the readings I got from Blake's objects," Des explains. "Just a glimpse of what I've seen, what I know, and a reminder that I've been entirely honest with you both. About everything. You already know that you have abilities that are not normal, I don't need to convince you of that. I'm only giving you context. What I'm telling you is the truth. I know it's not easy to hear, but you've just bloody well got to hear it."

Despite the fact that he didn't kill Blake, Layna no longer feels confident in her decision to trust Des. The story he fed them cannot be the truth, but she certainly doesn't want to give the impression that she doesn't believe him and get the same treatment as Blake. Des is looking at her. He can tell she no longer trusts him. She needs to break the tension—ask a question. Her mind latches onto one unfamiliar word he said, and she asks, "Um, okay, so what's Erebus?"

"Erebus is the darkness," Des replies.

Layna raises her eyebrows, waiting for further explanation. But Des just looks back at her blankly.

"That's it?" she says. "Wow, you really are bad at this."

"Right, sorry. Let's see. So you know how you might hear about multiple universes, parallel universes, and that sort of rubbish? Well, there are actually only two universes—our Universe of Light and the Shadow Universe. They're not so much parallel universes as they are inverse universes. Think yin and yang. Everything here in the Universe of Light—from single-celled bacteria to human beings to an entire galaxy—comes from *Aether*, the entity of Light. Likewise, everything in the Shadow Universe comes from the entity of darkness."

"Erebus," Layna concludes.

"Erebus," Des confirms. "And you remember the umbrae from the alley?"

"Remember?" Blake asserts. "Uh yeah...I think we can recall that traumatizing little adventure."

152

"Rhetorical question there, kid, but glad to know you've got your wits back about you. So the umbrae are humanity's counterparts from the Shadow Universe. Everything that exists in this universe has an opposite that exists in the other, matched atom for atom and planet for planet. So for every human being, there is an umbra being. And for each one of the aetherworlds in our universe, there are reciprocal netherworlds in the Shadow Universe. For each to exist, they both need to exist. It's quite a delicate balance."

"So...these umbrae, you're saying that's us, but just like, the opposite of us? From an opposite universe?" Blake asks, taking care not to sound entirely dubious.

"Aye, well, sort of. They're not like us so much as they are empty reflections of us. Unlike humans, the umbrae counterparts are not sentient. There is no sentience in the Shadow Universe, so the umbrae are just mindless extensions of Erebus. See, Aether gave itself to us—to the creation of the Kosmos, and that in turn created sentience. Erebus did no such thing. It doesn't create, it destroys. It hoards its energy and power—the power of Chaos. So umbrae, they have no consciousness, no free will, no sense of individual self at all. They're merely shadows of life. And as beings of darkness, their inherent drive is to consume light, to destroy it. Humans, as I said, are made of the stuff."

"So they want to kill humans?" Layna asks.

"They don't *want* anything. Light simply can't exist where there is shadow. For humans that means...well, you witnessed it yourselves today. With stronger umbrae, the damage can be much worse. The more darkness the human embraces, the stronger their reciprocal umbra gets, and the more power it has to influence them. Whenever a person enters a dark state of mind—rage, fear, hate, greed, despair—they are at risk of channeling their umbra, and the umbra will then influence them to carry out acts of chaos that destroy light. And darkness can spread from human to human like a sickness if the right conditions are met. History is chock-full of all sorts of ghastly events traceable back to the influences of a single, powerful umbra."

"And Nauts…they're supposed to stop all that from happening?" Layna murmurs, trying not to acknowledge how familiar that feels. The boys in the park. The men in the alley. The certainty that it was her responsibility to stop them.

"Aye, we are meant to fight against their destructive influences to prevent our world from tipping too far into darkness. It's impossible to keep out all of the darkness, mind you. But we don't need to. We only need to maintain the balance. We've had a few close calls in the past. The Mongol Conquests, the Rwandan Genocide, the Holocaust, to name a few. A secret war raged within the ones you read about in your history books. *Our* war—light versus dark." Des pauses and looks warily at both of them. "With me so far?"

"Well, we haven't run screaming from the train yet. I'd take the win, if I were you," Blake answers flatly.

Des responds with a monosyllabic chuckle and a faltering smile as he appears to gauge whether they are, in fact, about to jump from their seats and run from the train.

"Question though," Blake continues, raising a hesitant forefinger. "If the umbrae are from another—uh—universe, then how can they be here in ours?"

154

"Well…they're not really *here*. It's complicated."

"Well, un-complicate it," Blake demands.

Des glowers at him, muttering something under his breath about the lost art of respecting your elders. "When you saw them in the alley, they weren't in our world, or even in our universe. And, well, neither were you."

"Come again?" Layna replies.

"You—at least the 'you' that is your consciousness—had left this plane of existence and entered the dreamplane. That's what I meant by dream traveling. You are *cross-dimensional*. It's what makes you Nauts."

Layna tries and fails to conjure up a single, distinct emotional reaction to this information. But her mind is both emptiness and anarchy, a raging echo of numbness in a cavernous space. She looks to Blake to fill in the void, but his expression is unreadable. She tries to imagine that what Des has told them is true. Then she tries to imagine that he's crazy and this is all nonsense. Why do both seem equally plausible?

Des glances back and forth between the two of them as their silence continues. He throws his hands over his face and groans. "Yep. That was too much. A proper Guide would have known when to just shut his bloody gob. Knew this was a terrible idea. I'm not saying another word until we get there."

Layna has no desire to convince him otherwise. She has plenty in her brain to sort out before he says more words that make no sense.

Blake clears his throat. "Do you think you can at least tell us where 'there' is?"

Des looks relieved at his chance to offer a simple answer. "Oh, right, yes. We're going to North Carolina to see the *Senecta*, our eldest Naut. She'd like to meet you."

Layna almost slips right off her seat at the mention of her intended destination back in November. "Did you just say North Carolina?"

"Aye, I did."

Layna has given up on the concept of coincidences at this point. "Des, you said you took that train ticket from my house because it was evidence of me being activated," Layna remarks. "So that means you did a reading on it, right? You know I was trying to get to North Carolina?"

"I did read it, yes," Des grumbles, shifting in his seat.

"Yeah, wait," Blake interjects. "You said you experience what people were experiencing when you read their objects. Is that true even if they don't remember it afterward themselves? Because that would mean—"

"You'd know what I was thinking when I was trying to get to North Carolina!" Layna concludes. Layna and Blake both look at Des in anticipation. Layna will finally get those hours of her life back. She will finally know why she was so desperate to get to North Carolina and what she saw that pulled her there.

But Des shakes his head. "It doesn't work quite like that."

"But that's exactly how you said it works," Layna argues, examining Des as he refuses to meet her eyes. "You're hiding something. Tell me what you saw."

"I'm not hiding anything. I'm not a bloody magic eight ball, alright? I can't always just pop up any answer you want at any given time," Des grumbles, as he rises from his seat. "I need to go follow up on something. Just stay put."

Layna throws her hands up and sinks into her seat. "Why is he always running off?" she whimpers.

"He didn't even take his phone," Blake murmurs, picking up the phone resting on Des' seat. "He's definitely hiding something."

"Yeah, well, we will get it out of him, sooner or later," she huffs.

Blake turns to face her. "Layna...everything he said. I mean, he sounds absolutely, certifiably nuts, I know he does. But..." He hesitates, clearly unsure whether he wants to offer a condition to that statement.

Layna gives him an encouraging nod.

"Well, after what he just showed me, I don't know. I mean, he basically flashed my life before my eyes—like *everything*. He's telling the truth about all of that. And a part of me just..."

"Feels that it's all true?" Layna finishes.

"Yes," Blake breathes.

If it is true, it challenges everything Layna's ever known in her seventeen years of life. But it also means that she's not crazy and she's not alone. It means that she is a part of something...that she is meant for something more. She realizes she doesn't just feel that it's true. She desperately *wants* it to be.

157

Darkness has fallen by the time they finally reach the shoreline along the Inner Banks in the rental car Des picked up in Raleigh. After he disappeared for the latter half of their train ride, Layna eventually slipped into a light, uneasy sleep. Images of the umbrae chased her into her dreams, causing her to jolt awake each time for fear that she'd be trapped and abandoned in some alternate dimension. At one point, stuck somewhere between asleep and awake, she could swear she felt the comforting stroke of a hand against hers. It left behind a familiar tingling that soothed her troubled mind. When she next awoke, the train was pulling into the Raleigh station.

They've driven most of the last two hours in silence, Des and Blake up front and Layna in the back. Layna and Blake both made several unsuccessful attempts to engage Des in further conversation, but he seems to be sticking to his guns about not saying another word. Nothing other than, "The Senecta will help us." He repeated it over and over like a mantra until Layna and Blake gave up and resumed their game of Twenty Questions over the shoulder of the passenger seat. Blake was becoming a marginally better adversary.

As they pull up the gravel drive, Layna can see the structure of a house looming before them, outlined by the silvery moonlight. It is a magnificent, Victorian-style home spanning four somewhat frenzied and mismatched stories. White-washed porches wrap around the two lower floors, and here and there along the upper floors are a sprinkling of balconies. There are five distinct roof lines and rising from the center of the house is a rounded tower like the top of a lighthouse, which seems to stand guard over the rest of the construct. This house could well be the product of some giants' game of Jenga that its players abandoned midway through.

Imbalanced as it is, it is charming in its imperfection. And there is something else about it that captivates Layna. Something intangible…a pulsating deep inside its core. Like the house has a heartbeat that is calling out to her own heart. No matter what Des saw or didn't see from that ticket, she is certain this place has something to do with what happened last November.

"Wow," Blake exclaims. "This place is massive. Is it some kind of hotel or something?"

"It's a home," Des replies distractedly, as he gets out of the car.

"How many people live here?"

"Right now, just two."

Layna opens the door, and she is hit with the smell of saltwater so strong she can taste it on the back of her tongue. She hears the breaking of waves on the nearby shore as a gentle breeze rolls off the water and tickles along the hairs on her arms and neck. Before she even steps foot out of the car, she has already fallen in love with this place.

They climb the front steps, each one creaking beneath their feet in humble expression of their decades of steadfast dedication. Des opens the front door without knocking, revealing a grand foyer. A red, Persian rug lavishes the dark-stained, hardwood floors, with matching wood trim lining warm, mahogany walls. A crystal chandelier hangs above their heads in the center of the room, and a grandfather clock stands in the corner, ticking with zealous determination.

"Come on back to the kitchen. Y'all must be starving," shouts a pleasant voice from somewhere inside.

"Just drop your stuff on the landing for now and follow me," Des tells them, as he walks through the archway to a dining room rivaling the elegance of the entrance. As they follow Des through another archway, they find themselves in the kitchen, where a woman stands over the stove with her back to them. She is busy chopping herbs and dropping them into a large, metal pot.

The kitchen has a homier feel, with white-stained, wood-paneled walls and blue cabinetry and the pleasant scent of cooking spices, mint, and clove. On the other side of the large peninsula that cuts the room in half is an antiqued wooden table with bench seating. The back of the room is covered in floor-to-ceiling windows through which Layna can see the moonlight dancing across lively ocean waves. A back door leads out to a porch overlooking the private stretch of waterfront.

Des greets the woman at the stove by planting a light kiss on her cheek. She is a tall, willowy figure, nearly matching Des in height. Her long, coarse, silver hair is woven in a loose braid that hangs down her back. She chuckles at Des' greeting and gives him a gentle pat on the cheek. Layna notices that although she has the bearing of a young woman, her leathery hands tell the story of someone much older.

"Layna, Blake," Des says, "this is Lady Anora."

The woman drops the last of her herbs into the pot and turns to greet them with a smile. But as her eyes land on them, the cutting knife she is holding falls from her grasp and clatters to the floor. Des grabs her by the elbow as she takes an unsteady step backward. Layna tenses, unsure of why they have evoked this reaction from their hostess.

"Anora, what's wrong?" Des asks, voice edged with concern.

"Nothing. Nothing, darlin'," she replies in a voice like velvet. Des leads her around the peninsula and helps her sit down at the kitchen table. "Forgive an old lady, Desmond, I didn't mean to startle you. I just turned around too fast, that's all. Please, all of you, have a seat," she says, beckoning to Layna and Blake to join her. "The soup will be done shortly but help yourselves to the sandwiches."

Layna sits before a delicate platter of assorted finger sandwiches—ham and cheese, hummus and avocado, tuna salad, cucumber and cream cheese. Her stomach rumbles in sudden recognition of how long it's been since she's eaten anything. She takes several of the sandwiches and places them on the plate that's been set in front of her.

"Thank you so much," she says, as she looks up at the elegant woman across from her. Lady Anora returns Layna's smile, but with a glint of disquiet in her distinctive, grey eyes. Up close, Layna observes what a curious contradiction the woman is. An ageless antique, she is hale and radiant, though her skin is lined with untold decades of a fulfilled life. Her silver hair nearly matches her eyes, which both stand in striking contrast against her cocoa skin. And while her very presence commands deference, she exudes a maternal warmth that endears Layna to her instantly. It is not unlike the beautiful asymmetry of the house, and Layna concludes that never before have home and host complemented each other so completely.

"Lovely to meet you both, Layna, James—"

"Oh, actually, I go by Blake," he corrects.

"Ah, yes, that's right," Lady Anora says kindly. "You two must have a million questions."

"You aren't kidding," Des snorts.

Lady Anora looks at Des with amused disapproval. "What has Desmond shared with you so far?" she asks them.

"Oh, just that it's our destiny to join some ancient order that protects the world from a dark entity from another universe by crossing dimensions in our sleep and battling it. Or, you know, something..." Blake answers, his voice dripping with irony. Apparently, he is in no mood for pleasantries.

Lady Anora raises her eyebrows and gives a sideways glance at Des, who responds with a rueful grimace. "I told you they asked a lot of questions."

"Well, of course they did," Lady Anora says with a good-natured chuckle, turning her focus back to them. "We've upended your summer and whisked you away to some stranger's home in another state. Layna, I know your telesthesia told you it was right to do so, and so it was. But I thank you both for having the courage to come here and for placing your trust in us. And I do apologize for the haphazard introduction we have given you. These are unusual times. But while our Desmond may not be the most tactful Guide, what he has told you is the truth."

"Well, what if..." Blake wavers. "What if we don't want this to be our destiny? What if we don't have what it takes to be a...a Naut, or whatever? What if we want to, you know, opt out?"

Lady Anora and Des share a glance full of shared meaning and unspoken words. "Yes, Blake. People have denounced their power before. It is possible," Lady Anora replies. "However, it is no easy task. For a Naut to deny their destiny is to deny their very existence, their purpose for being. While some have chosen this path, they do so with a hollowness inside that cannot be filled with anything else. They float through life as lost wanderers, seeking fulfillment but never truly finding it. A number of those folks ended up returning to us, but they were not the same."

Layna looks at Des as Lady Anora speaks. He stares at his hands clenched together on the table, his face unreadable. Layna wonders if perhaps he is one of those who once chose such a path.

"Well, that doesn't sound like much of a choice," Blake remarks, his words barbed.

Lady Anora bows her head in agreement, unruffled by Blake's prickliness. "Truly, it may not be much of one, but it is still yours to make. All we can do is give you the information you need to make it. And I will say that while you are rather young to begin ascendance, you are both undeniably strong. And I believe you can do it."

"But how can you know we're strong?" Layna asks. "You don't know anything about us."

"I have a special sort of sight…I can see the true nature of things—of people. That is *my* gift. I believe you will move quickly through ascendance."

"What does ascendance involve? I mean, what do we have to do?" Layna asks.

This time, Des is the one to give an answer. "You need to train on the *Tripartite Powers*. And we need to begin first thing in the morning."

"Well, time is of the essence, yes," Lady Anora agrees, "but you two will need to get some rest. You've had a trying day, and you have another one ahead of you tomorrow."

"Before I even attempt to sleep again, I need to know more about what happened to us today," Layna protests. "Is it going to happen again? And if it really was only a dream, are we even in any real danger? I just still don't get any of this," she finishes, unable to keep the frustration from lining the edges of her voice.

"You will understand everything in time, darlin'," Lady Anora responds. "But for now, I will try to answer your questions thoroughly enough that you will feel safe here with us tonight."

Lady Anora stands and returns to the stove to retrieve three bowls of soup, and she sets them down before each of her guests before continuing. "Yes, you were in a dream. However, for us, dreams are not as you have heretofore known them. You're familiar with the fact that most dreams occur during REM sleep?"

Layna nods as she tries to focus on Lady Anora's words rather than the slurping sounds coming from the two boys devouring their soup next to her.

"Well, look out at that ocean. You can see it—the sand, the waves, the moonlight—even though you are separated by a barrier. The windows allow you to see through the barrier of this house to what lies on the other side. Dreams, in the simplest sense, are a window. A window through the many barriers of the human mind into other worlds, other dimensions, even other times. And though most humans tend to focus on the window's reflections of their own selves— their memories, hopes, and fears—dreams allow all conscious beings to glimpse the true nature of reality. This is all thanks to a connection that bridges the Universes of Light and Shadow called the *Ouroboros,* and it has existed since time immemorial. Colloquially we may refer to it as the dreamplane. It is an astral dimension that lies in between the inverse universes. You may think of it as…a wormhole, of sorts."

"Aye, see there," Des says, gesturing emphatically at Lady Anora with his spoon. "Better when she explains it, eh? You got it now?"

This time, Layna's nod is nothing but a lie. She remembers learning some stuff about REM sleep in health class. They must have skipped over the whole part about wormholes and other dimensions.

Lady Anora gives Des a demure smile as she continues, "So, now everyone has access to this window during REM sleep. But the important difference—what makes us Nauts—is what occurs during non-REM. Once we enter this phase of sleep, that window becomes a *door.* For ordinary people, the door is shut, and that is why they rarely dream during non-REM. But for us, the door is open. It is during these dreams that our consciousness can project into the Ouroboros. And it is there that we are able to encounter the umbrae as they attempt to destroy light in our world through the dark channels of human minds."

"So Layna and I were able to see those things happening in the alley and the park," Blake begins, "because our minds went through this door into the…dreamplane? And that means we weren't really *in* those places, which is why we could see people but they couldn't see us? Like a one-way mirror."

"Precisely," Lady Anora replies. "These experiences were the first times the door opened for you. We refer to this fondly as the First

Walk. Typically, Activates such as you have already been identified by a Scout and are well into their training by the time they have their First Walk. You two advanced so quickly that you were not afforded that luxury."

"But…if it was only our minds traveling into the dreamplane, and our bodies were asleep in our beds, what could the umbrae really have done to us?" Layna asks.

"You two saw for yourselves that we can channel light as a weapon against them, yeah?" Des responds. "Just in the same way, they can channel darkness. And…who rightly knows what they could do in their detached form like we saw today."

"Yes, well, today's anomaly aside," Lady Anora says, giving Des a pointed look, "this channeling of darkness takes the form of what we call shadowspears, and getting hit with one during dream travel *can* be deadly for us. You see, we Nauts are actually a unique balance of light and shadow, which is what allows us to withstand the forces of the Ouroboros. Shadowspears are not an attack on your body, they're an attack on your light. It destroys the balance and allows the darkness to consume your light."

"Basically, it can obliterate your consciousness," Des inserts. "But thankfully, there is the tell-tale vortex that appears just before a shadowspear is launched, and I'll be training you to evade their attacks."

Layna's alarm must be plastered on her face, because Lady Anora quickly adds, "That being said, Desmond and I will not allow you to project into the Ouroboros again without our supervision until you've undergone some essential training. For now, as veteran Nauts,

Desmond and I will be the ones called to defense, so you need not worry about facing the umbrae again until you're ready. I will even make you some of my special tea to make sure the door to the Ouroboros stays closed to you tonight."

With that, Lady Anora crosses to the massive walk-in pantry next to the peninsula and pulls out various jars, setting them each on the counter. She begins crushing herbs with what looks like a literal medieval pestle and mortar while the teapot heats on the stove.

Layna feels a killer headache coming on. Likely a combination of information overload and the beginnings of withdrawal from her meds. She probably should have weened herself off instead of making a stupid point to absolutely no one. She rubs her temples as she watches Blake, who is staring blankly into his half-empty bowl of soup. It evokes a fluttering of panic in her gut as she wonders whether he is planning on running like he'd suggested earlier. They started this together, and they need to see it through together. She doesn't know if she's strong enough to go back to being alone.

Blake looks up and sees Layna watching him, and he gives her a reassuring smile. There is no fear in his eyes, and as he clears their plates and carries them to the sink, his hands don't tremble. At least for now, they are in it together. As long as he doesn't go anywhere, she won't either.

Des joins Blake at the sink to help with the dishes, clapping him on the back to dismiss him from clean-up duty. He resumes his seat next to Layna just as Lady Anora sets two steaming cups of a dark green liquid in front of them and rejoins them at the table.

"This is an exceedingly old recipe, and I can promise you it will make sure that door stays shut tonight. It may make you feel a little woozy, but not to worry, you will wake up tomorrow feeling fresh as ever."

The tea has an earthy, sage-like flavor that is not entirely unpleasant, and it leaves an aftertaste of a kind of caramelized sweetness. As they drink the tea, Blake asks, "Can you answer one more question before we go to bed? What did you say or do to our families that convinced them to let us come here?"

Des turns around from the sink to face them as he wipes his wet hands on a towel. "Well…" He pauses to look at Lady Anora who nods her acquiescence. "Lucien, one of the Consulate Representatives of Region Four, possesses a form of telepathy called oneirokinesis. Basically, he can place people temporarily in a dream-like state and…manipulate their memory. In this case, he just gave your families and friends some memories suggesting you are away at a summer camp retreat," he finishes with a shrug. At their looks of dismay, Des smirks and adds, "Not to worry, he's one of our eldest Nauts, and he's a good bloke. He doesn't abuse his power but uses it only in the most limited sense for necessary situations."

"That's…sick," Blake mumbles. Layna notices the sluggishness of his speech, and she wonders if it's her hearing or his voice that's to blame. She looks down at her cup of tea, its rim now an indistinct blur, and sees that it's empty. She doesn't remember drinking the whole thing. But she has the sudden overwhelming urge to sleep.

"I think it's time for bed, you two," Lady Anora whispers. She stands to help Layna, and Des grabs Blake by the elbow.

"One more thing," Layna murmurs, so quietly that she's not even sure if she said it out loud or in her head until she notices Des and Lady Anora looking at her expectantly.

"My cat...can you have your guy go manipulate someone's memory to have them check on her and make sure she has enough food and water while we're here? Maybe play with her too. Moxie gets sad when I'm gone too long."

Des smiles at her. "Not to worry, kiddo. I'll pop in to see her myself. Cats love me."

Layna nods heavily, and allows herself to be led upstairs, where Lady Anora and Des point out their rooms and retreat back downstairs to finish cleaning up. Layna walks unsteadily toward her door and feels Blake's arm slide beneath hers for support. She leans on him gratefully, and as she reaches her door, she gives him a sleepy smile.

"Goodnight, Layna," he says, as he fails to suppress a yawn.

"Goodnight, Blake."

As he walks into his own bedroom and shuts the door behind him, Layna's mind immediately begins racing, as if he was the only thing keeping all her anxieties and fears at bay. She wishes he could stay with her as she goes to sleep like he did on the train. But trusting Lady Anora's promise, she takes a deep breath and walks into her room. In the emptiness and silence, Layna can once again sense the eerie pulsating somewhere below her. She has half a mind to go investigate and find out where it's coming from. But across the room, she spots the queen-sized bed dressed in plush, white linens. In her lethargic mind, it transforms into a fluffy cloud floating amid a dark night sky, and the promise of sleep drowns out any other thoughts in her head. She walks toward the cloud in a stupor, possibly asleep before tumbling into it with ungraceful appreciation.

CHAPTER

L ayna wakes early to the sound of ocean waves crashing against the shoreline.

Ocean?

She opens her eyes, and everything is dizzyingly out of place. No—her room is not hers at all. She's the one out of place.

Oh right. I'm in North Carolina. In the house of a total stranger who drugged me last night so that my consciousness wouldn't be murdered in my sleep. Cool.

She feels impossibly far from home. It's hard to believe the last twenty-four hours was not just some bizarre fever dream. And *dreams?* What even are they? She forces herself to sit up and scan her surroundings, which are, at the least, welcoming. The rising sun gleams through floor-to-ceiling double windows draped in white, casting a warm glow across the powder blue walls. The room, like all the other rooms she has seen here, is magnificent, though more modestly decorated. It has the same homey feeling of the kitchen, everything in soothing whites and pastel shades. Her duffel bag was brought upstairs sometime in the night and sits atop an antiquated, white vanity set, which matches the dresser and armoire on the opposite wall.

Layna is still fully dressed and didn't even make it beneath the covers last night. She jumps out of bed and throws open the double doors of the balcony. Stepping outside, she draws the cool ocean air deep into her lungs as she admires the orange and pink brushstrokes of sunrise. Lady Anora was right, she does feel incredibly refreshed. It's the perfect morning for a run, particularly since she has no idea what awaits her when the others arise.

She heads back inside to rummage through her bag for running shorts and a t-shirt. Before heading downstairs, she checks her phone to find an email from her mom. After regaling her with stories of zip-lining and hiking and sunbathing, and before signing off with her list of typical mom reminders—take your meds, brush your teeth, follow the rules, etcetera—she asks Layna how camp is going.

Though Des told them about this little mind trick, it's still shocking to see its effects in reality. To know that her mom now has this fake set of memories of sending Layna off to camp, even though Layna remembers clearly the *actual* conversations they had, the *actual* plans they made. It's unnerving, but impressive, what these people are capable of doing. She sends a vague but chipper message in response, including some clichés of what she imagines summer camp would be like. Tire swings, canoes, and three-legged races may have made their way into the description.

Layna closes her email and realizes she has a voicemail. Her stomach clenches at the sound of her best friend's voice on the message. "Hey there, weirdo," Kat says with forced cheer. "It's your long-lost besties, Kat and Suze. Um…just wondering how you're doing at your, uh, camp retreat. So, guess what? Hunter invited the three of us with him and Cam and some other grads to go see their buddy's band in the city on Monday night at this really cool underground spot. So, thinking maybe you want to escape from whatever whacked out stuff they have you doing there and come join us. So let us know—"

"Going to be epic!" Suzanne yells in the background. Layna doesn't miss the edge to her voice, and she instantly regrets embarking on this insane journey without making things right with the two of them first.

"—whether you can get away. Or whether we need to come rescue you. I mean seriously, Layna, who goes to summer camp? Are you seven or seventeen?" Then Kat's voice drops an octave as she whispers into the phone, "Are you actually at summer camp? Do I really need to rescue you? I can't reach your mom. Try to let me know if you're okay…okay?" Her voice drops even further, and Layna has a hard time discerning Kat's words through the muffled sound of her cupped hand over the phone. "Suzanne is driving me batshit. You know how she gets when you guys don't talk. I just can't with her right now. I miss you and I'm really sorry about last weekend. I know you've been going through some stuff. Just call me back. 'kay, thanks, bye."

The voicemail ends, and the comforting lilt of Kat's voice is replaced with a heavy silence that settles into Layna's chest like a gaping chasm. She fights the urge to run back home to them—to the normalcy and comfort of lifelong friendship. She settles on a compromise and decides to call back once she has come up with a realistic story to explain her whereabouts. Just realistic enough for a five-minute conversation so she can feel that a part of her life is still somewhere on this damn planet.

She places the phone back on the nightstand and bounds down the stairs. The house seems to still be asleep, and she heads less obtrusively for the back door in the kitchen. But before she even reaches the dining room, something stops her in her tracks. A thumping, pounding heartbeat that is not her own. She looks down the long hallway leading deeper into the house.

It's down there, she thinks. Whatever *it* is that has been calling to her since she arrived.

Without making the decision to do so, Layna finds she has already started down the hallway. A lavish, green runner trails atop the hardwood floors down the length of the hall. The walls are lined with a variety of intricate paintings ranging in style from portraits to landscapes to abstracts. She turns abruptly, letting her instincts guide her down a narrower hallway. There are no windows or lights in this hallway, and as she unsuccessfully searches the walls for a light switch, she realizes the hallway is also curved. As she picks up her pace down the hall, she can feel the closeness of the object, its pulsating now resonating throughout her body like the blood in her veins. Like it's a physical extension of her own self. But as she follows the arched path of the wall, she comes to the hallway of green carpet. Right back where she started. It's a circle—a circle in the center of the house.

She goes around again, this time carefully running her fingers along the walls in the dark, trying to find the crack of a door on the interior wall. She finds nothing. Back at the green rug again.

Thoroughly exasperated, Layna stomps her foot and turns down the green hallway back toward the entrance. Her headache from last night is threatening a return, and she is starting to feel jittery from the withdrawal. Now she really needs that run. She scurries back through the dining room to the kitchen, out the screen door, and onto the back porch. Jogging down the steps and onto the sand, she picks up speed as she rounds the large dune by the water's edge. She has time only to see the startled look on Blake's face before she barrels into him, throwing him into the surf as she goes tumbling onto the wet sand.

She gasps as the air surges back into her lungs and sits up just as Blake does, coughing and wiping salt water from his eyes. He looks at her as a smile creeps across his face and develops into laughter. That full, carefree sort of laughter, at once both deep and light. It fills Layna with an infectious warmth, and she gives him a cheerful smile in return.

"Are you making a habit of trying to run me over?" he asks between breaths.

She stands and walks toward him. "I'm sorry! I didn't expect anyone else to be awake this early." She extends her hand, but instead of pulling himself up, he yanks her down just as another wave rolls in.

Layna yelps in surprise as her body hits the chilly water.

"Jerk!" she sputters, splashing at his retreating body. His shoulders shake with silent mirth as he turns to offer her his hand. Layna tries to wipe the smile from her face as she smacks his hand away and bounces gracefully to her feet.

"I didn't know you liked to run," she says, as she wipes wet sand off her clothes. "You don't seem like the type."

Blake scrunches up his nose and asks, "What, just because I don't pop my collar, wear a letterman jacket, and go around flexing at all the girls?" He puffs up his chest and begins strutting along the sand, pointing and winking at invisible hotties along the way.

Layna giggles as the impersonation conjures up the image of several boys she knows at school. "No, I just meant...I don't know what I meant," she says, shrugging.

Blake gives a dismissive wave. "Doesn't matter. I do like to run. I try to do it every morning. It's the only way I can clear my head."

"Yeah, totally! Same here. Well, I mean, not the every morning part but—uh—the clearing my head part is the same...for me," Layna says, her voice trailing off. *Speak English much? What the hell was that?* Then she notices the way she's standing—weight on one leg, hands on hips, and head cocked to the side. *Oh, dear god, I'm flirting*!

She curses inwardly as she drops her stance to something less compromising. What would Suzanne and Kat say? She glances around in a pointless search for Caledon High's judging eyes, which she can somehow feel assessing her from hundreds of miles away.

She needs to get her head right. She and Blake may both belong to some secret, ancient order, but they also belong to another kind of order. The social order of Caledon High. She can't forget her place there, and she certainly can't develop *those* kinds of feelings for him. He's not even her type, so it shouldn't be difficult. She won't allow herself to get too close, and that way, it will be easier to break ties come fall. The decision makes her stomach twist up in knots.

Blake is looking at her, head tilted quizzically, and for a second, she worries that he is somehow reading her thoughts. Not beyond the realm of their new normal. But he straightens and says, "Cool, well, just don't go telling the jocks. They might try to recruit me. I mean, I am pretty fast," he says, wiggling his eyebrows.

"Oh yeah? Race you to the rocks," she says, pointing about a quarter mile down the beach.

"Challenge accepted. What are the stakes?" Blake asks, grinning broadly.

"Oh—uh, I don't know."

"Last one there has to ask Lady Anora how old she is," he laughs.

Layna smiles. "Deal. Shake on it," she says, holding out her hand. But when Blake reaches for it, she breaks into a sprint toward the rocks.

"Cheater!" he yells, as he lunges out after her.

"Opportunist!" she corrects over her shoulder.

She feels the muscles in her legs loosening, her strides getting longer and stronger as she moves her body with all her effort toward the stony finish line. As she closes in on the last dozen yards, she begins to feel the thrill of victory. But then she sees an amorphous shape out of the corner of her eye, and just as she reaches the rocks, Blake bolts past her with a final burst of energy.

Layna slows and drops to her knees to catch her breath. "Ugh!" she yells into the sand, pounding it once with her fists. "I totally had you."

"Hey now, sore loser," Blake says breathlessly, as he sits down cross-legged in front of her. "That's what you get for cheating." He wears a smirk that Layna would like to smack off him. But equally as strong is the impulse to lightly run a finger across those smirking lips.

Cut that out, she thinks, shaking the thought from her head.

"You alright there, champ?" Blake asks.

"I am just fine. We're totally having a rematch later. You were already stretched from running, and I won't take a head start next time."

"As you wish. You are really quick, though. I was almost afraid I wouldn't catch you. I've actually never been beat before, especially not by a girl."

"Oh-ho, here comes the misogyny!" she goads.

"And here comes the feminism!" Blake retorts with a laugh.

"Whatever, hater, be prepared for disappointment later," she insists as she stands up. "I'm going for a run down to the end of the beach. You can come if you're not too tired."

Blake answers by jumping up and breaking into a light jog. She joins him, giving him a playful shove as they fall into stride with each other along the surf. This is what she needed to start this day and this new life. This minor indulgence of control. The steady rhythm of inhale and exhale, pounding of feet on sand, waves rolling in and out of shore. A starting line and a finish line and the clear path between the two. The inevitability of it all is a symphony of solace and power, breath, and acuity, and she melts into it with all of her senses.

Layna and Blake collapse breathlessly into two of the white wicker chairs sitting on the back porch of Lady Anora's house. The temperature has climbed at least twenty degrees since Layna left this morning, the humidity hanging heavy on her skin like an extra layer of damp clothing. Sometime during their run, a pitcher of sweet tea, glasses, a fruit platter, and a plate of homemade cinnamon buns was placed on the glass table between the chairs. Blake pours a glass of tea and chugs it down in three or four gulps before instantly pouring another. Layna sips at the tea gratefully, noting how much better it is than the so-called Carolina sweet tea they serve at Izzy's. They didn't even get it close.

As she lifts her glass to take another sip, Des and Lady Anora suddenly materialize on the beach in front of them. Literally out of thin air.

Layna yelps in alarm, throwing the tea all over herself, as Blake spews his across the porch and jumps out of his chair. While Layna had suspected *something* after all those times Des seemed to have appeared and disappeared out of nowhere, now in the light of day, while she is fully awake, there is no denying what she just witnessed.

As Layna and Blake stare in gap-mouthed astonishment, Des and Lady Anora stride toward the house, speaking in hurried whispers. When Lady Anora looks up to see their audience, she holds a hand up to Des to quiet him.

"Oh my, I'm so sorry," she apologizes, as she reaches the steps of the porch, Des trotting up behind her. "That can be a little off-putting without explanation, I imagine. Desmond and I were just meeting with the Consulate to let them know we've got two new promising Activates staying with us," she says with a reassuring smile. "Please, take a seat a moment before we get started with training."

Despite the distinctive warmth in her voice and her smile, Layna's instincts tell her that Lady Anora is not being entirely candid about the subject of their visit with this Consulate.

Des pulls up a chair as Layna and Blake resume their seats and Layna tries to wipe some of the tea off her clothes. Lady Anora hops up onto the porch railing across from them with astonishing ease.

"Who exactly is this Consulate you guys keep referring to?" Blake asks absently, his eyes still on the spot where they'd just appeared.

"The Consulate of Augury. They are the leading members of the Order of Oneironauts," Des explains.

Blake responds with a lighthearted roll of his eyes. "Thanks, Des. I pretty much figured that part out on my own. I guess I mean like...*what* are they? Are they the ones who gave us these abilities? Are they...human? Or are we talking aliens or gods or mutants or something?"

Lady Anora smiles with consummate forbearance. "They're Nauts, just like us, here on Earth. Two elder representatives from each of the six regions of Earth, including the eldest living male or female Naut, the Senectus or Senecta, respectively. Lord Alden was our Senectus until about a decade ago when he passed, and I filled the role of Senecta. Now, as I was saying, when the Consulate comes together for a gathering, we meet in Athens—"

"Wait, you were in *Athens* just now?" Blake interjects. "As in, like, Greece. *Greece*...the other country on the other side of the ocean."

"Well, technically, we stayed in the Ouroboros," Des remarks. "At a spot *parallel* to Athens, Greece. If you want to get nit-picky about it."

"Oh, Desmond. Let's not unnecessarily confuse our young Activates, hmm?" Lady Anora scolds. "Last night we told y'all about using dreams to project our *consciousness* into the Ouroboros—the dreamplane—which, as we said, happens during deep sleep. However, over the centuries, Nauts have honed a different capability. We learned early on that non-REM not only occurs in deep sleep, but also just on the brink of sleep as our minds drift toward the dreamplane. A sort of wakeful dream state. By training our bodies to identify this moment, we can use it to project *physically* into the Ouroboros, meaning it is not only your mind crossing into the astral dimension, but your body as well."

"So, you did literally just materialize on the beach, and that was you...returning from another dimension? That just happened," Layna concludes.

"That did, indeed, just happen," Lady Anora says with a delicate nod.

"But that doesn't explain how you were also in another country," Blake points out.

"Well, Blake, therein lies the fun part," Lady Anora says with a knowing smile. "Because the Ouroboros is an astral dimension, it does not follow the same laws of space and time that exist here. Trips that would cover a great distance here in the physical world can be traveled instantaneously in the Ouroboros. When we enter the Ouroboros, we may reappear wherever we like."

Layna's heart soars at the thought. She's always desired to see more of the world, always felt that she belonged not just to Caledon, but everywhere. And *everywhere* has been calling to her. The farthest she's traveled was the Florida Keys when she was twelve. It is impossible to grasp the limitless freedom of being able to travel instantly to any place in the world, but now they definitely can't get to training fast enough.

"That…is…sick," Blake murmurs. He looks at Layna, eyes alight with exhilaration. "We can freakin' teleport."

"Yes," Lady Anora says with an airy laugh, "our vocation does have its perks. But it will take quite a bit of training to get you there. So, if you'd like to get started, please follow me to the athenaeum."

They follow Lady Anora inside as she leads them through the house and down the green hallway. Layna knows exactly where they are headed, and she has a difficult time not sprinting on ahead of them. Lady Anora comes to a stop about a third of the way around the mysterious circular hallway. She reveals a medallion hanging around her neck that was tucked beneath her shirt, black on one side and white on the other. She turns to the interior wall, sliding the medallion over an inconspicuous sensor. A hidden door swings inward. The hallway is flooded with the telltale sweet, musky scent of aging paper. The smell of knowledge and mysteries unbound, wafting outward to mix pleasantly with the saltwater air that permeates the house.

Lady Anora moves aside and daylight begins to pour from the room as though automated window shades are gliding open somewhere inside of it. Layna is peering in on a massive private library. The circular room is an archive holding four stories of books, records, maps, globes, telescopes, and aged artifacts. Atop the natural stone flooring to the right is an area of traditional Bohemian-style floor seating with a plush rug and a plethora of pillows and cushions surrounding a low coffee table. A spiraled staircase lies flush against the wall, encircling the room and rising to a ceiling made entirely of glass. Above it, Layna can see the roof as it finishes sliding open and clicking into place—an enormous skylight cover. The ceiling is the only window in the room. They are in the heart of the house.

Layna scans the space, trying to detect what it is that's been calling to her. It remains amorphous, indiscernible. But the moment she steps foot inside, she is overcome by a feeling—or rather, several feelings and sensations all at once—coming from outside of herself. Before she can warn the others of what she knows is coming next, it pulls her under.

The episode subsides—what her psychiatrist once labeled a fugue state but which she now knows to be something called telesthesia. By whichever label, the unnerving lack of control leaves her trembling with the same creeping sensation that her body does not belong to her.

She now stands in a dark room lit only by a thin sliver of light. For a moment, she has no idea where she is or how much time has passed. She whirls around, finding that the sliver of sunlight is coming in through a crack in the wall. As the crack widens, and she sees the stone flooring and wall of books on the other side, she realizes the wall is an enormous door. She is still in the athenaeum but in an interior room. Lady Anora, Des, and Blake walk through the doorway into the small, dark room to join her.

Blake and Des look stunned, but Lady Anora beams at her. "Well done, Layna. That is an impressive telesthetic ability you have. Not to worry, you were only under for about thirty seconds this time. But you found your way into this secret compartment all on your own, which I must say, makes me second guess the adequacy of my security measures."

"Impressive?" Layna trills, as she tries to stop quivering. "All this 'ability' has done is ruin my life. If it's a gift, then I don't want it. My mom, my best friends, now the entire *school* thinks I'm a total mental case. And I was! They put me on an *antipsychotic*. Do you know what it feels like to be diagnosed as a schizophrenic as a junior in high school when you're supposed to be planning your entire future? To have to go through each day waiting for the moment when suddenly you aren't *you* anymore? That's what this year has been. It's not impressive, it's tragic. It *sucks*." She feels a fuming heat in her cheeks as she allows herself to feel some of the betrayal that has lingered beneath the surface of her gratitude and awe. The damage that could have been avoided had these people just shown up earlier and told her that she's not losing her grip on reality but rather was gaining a grip on a new one.

Lady Anora looks at her—no, it's more accurate to say she looks *in* her. "I'm sorry, darlin', that was quite callous of me. I truly regret what you two have had to go through alone this year. I know how difficult it can be for young Nauts in the beginning. If we had only known sooner how far you'd each advanced...But we will teach you what this ability is, and in time, we'll help you control it so that you can use it to your benefit."

Layna opens her mouth to retort, or maybe apologize. Whatever it was flees her mind as something else pulls at her attention. A silent petulance, yearning to be recognized and known by her. Something else in the room with them. She turns away from the others and peers into the dark. Her eyes now adjusted, she can see the interior of the curved room. A circle within a circle, this one is small in diameter but immense in height, with limestone walls stretching up to a rotating, industrial-sized fan at the top. This must be the tower she noticed when they arrived. The only other thing sharing the space with them is the limestone pedestal rising from the center of the room, and the object that rests upon it. It's an enormous, archaic-looking book. Ordinary enough to the eye, it is still the most extraordinary thing Layna's sixth sense has ever encountered. Its presence pours into her, filling a previously empty void like the missing piece to a puzzle. The restlessness that has been with Layna for her entire life quiets and perishes, and she is finally still.

She notices Blake has moved up next to her. His eyes are on the book, voracious, as though trying to soak in its very essence. She can sense it filling him too.

"That is the reason you were drawn in here, Layna," Lady Anora says behind her.

"What is it?" Layna whispers without looking back at them.

"That, my dears, is *Oneironautica.* The Dream Book, as we colloquially call it. It is the world's most ancient and powerful text, and this tower was built to hold it for so long as I am the Senecta."

Layna and Blake simultaneously move closer to examine it. The binding is thick, leather or wood or metal. All of those or maybe none of them. The breadth of it is likewise inscrutable. It is most certainly vast, but it is an immeasurable vastness. Like trying to gaze upon a star in the night sky, the truth of it evades her direct gaze, skirting away and vanishing just when she thinks she has captured it. Despite this, she can see—or perhaps sense—the image that's been branded deeply into the cover.

At first, it appears as two overlapping circles. But as she hones her focus, she can see that one of the circles is actually a yin-yang, with the leather-wood-metal material a darker, burnt shade on one side and lighter on the other. The circle overlapping the yin-yang is the image of a serpent consuming its own tail. The serpent's body loops through the two smaller circles within the yin-yang, giving it a three-dimensional effect.

"What is the symbol on here? It's from like…ancient China or something?" Layna asks.

Lady Anora shakes her head. "No, darlin', this text and the symbol on it predate ancient China by many millennia. What similarity you may see is what they may have gleaned from *us.* You will come to learn that the histories of many ancient civilizations like those of Egypt, Greece, and China include many veiled references to our Order. The Consulates of those ages were not quite as strict about fidelity to secrecy as we must be now. After all, this is the information age, and it's quite a bit harder to stop speculation and fear of the unknown than it was in the past. Revelations that were relatively harmless back then could become catastrophic in today's highly-connected world."

"When I told you we belong to the most ancient order on Earth, I wasn't exaggerating," Des adds. "We were the beginning of civilization itself, before all of recorded human history."

"What do you mean, like the Stone Age?" Blake asks skeptically. "Nauts have been around since people were scraping rocks together trying to make fire?"

"Aye, well humans were a bit more advanced than that, but it was toward the end of what traditional history calls the Old Stone Age," Des replies.

"Damn," Blake murmurs. "So this symbol on here, that represents the Order?"

"That's correct," Lady Anora replies. "The light and dark sides of the yin-yang represent the Universes of Light and Shadow. The serpent that loops through the yin-yang represents the bridge between the inverse universes—the Ouroboros."

"If this book is that old, how does it even still exist?" Layna asks, as she impulsively reaches out a hand to the engraved image. But just as the tips of her fingers come near the book, it vaporizes. Layna gasps and pulls her hand back in shock.

Well, damn. I just destroyed the most ancient text known to man.

- Lady Anora lays a reassuring hand on Layna's shoulder. "Not to worry, darlin', it has only projected. It's still sitting right there, only now in the Ouroboros. The book still exists because it was created in the Ouroboros in order to withstand time. It has...unusual properties.

Should anyone attempt to hold the book, it jumps to the Ouroboros where only Nauts can reach it. Humans can never look upon its contents—not that they would be able to understand the language anyway."

"Sorry…you're not saying that Nauts—that we—aren't human. Are you?" Layna asks, her voice faltering.

Lady Anora's eyebrows knit together, portending an answer that Layna knows she doesn't want to hear. "Well, Nauts are human in the sense that we are carried by our mothers into this world in physical human form. But we are so fundamentally different from human beings that we cannot consider ourselves one and the same. Humans at their core are *ethereal* beings—children of Aether—and they have their nethereal counterparts, the umbrae. Nauts do not have umbrae counterparts because we are not ethereal beings but *astral* beings. Like the Dream Book, we actually come from the Ouroboros…we are born of dreams. I suppose it's accurate to say that we are, well, *semi*-human. The part in us that is Aether—light—that is the part of us that is human."

"Then…what's the part of us that's dark?" Blake murmurs.

Lady Anora sighs. "A necessary balance."

Layna and Blake respond with silence, which Des interrupts with a single clap of his hands as he plasters a smile on his face. "Well, I think we should get started, eh?"

Lady Anora brightens, too. "Yes, of course. I'm glad we could introduce you to the Dream Book before Des starts you on your training. Eventually, it will help you to understand our history better than I could ever explain. But, of course, you cannot read it until you learn *oneironautics*. So this will be the goal of your training," she says, looking sideways at Des, "to physically reach the book where it sits in the Ouroboros. Now I will turn y'all over to Desmond who has been waiting ever so patiently to begin. I will check in later today."

They emerge from the room back into the brightness of the library, and Layna sees that the massive door also serves as an enormous wall of books, a secret doorway to the compartment she'd involuntarily known how to enter. Des pushes the wall, which, despite its mass, glides smoothly closed until it clicks into place. It is impossible to tell now that it is anything but a wall of books.

"Woah," Layna whispers. "That is too cool."

Blake chuckles as he watches her. "Careful, Layna, your inner nerd is showing."

Layna smacks him on the arm as Des turns to face them. "Alright, kiddos," he says, rubbing his hands together as a wicked smile spreads across his face. "Time for some fun."

Des stands before them evoking the presence of an army general, straight as a pin and hands clasped behind his back. Layna and Blake stare up at him from the cushioned floor seating, awaiting his instruction.

"Ok, Activates," he bellows, flinching at the volume of his own voice. He continues in a softer tone more suitable to his two-person audience. "The first and most fundamental of the Tripartite Powers is oneironautics. The power of dream travel itself. You'll find that each of the three powers is sort of reflexive—like muscle memory, but muscles you've never used before and must build up slowly. So be patient with yourselves.

"As Lady Anora was explaining earlier, dream travel includes both conscious and physical projection into the Ouroboros. They each have their pros and cons, and we use them interchangeably. Conscious projection is the traditional way of fighting the umbrae, since it allows our physical bodies to rest while we fight, and it comes more naturally, as you will find. However, physical projection allows us to fight in our region during peak hours, and it poses less risk. Now—"

"How does it pose less risk?" Blake interrupts.

"Um, well, we explained that during conscious projection, shadowspears can obliterate your consciousness, yeah? Because it's your consciousness alone that is in the dreamplane. But our bodies are much more resilient than our minds. So during physical projection, it's more like getting shot with a bullet. It can be fatal or not, depending on what part of your body is hit. If a shadowspear hits a vital part of you, the darkness will begin to spread, and if that happens, you're nearly good as dead."

"Cool, cool," Blake replies tensely. "So the equivalent of bullets shot from a gun is the *lesser* risk."

Des laughs uneasily and gives him an apologetic shrug. His explanation reminds Layna of the dark marks she saw scattered about his body when she saw him in the dream yesterday. She now realizes they must be battle scars from being hit with shadowspears during physical projection, and it sends a chill of apprehension down her spine.

Des clears his throat and continues, "So, you're both quite a bit ahead of the curve for when training with a Guide usually begins, having already experienced conscious projection. So we're going to jump right into working on physical projection. Now, don't you go assuming you'll be picking this up lickety-split like you did with conscious projection. It's not *quite* so reflexive. It's really two separate skills combined in one. One being the actual physical projection into the Ouroboros—moving from one dimension into another—and the other being porting, which is moving from one location to another location in the *same* dimension. The concept of porting is that you're basically traversing the Ouroboros instead of entering it. Sort of like a stone skipping across a pond."

"And projecting would be like throwing the stone straight into the pond?" Layna asks.

"Aye, more or less. Naturally, you'll learn to do both simultaneously, but it's easier to start with porting, since it doesn't require you to remain physically in the Ouroboros. That, of course, being the hardest bit as it requires a more lasting change in your state of matter, rather than just a quick scrambling of it."

"Come again?" Blake says, his voice tremulous. "You're scrambling our matter?"

"Well…yes. Human bodies are just loose material form resulting from the high vibrational energy between your atoms, which are ninety-nine percent empty space. Well, not empty. Know what takes up that space? Scientists like to call it quarks. But it's Aether—light.

For us Nauts, both light and shadow. That's all we really are, all anything is. Not as crazy to think about traveling instantaneously anywhere when you think of it like that, eh? But we're getting ahead of ourselves. You aren't going anywhere today. Both of you lay down, bellies up and hands at your sides. Feet spread apart."

At their perplexed expressions, he adds, "Remember, you need to train your bodies to recognize that moment on the edge of dreaming when we slip briefly into non-REM. Today we're just focusing on identifying that moment through meditation."

They do as instructed as Des crouches on a cushion closer to them and continues in a softer voice.

"Now, your destination is the Tower. Eventually you'll be able to port to places you've never seen or visited, but in the beginning, you've got to know the space you're aiming for. Close your eyes and picture that room. Imagine every detail, everything your five senses can remember about it, and try to think of nothing else."

Layna pictures the small, dark room with the rotating fan on the ceiling. She thinks of the light stone walls and the pedestal that appears empty, but which holds the Dream Book in another dimension.

Des continues in a whisper, "Keep your mind on the room and relax your body, releasing all tension from your muscles. Allow yourself to grow heavy, sinking into the floor. Breathe deep into your stomach, steady breaths…Good. Now imagine you are standing in that room, convince your mind that you are already in there. Keep concentrating on that, and that alone. Dismiss any thoughts that exist beyond the details of the room. Breathe deep, concentrate…"

Layna imagines the blackness of the room on the back of her eyelids, hears the gentle whir of the fan, and feels the breeze brushing lightly against her skin. Eventually, she no longer senses her body on the floor. Only the rise and fall of her stomach on each inhale and exhale. Her mind laser focused, there is a dizzying moment when she actually believes she could be standing in that room. And then next to her, Blake begins snoring. Layna opens her eyes and turns to find him fast asleep, and she can't help but laugh at how ridiculous this all is.

"Oy, mate, wake up," Des says, giving him a gentle nudge.

They start over again. And again, and again.

"I'm sorry, I'm just really good at sleeping," Blake whines after he is awoken a third time. "I think I just skip right over this whole edge of dreaming thing you're talking about, man."

Thus far, Layna hasn't had the problem of falling asleep, but she hasn't gotten any further than merely pretending she's in the other room. But on the fifth or sixth attempt, as her mind gets fuzzy with sleep, she feels an abrupt tugging sensation right in the center of her stomach. It yanks her back to awareness, not unlike the falling sensation that sometimes jolts you awake as you're drifting off. "This is very frustrating," she murmurs without opening her eyes.

"Aye, it is. You're doing brilliantly though," Des encourages in a whisper. "Keep going and tell me if you feel anything out of the ordinary."

The task begins to feel insurmountable. How can you concentrate on tricking yourself into thinking you're somewhere else with sleep pulling at your mind and causing it to drift here and there? Layna lays there for some time, engaged in the battle between sleep and concentration. When the tugging sensation returns, it is not quite as jarring, and she is able to hold onto it without breaking concentration. Her fingers and toes begin to prickle, and there is a weightlessness that is not unpleasant, though somewhat disquieting. But when she feels a particularly strong, sucking pull in her center, her eyes burst open in alarm. Des sits cross-legged next to them, a hopeful look lighting up his face as he sees Layna's reaction. He opens his mouth to question her when, between them, Blake vanishes from sight.

Layna bolts upright, staring at the spot where Blake was just lying, unable to believe what he's done. Whatever Des was about to say escapes as a stunned croak, his mouth hanging open as though his jaw has come unhinged. Layna hears a noise from across the athenaeum, behind the wall of books. Then, Blake's muffled voice, "Hey…hey! Uh, guys…can you let me out of here?"

"Bloody…hell…" Des murmurs, unsteady as he rises to his feet. "Lady Anora suspected you two would be quick at this, but…" He looks at the watch on his wrist. "Bloody *hell*."

As Des rises to let Blake out, Layna lays back and closes her eyes in concentration, slightly miffed that Blake has beaten her for the second time that day. More determined now, she lets her surroundings melt away, and imagines again that she is in the tiny room, this time with Blake by her side. Inexplicably, the tugging sensation begins the instant she pictures him in there, and it's *strong*. She refuses to let it go, keeping Blake's face in her mind. There is a sound like rushing wind in her ears, and for a breathless moment…Layna no longer exists.

She has no body. She is the air. She is everywhere and nowhere, nothing and everything. She has no beginning or end. She is eternal.

Then she is all panic and exhilaration and arms and legs and bodily senses. The sunlight on the back of her eyelids has been extinguished, and she opens her eyes to darkness. She feels the cool draft from the overhead fan hitting every inch of her skin, an effective indication that she is, once again, her very contained self. She is standing inside the Tower.

Ha! In your face, physics!

Layna reaches unsteadily for the rock wall as she hears more astonished cursing coming from Des on the other side, and closer by, Blake's shaky breathing. "Blake?" she whispers, trying to contain the euphoria she feels bubbling up inside her. She hears him jolt next to her as he bumps into a wall.

"Ow! Jeez, I didn't realize you were in here, too. That was insane. But kind of awesome. But, really, really insane," he says breathlessly. "I'd really like to get out of this room now, though."

"What, afraid of the dark?" Layna teases. Her body begins trembling from the intensity of the adrenaline rush.

"No…more like confined spaces," he mumbles with an edge of panic in his voice.

Layna turns toward the sound of Des still raving like a lunatic on the other side of the thick stone. "Hey, Des, can you let us out of here now?"

Des' rant cuts off abruptly, as though, in his astonishment, he had forgotten entirely the subject of it. The wall unlatches and a ray of light falls across Layna and Blake. She can see little beads of sweat on Blake's brow as his expression shifts to wild relief.

Des enters slowly and silently, apparently having exhausted his ineloquent expression of shock. He clears his throat and looks back and forth between them. "Alright, so that was...unexpected. This isn't a trick, is it? You two aren't messing with me? Done this before or something?"

Layna and Blake shake their heads.

"Okay. Alright. I planned just to get into recognizing the physical *signs* of porting for the next few days not just...right into...I've just never...You know what? It's fine, this is fine. Just add it to the list. Brilliantly done. Lesson one through, er, five over. Would you like a break?"

Layna and Blake both shake their heads again. The feeling of having just skipped across another dimension is thrilling, to say the least, and Layna feels more motivated than ever to keep going.

"Thought you'd say that," Des answers. "Alright then, let's keep at it with porting."

For all of his moaning and groaning about being assigned as their Guide, Layna gets the distinct impression that he is disappointed at the ease with which they are picking this up. He said on the train that he could be out there helping, rather than babysitting kids. And now, it must seem to him that even that responsibility is nothing but a superficial assignment. Maybe it's not guiding them specifically that bugged him so much, but more the idea of being obsolete.

"We'll head back out to the cushions and, this time, I want you to focus on porting to the main staircase in the entrance. Then we'll try a bit farther, to the kitchen, and so on, until you start feeling comfortable doing it sitting up, then standing. The more you do it, the less you'll have to concentrate on getting yourself right to the edge of sleep and it will become instinctive. And we won't have to listen to Blake snoring anymore."

"Sounds tedious," Blake quips, unable to wipe the goofy, euphoric grin off his face.

"You're tedious," Des retorts, prompting a delirious cackle from Layna. "As they say, Rome wasn't built in a day. Now, let's get back out there."

CHAPTER

"So how 'bout Jesus, was he real?" Blake asks, as he shovels a hefty bite of Fettuccine Alfredo into his mouth.

"Don't you know not to bring up religion at the dinner table?" Des replies with a smirk. "You'll have to read that one for yourself, kid. No spoilers."

Lady Anora chuckles as she stands to get Des a second helping, giving him a good-natured smack on the shoulder.

"Okay, okay, give us another famous Naut then," Blake says with an encouraging grin.

"Hmm…" Des mumbles, eyes cast toward the ceiling as he gives a thoughtful rub of his chin. "Alexander the Great."

"No shit!" Blake cries, clapping his hands together once with satisfaction.

Their whirlwind weekend, of course, has been anything but tedious. Even now on Sunday evening after three full days of training, Layna still feels the same exhilaration she felt on Friday when she first leaped across dimensions. And she's had the added bonus of watching Blake become...well, Blake. It's amazing how animated and comfortable he's been over the past few days. It's like he knew who he was, who he was always meant to be, the second he laid eyes on the Dream Book that first day. Layna has felt it too. The ease with which she has slipped seamlessly into this life. With him, with them. The weightlessness of knowing who you truly are and where you belong.

By Saturday morning, she and Blake were porting from a standing position, and this morning, they passed the little pop quiz Des gave them as he called out locations around the house, where they'd port to on cue. That afternoon, they'd moved onto projecting, but it was proving more difficult. Each time they would try to enter the Ouroboros, it would spit them back out. As Des explained to them, "Our bodies are used to being here. But we Nauts are *from* the Ouroboros, and your bodies will recall how to exist in it, even though it might feel a wee bit...claustrophobic, at first."

That didn't make for the best motivation, particularly for Blake, who now seems to be perfectly content sticking to porting. Each day, they stopped training at dinnertime, when Lady Anora returned from her now daily meetings with the Consulate to prepare a homemade dinner with the three of them. As she would divvy up cooking tasks, they blasted old tunes from Des' vintage iPod through the kitchen's Bluetooth speakers.

This came about as the result of a friendly debate between Blake and Des on Friday night about what each considers 'music' after Des read his t-shirt and asked what a 'seether' was. Blake played one of their songs on his phone, which did exactly nothing to improve Des' opinion of them. When he learned Blake had never listened to *The Beatles,* he vanished from the kitchen without a word and returned a second later with an old iPod in hand. Des started them off by boisterously singing and dancing along to a song called *Eight Days a Week* while he chopped potatoes. Layna worked on the gravy, Blake on the ground beef patty mixture, and Lady Anora brought it together into a Salisbury steak and mashed potato dinner just in time for a funny little tune called *Ob-La-Di Ob-La-Da.*

Saturday and Sunday went by in much the same fashion, and *The Beatles* anthology became the soundtrack to their new lives. Tonight, Layna could tell even Blake was beginning to enjoy the music, his foot tapping to the beat as he dropped raw noodles into the boiling pot of water.

Over dinner each night, Lady Anora and Des regaled them with stories of their most memorable battles with the umbrae, or they would tell them about famous people in history who were actually Nauts— Layna's personal favorite being none other than Abraham Lincoln. Or they would teach them some basic Naut terminology, like *homeplane*, which is what Nauts call this plane of existence. Layna thought that one was kind of endearing. And *eclipsed*, which is the word for a human who is being influenced by their umbra, like the guy in the park and the men in the alley.

And although Layna gratefully soaks up every bit of knowledge they offer, she can tell Lady Anora and Des are taking care to keep things light. The heaviness in Lady Anora's shoulders each time she returns from Athens, the pointed looks she and Des share, they tell a different story. Her mentors are hiding the bigger truths, evading more specific questions about both the history and future of Nauts, and it casts a shadow over the thrill of this new adventure.

"Oh, I've got one," Layna interjects, as she begins clearing plates off the table. "What if two Nauts try to port to the same place at the same time?"

"Simultaneous combustion," Des answers flatly.

There is the briefest moment of shocked silence before Blake and Layna shout at once, "I call BS!"

Layna gives Blake a wry smile and a fist bump as Des chuckles at them. "No, of course not that," he clarifies. "Why don't you just try it out?"

"The best way to learn is by doing," Lady Anora adds, her grey eyes sparking with amusement. It's Layna's cue that whatever Des is proposing can't be that unsafe.

"Okay, Layna," Blake says, catching her eye. "I'm going to steal your seat."

"Just try," Layna says with a defiant smirk, carefully placing the plates she was holding onto the counter. She stares at her seat, and within the blink of an eye, she's vanished from where she stands and reforms right in her seat as Blake lands on his butt on the floor next to her. All four of them erupt in a fit of laughter.

"That's what happens," Des snickers, wiping tears from his eyes.

"That was super weird," Blake laughs, popping up off the floor. "It was like I felt matter being like, '*Nope!*'"

"More or less," Lady Anora replies with a smile. "Matter can't simultaneously occupy the same space. Physics won't allow it. So you get shifted to the nearest space where your matter can properly recompose."

"Wild," Layna adds, mystified.

They finish clearing the table and cleaning the dishes, and Lady Anora makes them tea before she and Des go for their usual nightcap on the back porch. Since Friday night, Lady Anora has included something in Layna's tea that has been helping with the headaches and jitters as her body readjusts to not being pumped with useless drugs. Layna and Blake down the contents of their tea and head upstairs to bed. Training begins with the sunrise tomorrow, as usual. "Good night, Blake," Layna says, turning back to look at him as she reaches her room.

"Good night, Layna," he replies, pausing at his door as though he wants to say something more. But after a moment's hesitation, he simply adds, "Good job today," before slipping into his room and shutting the door.

"You too," Layna replies softly.

She heads into her room and pulls up her mom's daily email on her phone. She drafts a reply as she's changing for bed about new friends and skills she's been learning in camp. More like cooking and music, less like teleportation. Strangely, although the emails mark the farthest departure from the truth with her mother, she finds it easier than it's been in a year to be honest with her feelings. She's *not* anxious, or feeling overwhelmed, or becoming unglued. For the first time in so long she feels…happy. Content. Hopeful. She's glad she can at least send that back to her mother, even if the details are a lie.

She climbs into her cloud of a bed, and while she's plenty exhausted to drift straight into sleep, she also feels particularly drawn back to the athenaeum. It's the Dream Book, calling to her still. It remains in the Ouroboros, where she has been unable thus far to reach it since she saw it on Friday.

Maybe just one more try before bed.

She can now conjure that tugging sensation in her gut within seconds. Then all she has to do is hold on as it yanks her like invisible reins across the Ouroboros and back out to the homeplane at the spot where she aims to be. So she finds herself downstairs standing in front of the limestone pedestal in her pajamas in the pitch dark. The Dream Book is right there, waiting for her to explore, reaching for her in the dark. All she has to do is project into the Ouroboros in order to see it. She concentrates as Des taught them, letting go of her fear and focusing on her desire to reach the book. It's easier, now that she's alone. Just she and the book on the opposite side of the dimensional barrier. This time, when the reins grip her, she grips them right back, harnessing the power and embracing it. There is a new, unsettling squeezing and whooshing sensation before she is returned to the confines of her body, now relocated to another dimension.

Oh, I'm going to die, one hundred percent going to die in this godforsaken alternate dimension.

She has successfully projected physically into the Ouroboros. And now she very much wishes she hadn't. A smothering blanket of dense air envelops her, squeezing the breath from her lungs. She can actually feel her joints crackling inside of her body with the weight of it. The world has become so alarmingly quiet that Layna's ears ring in the unnatural silence.

A wee bit claustrophobic, Des? A wee bit!

Her vision swims, but she realizes that the whole room is churning, swirling like some eerie Van Gogh portrait come to life. Every surface in the room is covered in a misty grey—the walls, the ceiling, the pedestal. But not her, and not—

The book.

Its beauty takes her breath away. It pulsates with a brilliant russet-orange glow, as though it is greeting her with a pristine sunrise. And then she sees something different. Not with her eyes but…inside her mind. A vision in which the book flips open to a specific page that flashes red, like a warning. Or maybe…a beckoning.

I need to read that page.

She takes a labored step toward the pedestal and the room takes a nauseating dip sideways. She tries to take a deep breath, but the viscous air burns her lungs, and she resolves to quick, shallow breathing as she moves closer. Now that she's viewing the book in the Ouroboros, she can see that the image on the cover is actually *moving*. The yin-yang is rotating counterclockwise, as the serpent turns through the yin-yang's smaller circles in an opposite, clockwise motion.

She reaches for the cover and opens to the first page. For a second, the inside appears to be only blank, glowing parchment. But as she focuses her frayed mind, Layna can see text appearing there, though not any kind of writing she's ever seen. These are small, discrete markings and patterns almost like Egyptian hieroglyphics but in much more elaborate detail. Each hieroglyph is a piece of artwork in its own right—a hundred little brushstrokes to comprise an image not larger than a square inch.

Layna concentrates on the row of the text at the top of the page, and inexplicably, she understands it. Or at least an English phrase pops into her head that she attributes to the text: *The History of Our Creation: The Last Oneiroi, Hemera and Nyx.*

She has never even heard the English version of some of those words. But there they are in her head. She looks at the next line, and more English words pop into her head:

In the beginning of time, there existed only two opposing Kosmic energies. One of Light and one of Darkness. These are Aether and Erebus. From them, the Universes were born. One created the Kosmos, while the other sowed Chaos. This was the Age of Great Harmony.

Her head begins throbbing, and the lack of oxygen makes the room start to spin. Survival instincts finally win out over curiosity. She needs to get out of here. She steps backward from the book, but her legs buckle beneath her and she falls in a heap. That's when she realizes that she may actually be suffocating.

She also realizes that she has no idea how to get back out.

Des! She shouts for him inside her head, willing him to come help her. And just when she feels everything inside her mind collapsing, it shifts, and begins expanding, searching outward like the radar on a ship. And then—a ping. It has to be the way out. There is an uncomfortably strong pull in her gut as the whooshing sensation consumes her, and for a moment, she is gone again from existence. But upon the reassembly of her matter, the heaviness of the air does not abate. She hasn't escaped back to the homeplane. She's only ported to another spot in the Ouroboros. As she tries to contain her panic, she looks around to find she is standing in the deepening night on a lonely, dirt road. And everything around her—the road, the plants, the trees, even the sky—is veiled in that same swirling, grey mist. Then, out there on her own, she feels suddenly…watched.

Something moves in the dark to her right. She is so exposed. And alone. And suffocating. She turns as quickly as the air will allow and finds them creeping out from a shadowed sideroad like demons from hell.

Umbrae.

Two eclipsed men, walking toward her with hunting rifles dangling in each of their hands. Except, for some reason, the men move in slow-motion. She knows from her experience in the alley and the park that the men can't see her while she's in the Ouroboros. Nevertheless, she gets the distinct feeling that their pitted black eyes are locked onto her. Des said the umbrae have no consciousness, that they are incapable of wanting. But Layna swears that it's the umbrae looking at her and that they want to kill. To kill *her*.

She notices around the center of the man closest to her, the shadow of the umbra begins swirling inward like a small vortex. Something about this is important, and though Layna's brain is fuzzy from lack of oxygen, she hears Des' words in her mind. *There is the tell-tale vortex that appears before a shadowspear is launched.*

207

Oh, right, that.

This umbra is about to shoot her with one of those shadowspear things, and if she doesn't move, she's going to die. But she just continues to stand there. Frozen like an idiot deer in headlights.

As the black vortex spins faster, she feels the air knocked out of her lungs and knows she's been hit. A shadowspear, moving so quickly she didn't even see it. She topples over onto the ground, but she's surprised when another person lands on top of her.

Des has tackled her out of the way, and the shadowspear whizzes over their heads as a dark blur. Without a moment's hesitation, Des jumps up and raises his hands, shooting bright bolts of light directly at the pair of umbrae.

How the hell is he moving that quickly in this place when I can't even breathe?

Another vortex appears around the second eclipsed man. Layna tries to shout a warning only to find that her voice doesn't seem to work in this dimension. Like trying to speak underwater. But Des doesn't need her warning. At the same moment the spear is launched, he leaps into the air, vanishing and porting to a spot just behind the men where he immediately resumes his barrage of light. The shadowspears begin raining down on him like arrows from a crossbow, occasionally colliding with the bolts of light between them and exploding mid-air.

Layna watches from the ground in awe as the crackling of electricity fills the night and Des strikes the umbrae again and again, rolling and spinning and porting to avoid being hit himself. With great difficulty, Layna pushes herself up to her hands and knees to attempt to help. But Des ports in between her and the umbrae and yells, "Stay down, Layna!" His voice is morphed slightly, both lighter and louder as it cuts through the air to Layna's ears like an earthquake.

Layna has no intention of staying down, but before she can even lift her hands in assistance, Des delivers a final blow, and the umbrae dissipate with a hiss of air and puff of blackness.

The two men blend back into the rest of the churning, grey world, emanating only a faint, white glow. Though Layna's never seen it before, she recognizes it as the natural light of ordinary humans. More pure and gentle than the light that Nauts channel.

Des scrambles up and helps Layna stand, frantically inspecting her for injuries. "Are you okay? Did you get hit?"

She shakes her head, unable to respond with words, and grabs hold of Des' arm. Not injured, but a bit unsteady. Those things could so easily have killed her, and she couldn't do anything to defend herself. She was totally useless. Just like in the alley when she just shut her eyes like some kid having a nightmare.

But these nightmares are real. These nightmares can kill.

"For mercy's sake, Layna. Let's get back. Lady Anora needs to know about this lot," Des says darkly, nodding toward the men.

Layna notices the men have now stopped moving forward. One has dropped his rifle, which hangs eerily in the air as it makes its slow descent to the ground. The other has started to raise his hands to his head.

"It'll be easier if you just travel back with me. Just hang on," Des suggests. Layna tightens her grip on his arm, and within a second, they are back inside Lady Anora's kitchen in the homeplane, and Layna can breathe again. She gulps in the air and arches her spine, stretching her aching bones as she tries not to throw up her Fettuccine dinner.

"How did you know where I was?" she asks breathlessly.

Des responds by shouting a single, powerful expletive that causes Layna to recoil in shock. She doesn't know exactly how she got out there, but Des is clearly not pleased with her. She's surprised by how much this bothers her. Coupled with the near-death experience and dwindling of adrenaline in her veins, she feels uncomfortably close to tears.

"I'm sorry, Des," she mumbles, as she tries to blink back the rising flood behind her eyes.

"Oh, Layna—no, that wasn't directed at you," Des urges, gripping her by the shoulders. "You did nothing wrong. This was entirely on me, alright?"

Layna nods as she hears footsteps approaching and Blake appears in the open doorway, rubbing the sleep from his eyes. "What's going on, man? Why'd you yell like that?"

"What's going on is I'm not fit to be a Guide, and I shouldn't have been made responsible for the two of you!" Des bellows. Knowing now that his anger is directed inward, it rolls right over Layna, but Blake flinches in the doorway.

"I should have known better, given how quickly you've caught on and how unusual the umbrae have been acting. I just didn't think you'd be able to sense the Limits like that already. You hadn't even projected yet!"

"What's he talking about?" Blake asks Layna impatiently.

"I sort of projected, and when I was trying to get back out to the homeplane, instead I ended up...away somewhere. And, uh, ran into some umbrae."

Blake's mouth drops open. "Seriously?" he says, turning to Des.

Des nods and runs a hand through his hair, trying to compose himself. "Layna, what were you doing just before you traveled?"

"I'm sorry. I just wanted to see the Dream Book, so I decided I'd try to project one more time before bed. I ported down to the Tower, and then, I don't know, I was just finally able to project. And it was *awful*, by the way, Des. And I was trying to get back out, and then all of a sudden, I was out there."

"I see," Des responds, his eyebrows knitted. "And did you feel anything strange beforehand? Like your mind was...expanding?"

"Yes, actually. That's exactly what it felt like. It's like it was searching and then narrowed in on this one spot—I thought it was getting me back to the homeplane. But it was something else."

"It was the Limits. You were sensing the umbrae within the area of patrol in your region—where you'd typically be called to defense. That's why you ended up in the same spot as umbrae. All Nauts have the ability to sense the chaos of an umbra's energy when it's close enough. When it's within your Limits. Except you're only an Activate, so you shouldn't have been actually called. Lady Anora and I were on patrol, and I was *here*. I'm just bloody relieved I got there in time. If I hadn't...I mean...I just don't get how they could have gotten so close with the defenses we have in place. And their umbrae were rather strong. Took a lot to expel them. I need to speak to Lady Anora and sort it all out when she returns from patrol," Des mumbles. "We'll just have to sit tight for a bit."

Layna collapses onto the bench at the kitchen table. Blake pulls the pitcher of sweet tea out of the fridge and pours Layna a glass as he takes a seat beside her. She accepts it with a grateful smile. But instead of sipping it, she presses the cool glass against her cheek to soothe her quaking body as it reels from being almost suffocated and speared. Projecting was nothing at all like the wonderful euphoric feeling of porting.

"Layna, I'm sorry," Des says with a sigh, sitting across from them with his head in his hands.

"It's okay, Des. It's not your fault I decided to project on my own. It was stupid of me. I guess I don't really know what I'm messing with."

"No, but it's not your fault that you don't know that. We've been trying to ease you into this as much as we can. But it's getting more difficult to ensure your safety with things the way they are. I just need to be more careful in protecting you."

"Things the way they are?" Blake asks.

"That's a question for another day, mate," Des sighs, exhaustion etched in every feature.

"Okay," Blake concedes with a nod. "So, Layna...you projected! Does she get a gold star or something?" he asks Des, clearly trying to brighten the mood.

"Yeah, I projected," Layna cuts in, "and it was literally the worst. How can we possibly survive in that? I thought I was going to die."

"Really selling this one, Layna," Blake remarks.

"Yeah, it's not easy at first," Des says with a sympathetic grimace. "Was hoping to be there with you the first time you were in. But I promise your body will get accustomed to the feeling, especially once you learn to control your fear."

"But I was in there for like ten minutes and it just seemed to get worse, not better."

"Well, for you it may have felt like ten minutes, but you were probably only in there for about a solid two minutes," Des adds. "Really well done for your first projection, actually."

"Wait, *what*?" Blake gasps. "Time moves faster in the dreamplane?"

"Well, sort of. *We* move faster…than time. Time is just an illusion, after all."

"But no, everything was like real time when we were in Trent Park and in the alley," Blake argues.

"That was *conscious* projection. You weren't experiencing the Ouroboros with your bodily senses. Our minds are able to sort of go beyond time. Just how in that alley, you felt the rain soaking your skin, heard the thunder with your ears. But your bodies weren't there. It was your consciousness projecting your 'self' to allow you to fight. Our bodies, though, they've got to observe the laws of physics regardless of what dimension we're in. So when we're physically in the Ouroboros, it'll be like watching a movie in slow-motion."

"Slow-motion…" Blake murmurs, his eyes widening. "So guess that has something to do with why Layna and I would randomly feel like time would slow down?"

213

"Aye, did you now?" Des says, as he scratches the back of his head. "Well, I have heard of that sort of thing happening during activation. Just like night terrors and sleepwalking, your abilities are a wee bit haywire during that time. Your minds were likely reacting to certain stressful stimuli by shifting toward the Ouroboros, like a super-reflex, or…" Des turns toward the back windows. "Hold on, I think Lady Anora's just returned. I'll be back in a few."

Once the back door slams shut, Blake turns to Layna and asks gently, "So…you okay?"

"Yeah," she sighs, nodding slowly. "Des had to fight them while I just lay there like a useless slug."

"Hey, don't feel bad. We don't know what we're doing yet. I haven't even managed to project into the Ouroboros, let alone try to fight in it."

"That's what I'm worried about. I don't know why, but I feel like something big is about to happen. I can sense it. And you and I…we're *so* not prepared. Des and Lady Anora are amazing, but they're keeping things from us. We need to be ready."

Blake examines his hands and nods. "Okay. What do you think we should do?"

"Well, I think I know where to start. A page in the Dream Book. We need to go read it."

"What is it that we're reading?"

"I'm not sure exactly, but I do know it's been, um, calling to me."

"How do you mean?" Blake asks, leaning in closer.

"The book, it's been reaching out to me since we got here. And when I projected into the Tower before, I saw a vision of the book opening to a specific page. The page was glowing red. Like a warning."

This catches Blake's attention, and he sits up sharply. "You said the page glowed red?"

"Yeah, why?"

"Hold that thought for a second," he closes his eyes and vanishes in front of her, returning a moment later with his backpack. After rummaging through it, he pulls out his sketchbook and thumbs through the pages. "Here!" he says triumphantly. "I got this flash during finals and sort of forgot about it with everything that's been going on. But it was a weird one...Look, it's just like you said."

Unlike most of his sketches, which are done in pencil, this one has spots of color. And also unlike the others, it is lacking in exact detail. More like an abstract. But she can make out the outline of the Dream Book sitting open on the pedestal, drawn with orange pencil except for the right side, which is drawn in bright red. The date on the sketch is six days ago.

Layna taps the picture with her finger. "This is it. This is what I saw. It's like it was calling to you too," Layna says.

"Right, and now I'm guessing maybe it came in so fuzzy because it was of an image in the dreamplane. But look at the bottom."

Layna looks at the sketch again, and she sees one set of hands on the left of the book and a second set on the right.

"Your hands and mine...This hasn't happened yet," she concludes. "It's both of us reading the book. And it's supposed to happen today."

Blake looks at her, raising his eyebrows suggestively.

She nods and takes his hand. It's warm and comforting in hers, and they wordlessly disappear from the bench together and reappear in the Tower. The near-pitch blackness greets them, the only tendrils of moonlight dancing far above their heads interrupted by the whirring blades of the fan. As their eyes become more accustomed to the darkness, they approach the pedestal in the center of the room, seemingly empty of the Dream Book which waits for them in the other dimension.

"Ready?" Layna asks, as she prepares once again to project into the suffocating dreamplane. "Let's try holding the image of your sketch in our heads. Maybe it'll help."

Blake takes a deep breath and nods while still clutching her hand. They close their eyes in concentration. Layna is shocked by the strength of the tugging at her center as she pictures the details of the sketch, stronger this time than it was when she did this alone. And *she* feels stronger, more capable of this, with him at her side. In less than two minutes, they project as one into the Ouroboros.

Without being able to speak, Layna immediately finds Blake's frantic eyes with hers and tries to speak comfort into them. She squeezes his hand and signals deep breaths, even though it's laborious to do so. She doesn't want to start hyperventilating like last time. He seems to calm down slightly as his eyes remain on hers, but it takes a minute of coaxing before they find themselves standing over the book.

The moment Layna focuses on it, she sees the vision again. This time, she notices that the book opens to somewhere in the second half. It takes both of them to lift the pages to get to that section, and Layna notices the difference in the text there immediately. The brushstrokes are airier than the exacting, harsh lines of the markings she'd seen in the beginning of the book. She focuses on a page and gibberish pops into her head, scattered words and non-words she can't make sense of. Maybe this isn't going to be as easy as she thought.

As they flip through the pages, Layna glances at several passages, each one more indecipherable than the last. The weight of the air is draining her energy, and Blake lays his hand on hers as he motions toward the athenaeum with weary eyes. She's impressed he's lasted even this long on his first try and starts to nod in agreement, but an abrupt spike in her telesthesia changes her mind. The Dream Book…it's as if it's helping her. She closes her eyes to focus, running her fingers down the right side of the book until she feels it. A sort of vibrating beneath her pinky finger. She slips her fingernail between the pages there and flips it open, revealing a page that flashes briefly to red. She glances up at Blake who nods, his eyes wide and fixated. He saw it too.

They both lean over the page as the writing begins to appear. There is no title, and the glyphs that begin to form are faded, barely visible, and smaller than any of the others she's seen. And yet this passage is loudest in her head, every word crisp and identifiable. But with each word, Layna's heart sinks more and more.

Bound as one, twin fates are sealed
Neither light nor dark may yield
A balance broke by Phantom's spark
The mists of Chaos beget the dark
When of Aether and of Blood

217

Lends passage to the shadowed flood

The universes distend and rip asunder

The Light of Kosmos forever smothered

Just when Layna thinks it's finished, the page glows red again, weaker this time, and a final stanza appears, its glyphs slightly less faded than the rest.

Once Eskhatos is eclipsed

Then it can end in only this

Unless Day joins Night and Night joins Day

As one to close the Gateway

After she's sure no further text is going to appear, she grabs Blake's hand and they project back into the homeplane together. It happens almost instinctively, as though their bodies were just waiting for their cue to escape the agony of the other dimension. They port back to the kitchen, which remains empty. It seems Des and Lady Anora are still outside discussing what happened. Layna sits and slumps forward against the table as she goes over the words that have somehow burned themselves into her memory. It was a prophecy. And an ominous one at that. Layna shudders as the words nestle deeper, imprinting on her heart the allusion of a dark fate.

"Well…that really cleared things up," Blake finally says, his tone lighthearted.

Layna can't help but laugh at this, and she gazes at him in wonder. "How do you always do that?"

"What?"

"Just say something random and it makes me feel like maybe everything isn't doomed."

Blake gives the table between them an endearingly bashful smile and scrunches up his nose. "I'm just really good at saying random stuff, what can I say?"

"You are," she replies with a giggle. "So you think we should tell Des we read it and try to get more information out of him?"

"I'm not sure," he says, as he glances through the windows. "Why don't we wait until tomorrow? They seem to have a lot going on right now."

Layna nods in agreement just as Des swings open the screen door and is followed in by Lady Anora.

"Layna, darlin', are you alright?" Lady Anora asks, as she comes to sit beside her. She pushes Layna's hair back behind her ear just like her mother would do. The gesture, though still a comfort coming from Lady Anora, makes Layna feel suddenly very homesick.

"Yes, I'm fine," Layna answers with a smile. "Des saved my life. Again."

Blake shifts uncomfortably in his seat as Lady Anora glances at Des. "Yes, Desmond tells me you ran into two eclipsed. On the road that leads directly to this house, no less. This is likely an unfortunate coincidence, but we are going to need to take more precaution with the two of you."

"Why? You think maybe they were coming *here*?" Blake asks. "Like, to kill us?"

"It's not a coincidence, two very strong umbrae marching toward the house of the Senecta. The house that contains the Dream Book," Des says darkly. "This house is well protected. We're not supposed to get eclipsed people just walking down the road like that. With guns."

"Like I said before, Desmond, it is impossible the umbrae are capable of what you're suggesting," Lady Anora says to Des, her voice edged with restrained impatience. Then turning to Layna and Blake, she explains, "When a human is eclipsed, the umbra is not capable of influencing them beyond any acts they were already contemplating or in the process of carrying out. An umbra could not gain *control* over a human's conscious decisions. Such a thing would imply intent and we know full well that the umbrae are not capable of such intent, as they are not sentient. But, regardless of the reason they were here, I will continue to do a full sweep of our region to be sure we're not missing anything. First thing tomorrow morning, I will call a meeting with the Consulate to discuss this."

"Is there anything we can do to help?" Blake asks.

Lady Anora pats him lightly on the arm. "You two have worked hard enough this weekend, and I'm extraordinarily proud of how you've progressed. Why don't y'all go enjoy some fresh air on the porch while I make you some special midnight tea before you head back to bed?"

Blake and Des walk out to the porch, but Layna remains planted in her seat. She keeps silently repeating the prophecy's words, willing herself to understand their meaning.

Lady Anora crouches in front of her and clasps Layna's hands in hers. She doesn't say anything at first, but she looks into her eyes, drawing her feelings out like a magnet. "I know tonight must have been awfully frightening, darlin'. You must feel like you've simply traded one burden for another, and I wish that I could carry that burden for you. Though I can't promise the weight will ever grow lighter, I can promise that you will grow stronger, more capable of bearing it. It is who you are, and you will come to embrace it. And Desmond will always be there to help you. He is your Guide for life, as I am his."

"Really?" Layna says, brightening. She assumed after training was over that she and Blake would be back on their own. The fears and doubts that were beginning to rekindle inside her mind dissolve into a familiar warmth. The feeling of *home*. Not only does she have one waiting for her back in Caledon, but she is fortunate enough to have found another one right here with this enigmatic new tribe of hers. As nonsensical as all of this may be, it is also right.

"I know he can be a little volatile at times," Lady Anora chuckles, her grey eyes melting with affection. "He has seen more than his share of pain at such a young age, but he has the biggest heart of anyone I've had the privilege to know. He is very devoted to carrying out his purpose on this Earth. It is everything that he is. And as your Guide, he will do everything in his power to protect you and Blake. As will I."

Lady Anora wraps her in a hug, and Layna gratefully returns the embrace. Despite the substance and vigor with which Lady Anora carries herself, Layna is struck by how delicate her mentor feels in her arms. Like the bones of a hummingbird, as light as the air around her. It awakens a protective instinct inside her. One that she recognizes, for the first time, as a Naut. Just as Lady Anora has vowed to protect them, she silently returns the vow.

Lady Anora rises to set about making tea. Through the screen door, Layna hears the lilting voice of Ringo singing *Good Night* through a phone speaker with some vocal backup by Des. She smiles serenely as she heads out to the back porch.

"So, Layna, you officially met Oneironautica, eh?" Des asks, as the screen door creaks closed behind her. He is rocking gently on the porch swing, head back and eyes closed. "Some book, isn't she?"

"*She* is incredible, yes," Layna replies, as she takes the wicker seat next to Blake. "And, while we're on the subject, could you tell me what 'The Last Oneiroi, Hemera and Nyx' means?"

"Ah, so you opened it," Des says, leaning forward with a pleased smirk. "Not bad, eh? No practice required to read it. It's written in the language of the Oneiroi. We have the natural ability to read it since it's sort of coded into our DNA, so to speak."

Layna thinks of the numerous passages of gibberish and asks, "So we could read the whole book if we wanted to?"

"Not exactly. It's still writing itself," Des replies.

Blake gives him a disbelieving look. "Seriously, man? It's writing *itself?*"

"Well, Layna, you saw the text. Do you think a person could have made those glyphs? Bugger that, they're perfect. And not hyperbolically—I mean the shape and size and symmetry of them are *actually* mathematically, geometrically perfect. We have scribes who can replicate it enough for record-keeping purposes, but they're not considered authentic writings. The book writes our history as it happens—which is the first half of the book. The second half we refer to as the mysteries, which are quite cryptic, and to be honest, we still don't fully understand the whole of it. You don't know what it's even bloody talking about unless you know exactly what you're looking for. And that's not easy considering it is constantly changing. The only part of the mysteries we know for sure never changes is the Phantom's Prophecy."

The second the name escapes his lips, Layna sees the image of the glowing, red page, and she realizes that it wasn't just the book but that prophecy itself that's been calling to her since she arrived here. Since before then, even. Maybe for her whole life.

"What is that?" Layna urges. "That prophecy?" She can sense Blake's apprehension next to her—his wordless suggestion not to push too hard.

Des grimaces, apparently uncomfortable with his hapless introduction to this topic. She can tell it's something he'd rather not discuss. Or maybe he's not supposed to.

"It's the oldest part of the Dream Book, the oldest record of anything ever. The book—hell, the language itself—was created *for* the Prophecy. Every aetherworld has their own Dream Book, and every single one began as that prophecy alone. Legend has it the books were all forged from a single star, so strong that its energy broke through to the dreamplane, where it was collected and formed into text. Each book grew and matured differently alongside the development of its home world."

"Why is the prophecy so important? What actually is it?" Layna presses.

"It's…you know, the final prediction. End of worlds and all that. You'll be able to read it eventually. When the time is right."

"You can't tell us what it says?" Layna asks.

"No can do, kid. The first Tenet of Hemera and Nyx is that every Naut must read the Prophecy for themselves. It's not as easy as you might think. Not like flipping open a page of a textbook."

Layna and Blake cast each other a coded look.

"The Prophecy chooses when to reveal itself to each Naut. It's sort of a rite of passage as deemed by Hemera and Nyx."

"But who *are* Hemera and Nyx?" Layna repeats again.

"Sorry, yeah, you asked that. I keep forgetting how little you two know at this point. Usually by the time you can see the book in the Ouroboros, you've already been taught the basics of our history. Hemera and Nyx were the first two Nauts of Earth. They were also the last beings on any world who were gifted the power of dream travel by the Oneiroi. Earth was the last aetherworld."

"Why?" Blake asks. "What happened to the On...On...Onei—"

"The Oneiroi. They perished, after some billions of years of existence. Now all Nauts get their power by inheritance. Not genealogy, mind you—it's inherited from the balance in the Ouroboros, not from kin. The Oneiroi were not eternal, formless entities like Aether and Erebus, but actual beings. The *first* sentient beings, created in tandem by Aether and Erebus somewhat unintentionally."

"Unintentionally?" Layna encourages.

"Aye, see, when the universes were formed, there was no way between the two, and it was the natural instinct of Aether and Erebus to spread and be limitless. So eventually between them they created these beings comprised of both light and dark—the Oneiroi—who could exist in both universes, and from them grew the Ouroboros. The way between. Their sentience was just an unintended side effect. And of course, as it turned out, freeing Light and Dark to travel all willy-nilly between universes wasn't the greatest plan. Plunged all of existence into chaos and almost ended everything right there."

"What kind of chaos?" Blake asks, raptured. "Like…what happened?"

"Well, where there is shadow, there can be no light, right? But without light, there can't be shadow. Bit of a catch-twenty-two. So when Erebus used the Oneiroi to spread to the Universe of Light, the first few fledgling aetherworlds were destroyed in its shadow. And as a consequence, so were their netherworld counterparts. In their place, a vacuum of nothingness—black holes, as they're now referred to by Earth's scientists. The destruction was accelerating exponentially, and had it continued to spread, both universes were at risk of being torn apart and becoming one big black hole. The Oneiroi had no choice but to turn on their creators. They shut the door and become gatekeepers of their dimension. Worked great for a few billion years, until there was a slight hiccup. The Dream Book calls it *Saa*."

"And what is that?" Layna asks.

Des runs a hand through his hair, his expression pensive, as Lady Anora steps out onto the porch carrying a platter holding a tea set. Looking relieved, Des rises to help her set it down between Layna and Blake. "Anora, I need an assist with this one," he pleads.

"Saa? Well, I suppose it is most easily described as spontaneous evolution—or more specifically, spontaneous sentience," Lady Anora explains, as she sits with Des on the swing. "Essentially, life on the

225

aetherworlds across the Kosmos started to become self-aware, to think and feel and comprehend anew."

"So, to be clear..." Blake hesitates. "All this about other aetherworlds and other dream books and sentient beings and all that, that's not like metaphorical or mythological...you're telling us there is actual other intelligent life in the universe. As in, aliens."

"Well, of course," Des chimes in. "Didn't think we're the only beings on the only planet in all the Kosmos that can think for ourselves, did you? We are the youngest and least advanced of them all. It would have happened a lot sooner here if that asteroid hadn't hit and destroyed all the dinosaurs. Another million years or so and it'd have been dinosaurs walking around in clothes, eating cereal, building cities, and snapchatting each other all day."

Lady Anora laughs into her teacup as Blake drops his head in his hands. "This is nuts."

"So what was the problem with this, um...Saa?" Layna interjects, desperate to get as many answers out of them as possible.

"The problem was what evolutionary sentience invited," Lady Anora replies. "It is, quite simply, the key to our universe. The sentience of the Oneiroi was what allowed Aether and Erebus to flow between the universes, and Saa provided Erebus with another way in, limited though it was. But unlike the Oneiroi, who were granted sentience by Aether and Erebus, once ethereal beings evolve to become fully sentient, or in other words, *sapient*, they forget who they truly are. They forget that they *are* Aether, that they are from the same light as everything in the Kosmos.

"Becoming 'self-aware' really means becoming aware of a new self. An individual self in an individual body wholly separate from all else. It is as if a dark veil descends over their true identity, masking their true nature. This veil is what some refer to as the ego. And it is through the ego that the reciprocal umbra is able to influence the sapient mind to inflict chaos and destruction on an aetherworld. Homo sapiens were the first species to become sapient on Earth, hence the name. The Oneiroi referred to such species as worldlings, roughly translated. Once an aetherworld developed worldlings, it began to tip into shadow due to umbrae influence, and it is then that the Oneiroi would come. Tip too far, and the balance breaks, opening the floodgates to a darkness that would snuff out all light across the Kosmos."

"On that light note, pun intended," Des quips, downing the remaining contents of his tea, "I think we should call it a night. Tomorrow we'll wrap up oneironautics and start training on the second Tripartite Power. Get excited." He stands up and stretches, offering Lady Anora a hand. "Now, Anora, where's that chocolate stash of yours? All this talk of sentience makes me peckish for sweets."

As the others head inside, Layna walks over and leans against the railing, peering out at the ocean. She notices the rock wall that she and Blake raced to on Friday morning, which feels like a lifetime ago. She closes her eyes and listens to the waves tumbling into shore, the cyclical certainty of it, in and out, round and round. She breathes deeply, relishing the fresh sea air as she allows herself a moment to just be *Layna*. No destiny, no mysterious prophecy, no special powers or aliens or black holes or other dimensions or talking dinosaurs. Just

227

regular, seventeen-year-old Layna, who would be going to the beach, and the movies, and maybe a house party or two with her friends this summer. Who would be going back to school in the fall for her senior year, and then maybe design school after that. That's who she is, all she is, contained in this small body in this small life, and nothing more.

It's a cloudless night, and she looks up at the stars stretching out above the horizon. *But I am a part of that. I am more.*

The shift in thought is disorienting. Like the world has grown and she has shrunk, or the world has shrunk, and she has grown. There is so much actually out there. Not just their universe, but a whole other universe. Two whole universes, and a bunch of other sentient species. And all of it could potentially be destroyed someday by some primordial, eternal darkness. The end of all worlds. And she is part of a secret order that spans all of the Kosmos meant to help prevent that.

The knowledge of it all drags on her, strips her of the ignorance that preceded it. But in its place, she feels a new resilience taking form. As she straightens from the railing and follows the others inside, she leaves the young girl who once was Layna Emery of Caledon, New Jersey out on that porch. She floats away on a breeze, drifting out to sea and evaporating among the waves.

CHAPTER

Layna sleeps later than usual and is greeted with an ominous, orange-grey Monday morning. She changes quickly into a white cotton shirt and mesh shorts and pulls her hair into a ponytail. She slept too late to have time for a run, but maybe she can get in a quick walk by the water before Des wants to start training. She slips on her purple Keds and heads downstairs.

A dense fog hangs over the water, swirling around the shoreline where the waves break against the sand. It reminds her of the Ouroboros, and she finds it somehow nostalgic, though she only just became acquainted with the other dimension yesterday and had no measure of fondness for the place until now.

As she heads down toward the water, she starts to wonder if maybe this isn't the best idea in light of yesterday's events. As if in answer to her thoughts, through the fog she notices two dark figures moving erratically a little ways down the beach. She stumbles to a halt and drops to her knees behind the sand dune.

Oh god. It's more eclipsed. We're under attack.

She's no match for men with guns. She has a better shot crossing into the Ouroboros and trying to fight the umbrae themselves. Des and Lady Anora would not approve. She should port back inside for help. But she can feel her Naut instincts kicking in, and she almost yearns for the fight. For the chance to prove herself and fulfill her purpose. Fight or flight—her feet are itching to move, but toward the fight or back to the house for help?

Then she notices the two figures are not moving any closer to her. They are circling each other, lurching forwards and backward in sporadic movements. Then she hears a laugh. It's a laugh she knows, boisterous and carefree.

Layna releases the breath she was holding as her tense muscles relax. She pops up from her hiding spot and moves silently across the sand toward them. As she gets closer, she realizes Des and Blake are engaged in some sort of hand-to-hand combat in the surf. Blake is soaking wet from head to toe, and Des is, of course, still mostly dry. They both have ridiculous grins on their faces as Des taunts Blake to make another move.

Blake may not have Des' strength or skill, but he sure is quick, darting here and there around Des like a cat. Layna silently observes their virile dance until Blake goes down again, yelping as he hits the cold water. Layna bursts into laughter and they both finally notice her standing there.

"Layna!" they shout in cheerful chorus as Blake rises from the ocean and starts wiping water and sand from his running clothes.

"Blake was just teaching me a thing or two about slap-boxing," Des quips, as he reaches an arm sideways around Blake's neck and tosses him back into the water. He lets out a deep chuckle and deftly jumps out of the way of Blake's leg sweep.

Layna smiles and shakes her head in mock disapproval. "How long have you guys been out here?"

Des clears his throat, becoming serious as he responds, "Right, I was out here a couple hours ago to find this kid just returning from a run. You two can't be going off running on your own anymore. At least not for the time being. Got it?"

"Got it," Layna answers glumly.

"On a lighter note, Blake and I got in a little oneironautics practice this morning and I'm happy to report that he's successfully projected. A couple of times, actually," Des says, a proud smile etched on his face.

Behind Des, Blake looks guilt-ridden as he flashes Layna an uncomfortable grimace. It's amusing how bad he is at lying. She's actually kind of surprised he didn't already spill the tea.

"So, since everyone's on the same page now, why not have a bit of a friendly competition, eh?" Des suggests.

"Meaning?" Blake asks, scrunching up his nose like he's smelled something foul. The gesture strikes Layna as characteristic Blake, and she decides she very much likes it.

"Meaning it's time for you to combine oneironautics with the second of the Tripartite Powers—the *lucetelum*. Good news is that the next two powers are a wee bit less complicated to learn than oneironautics. Bad news is, they normally take much longer to totally master. More good news? You both happen to have a loose handle on the basics already!"

"Starting *and* ending with the good news. I like your style," Blake says, as he shakes wet sand out of his hair.

"Aye, well, I've got lots of it," Des says with a smirk. "Anyone want to guess what I mean by lucetelum?"

"Are you talking about the light?" Layna asks.

Des nods once. "Right you are, Layna. Lucetelum is the light we emit when we are in the Ouroboros—the auras you saw around each other there. More specifically, as a Tripartite power, it refers to our ability, when we're in the Ouroboros, to gather that light and discharge it like lightning at the umbrae."

"Cool, so…what's with my aura, then?" Blake asks. "I mean, why's my lucetelum, um, darker?" He awaits the response as he begins an intense examination of the hole his foot has been idly digging in the sand.

"Oh, well, now that's nothing to worry about, mate. Technically it's not darker in the slightest. It's just how we perceive it when we're in the Ouroboros. Because you're a nyx."

"Say what now?" Blake replies.

"By design, there are two different lines of Nauts. Descendants—if we can use that word loosely—of Hemera and Nyx. Layna and I are hemera, and you're a nyx."

"But what's the point of having two different kinds of Nauts?" Layna asks.

232

"Remember Lady Anora said that the Ouroboros is like a wormhole—a sort of five-dimensional tunnel. It's not only an entrance, but an exit as well. That means there are two ends that must be guarded. We're meant to fight in hemera-nyx pairs, which is why the two of you were both called to defense at the same time back in New Jersey. It's also why each of the Earth's six regions will generally have an equal number of hemera and nyx, and why each region's two Consulate representatives are one of each. Even though we aren't capable of perceiving it with our limited senses, all hemera enter the Ouroboros near the entrance to the aetherworld, while all nyx enter closer to the exit to the netherworld."

"So the one who guards the netherworld has a darker aura, because they are closer to the darkness, in a way," Blake concludes.

"Exactly," Des responds with a nod. "Their light is tinged with the darkness."

"So, Lady Anora, she's a nyx?" Layna asks.

"Well, no, actually, she is also a hemera."

"But you two fight together so shouldn't you be one of each?" Blake adds.

"No," Des says, suddenly defensive. "We aren't partners. She's my Guide."

"But—"

"Let's get started on lucetelum, shall we?" Des chirps, interrupting Layna's question. "Follow me back toward the house." He vanishes, reappearing on the other side of the dune between the house and the water line. After a moment of concentration, Layna and Blake reappear one after the other beside him. "Now," Des continues, "although there are a number of advanced methods, the basic way of using the lucetelum against a single umbra is to focus your energy, channel it, and sort of push it out through your hands. It's like…you're trying to push a heavy object that isn't there. Like this." He places his palms on Blake's arm and shoves. Blake stumbles back several steps before he can put up any defense.

"Hey," he objects.

"Sorry not sorry," Des mocks with a laugh. "Now you do it to me."

Blake puts his palms against Des' arm and pushes with all his might.

"Not quite," Des corrects. "You used the momentum of your whole body to move me. You've got to force all the energy out through your hands. Do it again, keep your core stable when you push, and try to notice the difference."

After allowing them both a couple minutes of practice, Des claps his hands for attention. "Okay, that's pretty much it. So, who wants to practice for real?"

"But there are no umbrae. What would we be targeting?" Layna asks.

"Each other, of course," Des replies, as a smirk plays at the corners of his mouth.

"Each *other*?" Layna blurts. "You mean we have to hit one another with the lucetelum?"

"It's precisely what I mean. Not to worry though. The lucetelum is a powerful weapon, but not against Nauts. What it does is cast the umbrae back into their netherworld. While they may seek to destroy light with their shadowspears, we Nauts do not destroy. We can't kill the umbrae because we'd also be murdering their human counterpart— one can't exist without the other, remember? That's what makes us gatekeepers, not warriors, as I'm so often reminded by my elders," he says with a role of his eyes. "So the lucetelum doesn't destroy an umbra but simply weakens them, and it'll be some time before it can gather strength to influence its human counterpart again. The most it'll do to a Naut is knock him or her out of the Ouroboros and back into the homeplane. Oh, and it'll sting like a...well, you get the idea. Stick around the house and try your best to not get hit."

Blake and Layna stand there looking at each other, not sure what to do next.

"Well, don't be daft...off you go!" Des shouts.

Layna turns to face Lady Anora's towering house, closing her eyes and concentrating on the image that still remains etched on the back of her eyelids. She imagines the swirling grey of the Ouroboros, the weight of the air. In under a minute, she has projected into the Ouroboros, standing in the same spot as she was in the other dimension. She feels briefly triumphant until she sees Blake's deep, blue glow about fifty feet away. He has already projected and is on the move, leaping awkwardly through the heavy air of the Ouroboros and around the side of the back porch.

Des was right. Already the Ouroboros feels less suffocating, her body already becoming used to the viscosity of it. Layna follows Blake as Des pops up next to her and takes a seat in the sand, preparing to watch the coming battle.

Blake has turned around to face her, peeking out from around the side of the porch. His body protected, he has a clear shot of her, but he seems stuck between action and inaction.

Layna uses the opportunity to dive behind the nearest sand dune to the left of the house. She lifts her head and hands over the top of the dune and aims at Blake, concentrating on channeling her energy. Unlike in the alley, she can now see the faintest light shoot toward Blake from her palms as the air crackles with electricity. He looks momentarily shocked as the light meets a mark about a foot above his head, and then he hits the dirt.

"Good, Layna!" Des shouts. "Blake, move around! Remember, you can port around here too to get around faster, just like in the homeplane."

Oh, sure, piece of cake, Layna thinks as she remembers how Des was porting wildly around those two umbrae yesterday. She focuses on the space right behind where Blake crouches in the sand, reappearing there a moment later, but he is gone. She looks around to find that he is now behind the dune. They've traded places.

Layna hears a deep belly-laugh from Des' spectator spot. "Brilliant! Now try and actually hit each other!"

Layna grins at Des' joviality in spite of herself. She takes aim again at Blake, but he vanishes again before she can channel the lucetelum. She spins around, trying to locate him.

Then she hears the crackle of lightning as a dark shot of light whizzes past her head into the sand by her feet. She looks up and sees Blake standing on the roof of the back porch, smiling down at her apologetically.

She ports to the second-floor balcony, now looking down at him. He spins around to find her, and they raise their hands and fire lucetelum simultaneously. Layna sees a small explosion of light between them as their lucetelum meet in the air. There is a laugh in Blake's eyes as he disappears. He is fully enjoying himself, just like Des. She tries to give herself over to the thrill of the game, too, but something is holding her back. Something is nagging at the back of her mind.

Layna crouches low on the balcony, surveying her surroundings, but she doesn't see Blake reappear anywhere. She ports back down to the beach to try to get a better vantage point of the house. She scans every level of the house, the sand, the dunes, and she catches Des' eye as he nods to a spot behind her. She spins around just in time to catch a flash of light as a sharp, biting pain tears through her right hip, and she is thrown backward.

In the split second that she is airborne, the whooshing sensation thunders involuntarily across her body and she's spit back out into the homeplane. She lands hard in the sand and sucks in the air to replenish the breath in her lungs. The stinging pain in her hip subsides almost immediately once she's back in the homeplane, and Blake materializes in front of her as she sits up.

"Sorry," Blake says with a remorseful grimace. "Are you alright? Did it hurt?" he asks, crouching down next to her.

She laughs breathlessly and yells, "Of course it hurt, you idiot!"

"Guess you've got to be a little quicker, then," he says with an impish grin, offering her his hand.

As she rises to her feet, Layna sees Des is back in the homeplane too and is making his way over to them. But she's not ready to admit defeat. "And you'd better watch your back," she retorts with a wink, as she projects back into the Ouroboros.

Before Blake can have time to follow, she instantly ports to the second-floor balcony and aims at his still frozen figure down on the sand, waiting for him to cross over. But when he vanishes from the homeplane, he doesn't reappear in the same spot in the Ouroboros. He's just projected and ported at once. There is the faintest pop right next to Layna, and she whirls around to find him behind her on the balcony, so close she can feel the breath of his soundless laugh in her hair. She squeals in surprise and loses her balance, grabbing at his shirt so that they fall together against the wall of the house. There is a distinctive tingling of electricity where her skin meets his, and she can feel his heart pounding in his chest. Or maybe it's hers. Her mind is cloudy as she looks into his cobalt eyes. He doesn't look away. He doesn't attempt to move off of her. She doesn't want him to.

Stop it, get your head in the game.

She takes advantage of the moment to concentrate on the third-floor balcony above them, porting there and then immediately back down to the sand before she can even fully get her bearings. She spins down on one knee to aim her palms at the third-floor balcony where she just stood. As she suspected, Blake's deep, blue light appears on the third-floor balcony not a second later. She fires a lucetelum at him before he can pinpoint her new location.

This time, Layna can clearly see the lucetelum leave her hands, and it hits him dead in the chest. His puckish smile is replaced with an expression of shock as he is flung through the air. And in that moment, Layna knows that he is going to go over the side of the balcony.

He is going to fall to his death all because she couldn't let him win the stupid game.

Her cry comes out as a helpless whimper, and she watches him tip over the railing. He is almost doubled backward over it when his body pops back out to the homeplane from the force of the lucetelum. It slows his progress just enough for Layna to hatch part of an idiotic plan that will require her to do what Blake just did—project and port at once. She will need to be one hundred percent accurate, but she has no time to think about the odds.

I've got you, Blake.

She concentrates on him, only on him. And as she feels the whooshing sensation, she pictures her arms outstretched toward him, her legs straddling the railing so she can grip it with her thighs. She doesn't know physics—that's senior year—so instead, all she can do is pray that she will be strong enough to stop his momentum.

She pops out in the homeplane right by his side, instantly bringing her arms together around him. The fabric of his shirt is sliding through her arms. She tightens both the grip of her arms around him and her legs around the railing.

The pull on her is too great. He is moving too fast. She knows what it means, but she can't let him go. She won't. Instead, Layna feels her legs yanked from the railing. And then they are both falling.

The sensation of free-falling through the air is a strange, panicky blur. Your body hurtling toward death as though time has decided to just fast-forward to the end of your life.

As the ground approaches at an alarming rate, Layna squeezes her eyes shut and braces herself for impact. Every fiber, nerve, and muscle in her body prickles in anticipation of bone-crushing pain. There is a small pop in her ears and a tightening around her waist. But rather than the solid, unforgiving ground, she and Blake sink into a body of chilly water.

Underwater, her mind is a jumble as she untangles herself from a mess of arms and legs and instinctively kicks toward what she hopes is the surface. Her head breaks over the waves of the ocean to see a stunned Blake emerge after her, glasses askew on his face and the shoreline well beyond him. She opens her mouth to speak, but it is instead filled with a mouthful of saltwater as a wave hits her from behind. She sputters and coughs as Des breaches the surface next to them. They stare at him for a long moment as they bobble there atop the waves.

"We're in the ocean," Blake observes.

"Aye, thanks for clarifying," Des grumbles. "Now port your bums to shore before the sharks get us."

He disappears from the water, leaving them floating there on their own. But nothing could have motivated Layna more than the idea of a shark lurking in the dark water beneath her. She quickly reigns in the frayed ends of her mind to concentrate on porting to dry sand. Des is already pacing in front of the house, and as soon as Layna and Blake appear next to him, he goes off.

"You two will be the death of me yet, I know it! My nerves—I can't—you're too good for your own good, you know? I couldn't keep track of you, popping in and out. How's anyone supposed to *guide* the two of you? I mean, even a great Guide, hell, even Lady Anora herself would…"

Layna's attention drifts from his outburst as she catches her breath and tries to comprehend what exactly happened in the last thirty seconds. She only now realizes how fast she and Blake had been moving through the Ouroboros. With the time lag, Des probably wouldn't have even had time to project back into the Ouroboros after them before they were falling from the balcony. He must have seen them fall, ported into mid-air, caught them, and then ported them safely into the water, all before they could fall three stories.

Her jaw drops as she looks at Blake, whose face mirrors her own. His glasses are still lopsided, and his eyes dart between the balcony, Des, and the ocean. He finally settles on Layna, and his shock turns to an expression that seems to border on anger. Is he mad that her competitiveness almost got him killed? She doesn't like the panicky way it makes her feel, and she turns away from his glare to find Des still raving like a damn lunatic.

"…be more careful! When I said try porting to get around faster, I didn't mean all the way up the side of the bloody house—"

"Des!" Layna finally interrupts. He is surprised, again, to find that he is actually conversing with someone.

"Sorry," he mutters. He takes a deep breath and squeezes his eyes shut for a moment, like he's trying to bury some errant emotion or memory attempting to break the surface. "Are you both alright?"

Layna and Blake nod, the ends of their hair and clothes dripping with the sea. "Man...how the *hell* did you do that?" Blake cries.

Des swallows hard and responds, "Practice, kid. Lots and lots of practice. Although at the rate you two are going, you'll surpass me before you even complete ascendance. I mean, your *speed* already, and, Layna, what I believe you did up there, that was quite brilliant. Maybe not the *wisest* plan, but brilliantly executed. To get as precise a position as you did, and under pressure too."

Layna gives Des a smile of thanks, but she doesn't miss the way Blake is staring indignantly at the ground, aggressively wringing out his sodden clothes. Maybe it's jealousy?

"Why don't we take practice inside where neither of you will have an opportunity to fall to your deaths, eh? And tell you what, seeing as it won't be quite as much of an unfair advantage as I initially thought, I'll join you for this round. You two versus me, and we'll make it interesting and play resurrection style."

"Resurrection style?" Layna wonders aloud.

"Oh, come on," Des says as he crosses his arms in disbelief. "Haven't you ever played dodgeball?"

Blake laughs as he responds, "Don't you know who you're talking to? She wouldn't be caught dead playing dodgeball. She's too cool for that. I played all the time back in Philly," he says with a smirk.

Layna pulls her dripping hair into an angry ponytail as Des and Blake go over the rules. She doesn't care why Blake is mad anymore, and she kind of wants to punch him in his stupid, lovely teeth. There is a sort of nostalgic childhood excitement between the guys, but she still can't shake the feeling that something is wrong. She decides she should probably mention this to Des, when he bellows, "Alright, on my count, then. One, two...three!"

With an aggravated sigh, she ports to a spot in the hallway outside the study near her bedroom. There she finds that Blake has chosen the same spot and stands right across from her. They share an awkward laugh, and Layna senses his anger melt just a little. She opens her mouth to ask him what his deal is when, without warning, the slight nagging feeling at the back of her mind explodes across her skull with such power it feels as though it could tear her soul in two.

Her body goes rigid, spine arching violently as the breath is forced from her lungs. She gasps desperately for air, and her knees buckle as she collapses under an unidentifiable weight.

Blake lunges forward and catches her before she can hit the floor. She can hear him saying her name, but he sounds so distant. Her vision swims and she senses something pulling her away, her mind warring between here and there. Something horrible is happening, and she can't get a clear enough sense of what it is.

She hears Des' voice from somewhere too. "Oy, come on! You two aren't even trying to..."

Layna sees his figure appear above her but trying to focus on him causes a mixed wave of nausea and doom to wash over her. It's pulling her under, and she wants to let it. She knows it's important, but terror causes her to cling desperately to reality. Her eyes roll back against her will, and she sees the flash of an image in her mind—too fast, and it's gone.

"Blake, what happened?" Des says, as she feels his fingers press against her neck.

"I don't know. She just went all rigid and collapsed!" Blake cries. Layna feels him trembling and wants to tell him that she is okay, to just keep talking so she can stay there with him, but her mouth won't work.

"Damn, her pulse is way too fast. Get her on her side, I need to grab a pillow from the study," Des instructs. She feels herself being turned, and at the same time, she stands in front of a screaming, black sea somewhere far away. She senses Blake sitting next to her, holding her hand, and Des putting a pillow beneath her head. But she is also alone on a cliff, a harsh wind biting her cheeks, surrounded by darkness.

"Layna, talk to us," Des commands, as he snaps his fingers in front of her eyes. "She's not responsive. I think she may be having a seizure. Layna, can you hear me?"

Layna tries to answer but instead finds that her lungs are no longer pulling in air. Something is crushing her chest.

"Des…her face is turning…I don't think she can breathe!" Blake yells.

Des shoves Blake away and pries her mouth open. As he rolls her onto her back, she feels the weight come off her chest and she gulps hungrily at the air. The 'there' fades away as the world around her settles back into place and she becomes whole again.

"Layna! You can hear me now? Are you alright?" Des asks, as Blake reappears over his shoulder, his eyes filling with relief.

"I—I'm not sure," Layna stammers, as her teeth begin to chatter.

Des picks her up and carries her to the leather couch in the study. Blake sits down next to her as Des grabs the knitted, wool blanket from the desk chair and throws it over her. Her whole body is shivering with a coldness that comes from deep inside her. "I think it was my telesthesia," she whispers.

"I've never seen anyone react that way to a telesthetic impulse," Des says, shaking his head. "Are you sure? It seemed like you were having a seizure. In which case, we would need to get you to a hospital."

Layna thinks about the horrible sensation of dread that gripped her, and that nagging feeling she had earlier that something was wrong. The glimpses of the 'there' that have already faded from her mind. She should have gone with it into the dark and not been such a coward.

"Yes, I'm sure," she answers definitively.

"Alright, well try to relax a second. Blake, stay with her. I'm going to go pull Lady Anora from the Consulate gathering."

"Are you allowed to do that?" Layna asks weakly.

"For emergencies, yes. And if that really was a telesthetic impulse, it was the strongest I've ever seen, which can't mean anything good."

Des vanishes to Athens to retrieve Lady Anora. Blake takes Layna's hand again, squeezing it reassuringly.

"Not mad at me anymore?" Layna murmurs, trying to sound lighthearted but leaning more toward pathetic due to the trembling in her voice.

"Mad?" Blake gasps, sounding almost hurt by the accusation.

"You know, for almost killing you?" she guesses.

"Wait," he says, shaking his head in confusion. "You think I was mad at you for hitting me with the lucetelum?"

"You weren't?"

"*No*. No, that wasn't it, Layna. It was just…" He pauses and looks away. "I was mad that you almost killed *yourself*, okay? I mean, what the hell were you thinking throwing yourself over the railing like that?"

"You must be joking. First of all, I'm the one who sent you over the railing. Seriously, Blake, what was I supposed to do, just sit there and watch you fall to your death?"

"*Yes*. Better than both of us falling. It was a really dumb thing to do, no matter what Des says."

"It was the *only* thing to do. I mean, I'm sorry if you think your life is not worth saving but—"

"It's not."

"*Blake*," she rebukes, alarmed at the conviction in his voice.

"It's not," he repeats firmly, as he looks into her eyes. "Not when it means risking yours. I don't want people dying for me, okay? Just please don't do that again."

She has clearly hit a nerve and doesn't know how to respond. But their silence is broken as Lady Anora and Des return from Athens. Blake jumps up and steps away as Lady Anora crosses the room to

Layna, her mouth set in a tight line. Layna scoots into a sitting position as Lady Anora sets herself at the edge of the couch.

"Are you alright?" she asks tightly.

Layna nods and attempts a composed smile.

"Are you able to tell me anything about what you felt during your experience?" Her voice is calm, but her grey eyes are a storm.

"I don't really know, but I was here and also very far away, somewhere dark and cold. Mostly it was just this overwhelming sense of dread. Like it was too big for me to really grasp. It was…suffocating me," Layna responds with a shiver.

Lady Anora places a hand on Layna's knee and gives Des a guarded look.

"What is it?" Blake asks.

"I'm afraid what Layna felt may be related to the Consulate's decision today. Layna, do tell us if you remember anything else."

"I promise I will. I'm sorry I can't be more helpful."

"Please don't worry about that, darlin'. You are doing your absolute best with a very new, very powerful ability you don't yet know how to control. You did just beautifully. Perhaps though…being new Activates, I do wonder if either of you could shed some light…" Lady Anora says, glancing at Des. "We know about your First Walk in the park, and your next experience with Des in the alley. But did either of you have any other experience with umbrae prior to your arrival here?"

"Layna did," Blake replies warily. "You'd seen it a few times by the time we had our First Walk, right?"

"Yeah, well, there was the time during my telesthetic impulse in November I've told all of you about, which I don't really remember.

Then there was this other time when I was completely awake. This guy was being aggressive with me, and it was only for a few seconds, but I'd swear he was eclipsed even though I was in the homeplane when I saw it."

Lady Anora visibly relaxes. "For those in the throes of activation, thankfully it's not too unusual to glimpse the presence of an umbra when you're awake and have a sudden spike in adrenaline. Similar to what Des told me about how you two experienced moments in which time felt sluggish. All relatively normal incidents of activation," Lady Anora explains.

"What about seeing yourself be eclipsed while you're awake?" Layna asks.

Des jumps up from the desk chair, knocking it over behind him. "*What?*"

"Layna, did that happen to you?" Lady Anora urges.

Layna balks at their sudden intensity and has a hard time finding her voice. "I—I mean, I don't know. I was arguing with my friend, and one second, I was in my body and the next second, I was looking at it. And it looked eclipsed. It only lasted a second."

Lady Anora and Des look at her in stunned silence, and then Des walks toward the door and punches a hole clean through the drywall alongside the doorframe. Layna and Blake jump in surprise.

"Desmond," Lady Anora pleads.

Des turns to them, a tormented look on his face. He stands there panting a moment and then vanishes.

"What the hell was that about?" Blake asks. "And what does all this have to do with what happened to Layna just now?"

Lady Anora closes her eyes, her brow knitted with worry. Layna has never seen her wear such a look of distress, and it leaves her feeling even more unsettled. She realizes only now how much she has relied upon Lady Anora's steadfast composure in shepherding them through the uncertainties of this new life.

"It's one of the things the Consulate has been investigating," Lady Anora murmurs. "It's as Desmond has feared for some time, and none of us wanted to believe it."

"Believe what?" Layna presses.

Lady Anora hesitates, seeming unsure of how much she wants to say. "Well, I suppose it's about time I told you about Darcie."

Blake takes a seat in the desk chair as he shares an apprehensive look with Layna.

"Desmond didn't go through ascendance alone either. Like you, he had a training partner, and I was Guide to both of them. Desmond didn't have any family when he arrived in this country at eighteen, and I found him by happenstance even before he was activated. But I knew he was one of us, and I could see he would be powerful. He took up residence here and worked as an EMT until his activation began when he was twenty-two. When we discovered Darcie, she was already thirty, which is extremely late to be activated. It makes it significantly harder for someone to accept, as you can imagine. Desmond had just started his training when Darcie lost her marriage. Keeping this life a secret from her husband put too great a strain on them. She moved in and the three of us lived here together for two years. But Desmond and I both saw Darcie slowly slipping into a state of despair. We did what we could, but one day we woke up and she was gone."

"She was one of the Nauts you mentioned? Who tried to leave?" Layna asks.

"Yes, darlin'. Desmond took it hard when she left. You see, as she was his partner, Desmond read many of her objects as part of his training. And when he reads a person's objects, through that sliver of their life, he gets to know a part of them on a deeper level than any other person ever could. The empathy he gains in doing so, well, it can turn into a profound love. Like the person is an extension of his own self. He becomes very attached to those he frequently reads, which is why he now typically tries to avoid it when he can. It's too much for him.

"He wanted to go find Darcie, talk some sense into her. But I forbade him from trying. I told her she would come back to us one day on her own. And when she did come back nearly two years later, she was a different woman. She had a darkness about her, a hollowness inside. For that first year back, the only time she ever seemed alive was when she and Desmond were fighting the umbrae. But I saw her slowly brightening the more time they spent together. Desmond brought her to life again. It was during that time that they fell in love.

"Then one day late last year, Desmond and I were in Athens on an important matter. He abruptly said he had to go—that he felt Darcie was in danger. He went back to the house but couldn't find her. He went outside and she was there, standing on the top of the tower. Before he could do anything...she jumped. He tried to catch her in the air, but it's extremely difficult to port to a moving target. He missed, and Darcie fell to her death."

"Oh, god," Layna gasps in dismay.

Blake curses under his breath as he stares absently at the floor. Des saw Darcie fall and couldn't catch her. Couldn't catch her the way he caught them today. He must have absolutely tortured himself practicing after what happened. Layna's heart aches for the pain they must have caused him in dredging up those memories.

Lady Anora sighs and closes her eyes, the remorse etched on her face. "To make matters worse, Desmond was convinced that she was somehow eclipsed when she fell. It was a ludicrous assumption of course, as Nauts have no umbra counterpart and are therefore insusceptible to Erebus's influence. But he swore he sensed it, swore she wouldn't have jumped unless under the control of darkness. I tried to convince him that what he was saying was not possible, that she had always struggled with accepting her destiny, and I had failed as her Guide. But he wouldn't hear it. He insisted that she had been getting better, and they were happy. I thought it was just his grief," she says, shaking her head.

"He brought the matter before the Consulate, warning them that this was a sign of something more nefarious. He asked them for a vote to form a task force to investigate. The Consulate, of course, voted him down. Myself included. Desmond would not speak with me for some time after that. And now…I fear that he may have been right all along. There have been a few reports of late—young Activates who felt they had been momentarily eclipsed. Layna's experience is further confirmation of their accounts. Among other anomalies, not the least of which was the detached umbrae you two encountered in the alley, there is mounting evidence of…well, I'd like the four of us to talk this over together. Why don't we reconvene in the athenaeum in a few minutes?"

As they stand to head downstairs, Lady Anora leans over to Layna and whispers, "Layna darlin', would you mind retrieving Desmond from his room before you come down? I'm afraid he may not want to see my face right now, but I'm sure he'd be open to seeing you."

"Why would he want to see me?" Layna asks dubiously.

"Because you're the only other person who's ever sensed he was right about the circumstances of Darcie's death," she replies.

"What? But I only just—" Layna stops speaking as everything falls perfectly into place.

"His room is on the third floor, second door to the left," Lady Anora instructs. She barely finishes speaking before Layna ports upstairs, now anxious to talk with Des.

Layna doesn't know what she was expecting Des' room to look like, but it wasn't quite this. Every surface in the room is covered with a mass assortment of items. From trinkets and knick-knacks to clothing, books, and paintings, to receipts, old newspapers, and other junk. And on the floor in the middle of it all sits Des, staring at an object in his hands and looking forlorn.

He looks up when Layna enters, his eyes wet and bloodshot. He clears his throat and sits up straighter as she makes space on the floor across from him. The room reminds her of something she saw on television once about hoarders. She begins to feel slightly uncomfortable, like she is intruding into an area of Des' life that is deeply private.

If this is the case, he doesn't let on, giving her a melancholy smile as she kneels down to face him. "Sorry about before," he mumbles. "Got a bit carried away. I just—"

"You don't need to explain yourself, Des. I know why you got upset."

"You do?"

"Yes…Lady Anora filled us in. And now I also know why you took that train ticket from me."

Des looks absentmindedly to an indiscriminate pile of things on his nightstand, but he doesn't respond.

"I was trying to get to Darcie, wasn't I?"

Des looks at her, and all she can see in his eyes is anguish. No more pretending. No more mask of indifference he once wore with them. After a moment, he nods heavily. "When I picked up that train ticket, I felt what you felt. Why you were trying so desperately to get to North Carolina. I'm sorry I kept it from you. But…you saw her. My Darcie," his voice breaks as he says her name, and he looks back down at the item in his hands.

"What did I see?" Layna probes gently.

"Well, at first you just sensed something was going to happen, like some dark plan was about to unfold. That's why you left school and got on the train." Des takes a deep breath, and the rest of his words come out in a rush. "Then you saw her in town, fighting a group of

253

eclipsed—five of them. All by herself. You saw her see something that made her panic and project back to the homeplane. Now I think it must have been a detached umbra. And then you saw it taking her. The shock on her face, her eyes going black. An umbra *had* her. I was right. You saw her on top of the tower. You saw her…seeing me. You heard her say my name. Like she was saying goodbye. And then you saw her fall."

Layna stares at him in dismay. If only she had been able to get there. What if she could have stopped it? "Des…I—I'm so sorry. I wish there was something I could do."

"You did do something," he insists, as he lifts his head to look at her again, his eyes intense. "You gave me proof that Darcie didn't take her own life. That it was Erebus who took her from me. You gave me a reason to keep fighting and shut that voice up in my head that plagued me every day. That maybe there was something more I could have done to bring her out of the darkness before it was too late. Layna…you gave me back a little piece of my life. And what's more, you tried to save hers."

The sincerity of his gratitude makes Layna uneasy. She doesn't deserve it. "I didn't even know what I was doing," she mumbles, inspecting her hands.

"You did. A part of you did know. If you didn't, then I wouldn't have been able to read it. I could feel what you were feeling, and you felt fearless, determined to save her. And somehow, you could also feel her…her goodness. The lightness of her being. It's something I've never experienced in any of my readings of her, or anyone else for that matter. It was a rare gift you gave to me. I can't begin to describe it." A rogue tear rolls down his cheek and he quickly wipes it away.

Layna feels helpless and speechless in the face of his pain. She hates seeing Des hurting so badly. He's their Guide, their protector, who shields them from danger. But how can she shield him from this? This is the kind of pain that no safeguard can prevent and no remedy can fix. So, she does the only thing that feels natural. She kneels forward and wraps her arms around his neck. He lets out a soft chuckle and hugs her back tightly.

"Anyway," he says, sniffling as he pulls away, "after I got that train ticket as proof Erebus could get to us, I went straight to Lady Anora with it. That is, after you and Blake tried to attack me with a bat and a bit of mace," he finishes with a lopsided grin.

Layna smiles at the memory. It was not even a week ago, but it feels like months had passed since that night. How silly they must have seemed to him then. "What did Lady Anora say when you brought her the ticket?"

"We took it to the Consulate to re-open the matter of Darcie's death. That's why I was late the next morning meeting you two. The gathering went on for over a day in Ouroboros time. They can be downright pigheaded sometimes, but voting is a serious thing to the Consulate. Can't do it until all the evidence is out on the table and everyone has a chance to make a statement. And the decision needs to be unanimous."

"What did they decide?" Layna asks.

"They didn't," Des responds with a roll of his eyes. "They said they needed more evidence and more time to deliberate. It's since turned into a much bigger deliberation as more evidence has been coming out. That's why Lady Anora has been going over there so often. I told them about the detached umbrae we saw, and I told them that was what I thought Darcie saw too. Last I know, it was still being discussed. But I think something happened today at the gathering."

"Oh, yeah, Lady Anora wants to talk to all of us. I came up to get you."

"Guess we should get down there, then," Des sighs, rising stiffly from the floor. He places the object he was holding gently onto his nightstand. Layna sees now that it's a woman's necklace.

Des follows her gaze. "It was Darcie's. Everything in this room was. I gave it to her a few months before she died," he says, picking it up again and handing it to Layna.

It's an oval-shaped, silver locket, about an inch and a half in length, hanging on a long, delicate chain. An embellished, Celtic design borders two initials in the center—D.H. & D.N. Layna unsnaps the latch on the side and opens it carefully. On one side of the locket is a tiny picture of Des and Darcie. Layna is struck by the familiarity and fondness she instantly feels for the woman in the photograph, and with it, the unexpected heartache of loss. Though she still recalls nothing of her Delaware episode, a part of her consciousness must remember, like a lost dream from long ago. Darcie is beautiful, with raven black hair, dark brown eyes, and olive-colored skin. She and Des are smiling at each other, and she certainly looks happy, not at all the way Lady Anora described her. On the other side, three words are inscribed: *I love you.*

"It was cheesy, I know. But that was my way of telling her. It was the first time I said it, to her or anyone. It was hard for me at first, saying it out loud. I wish I had said it to her every day. I must have done a reading on this thing a million times by now. When I do, I can feel how happy she was to know that I loved her, and I can feel her love for me balloon inside of her. And because she never took it off after that day, I can fleetingly relive the last few months of our life together through her memories. And I never do feel despair from her. It was what I was holding onto for hope that I didn't fail her. Until I found your ticket."

Layna puts the locket back on the nightstand and looks at the rest of the pile there, and on the desk, and floor, and bookshelf. "So, all these things were hers, and you've read them all?"

"I have. Every last one. She used to give me things of hers, as little gifts, you see. A receipt, a piece of clothing, didn't matter what it was. She'd give them to me so I would know her. She told me she didn't want to keep any secrets from me. I saved everything she ever gave me. And after she died, I took everything else that was in her room. Wouldn't let Lady Anora throw anything away. Quite the collection now, I reckon," he says, looking around the room. "You must think I'm completely mental."

"Not at all," Layna replies, as she shakes her head. "It makes sense that you'd want to hang on to her in any way you could. But...doesn't it hurt?"

"It hurts something awful. But generally, I'd rather spend every day up here with her than be out there in the world without her. Even if it is just a phantom of her. For a while, it was the closest thing I could get to happiness."

Layna thinks it sounds tortuous. How impossible it must be to move on from such a tragedy when he can relive pieces of her life every single day. Like being stuck in time.

"Come on," he says, as he claps her lightly on the shoulder. "We better get downstairs."

Des shuts the door behind them, and she can almost sense him getting lighter as he puts a barrier between himself and his former life. She gets ready to port, but Des begins walking down the hallway.

"Why don't you just port?" Layna asks curiously, as she speeds up to follow him.

Des chuckles. "Kid, it may seem like the most exciting thing in the world to you right now. But I'll tell you, the more time you spend as a Naut, the more you'll appreciate any little thing that makes you feel human."

CHAPTER

When Layna and Des get down to the athenaeum, Lady Anora has set out sandwiches around the coffee table. She and Blake sit cross-legged on the floor cushions, leaning across the table and speaking in whispers. Blake looks up at Layna and Des as they walk in, but quickly averts his eyes.

"Ah, good," Lady Anora says, as she turns to see them.

Layna takes a seat next to Blake as Des walks over to Lady Anora. He bends down to plant a kiss on her cheek, adding, "I'm sorry about your wall. I'll patch it up tomorrow."

Lady Anora smiles and pats the side of Des' face. "No matter, darlin'. Come, sit."

"Now, as we were saying upstairs, it's my assumption that Layna's telesthetic impulse was related to the Consulate's discussions today, which I believe I now must share with all of you," she begins. "Thanks in large part to Desmond's vigilance and determination, we have had an extensive debate about the possibility that Nauts may have somehow become susceptible to the influence of Erebus and, thereby, the umbrae. After gathering evidence on this matter for some time, today we were able to finally get a unanimous vote. We have concluded that the evidence does indeed suggest that Erebus has developed the ability to eclipse Nauts."

Des balls his hand into a fist and pounds his thigh, a look of pained vindication in his eyes as he mutters, "'Bout time, bloody pigheaded augurs."

"My dear friend, Thaddeus, a Region Two representative, hypothesized that whatever has allowed the umbrae to detach from their human counterpart and fully enter the Ouroboros must also make them capable of essentially jumping to Nauts who are in the homeplane. There's no evidence yet they can do this while we are in the Ouroboros with them. From the various accounts, it seems that we may perceive the intrusion as a sort of out-of-body experience. Layna, this coincides with your own experience of it.

"The fateful truth of this, I proposed today, is that these incidents have been tests—small, experimental attacks by Erebus. A sort of scouting of Earth's weaknesses. And we further determined today that when taken together, these unprecedented abilities of the umbrae are, undeniably, harbingers of the Phantom's Prophecy."

"Oh, *shit*," Blake breathes, raising a hand to his mouth. Layna instinctively grabs his other hand, gripping it like she's trying to squeeze courage from him.

The world is ending. The thought sounds ridiculous in her head. Some sick joke. Des looks unsurprised by the news, but simply resolute. A part of him must have known this was coming.

"I believe Desmond has mentioned the enormity of this prophecy, and I'm sorry to tell you like this. I know you haven't had nearly enough time to process all of this yet. When Desmond came for me earlier in Athens, we were discussing what should be done. Maven and I suggested that we weaponize our Order. It was not an easy suggestion to make and it was not lightly received. After all, we are gatekeepers, not warriors, and it is not in our nature nor is it our calling to go to war."

"We're already *in* a war," Des moans, exasperated. "How can they not see that?"

"It's not as simple as all that, Desmond. Remember that most of us on the Consulate are from an old generation with traditional ways of viewing our role in this world. It's not easy to suggest that our customs, as old as humankind itself, should be reformed. Nor is it easy to conceptualize such a reform."

"Well, what's the alternative? Let the universes be torn apart? Allow the end of the Kosmos and all life everywhere to just *happen*?" Des demands.

"Of course not," Lady Anora answers with a sigh. "They simply wish to focus our efforts on finding a way to prevent the Phantom's Prophecy from coming to fruition, rather than letting it get to all-out warfare. You know what it means for this world, Desmond, should we choose to weaponize. It is not a decision we can make lightly." Des gets up and starts pacing as Lady Anora implores, "Even if we did vote to weaponize, there's the small matter of how on Earth to do it. To our knowledge, no Naut has ever made a weapon to fight Erebus. We will have to consult the mysteries, and you know it could be months, *years* even, before we—"

"It will be too late by then!" Des shouts.

It's the first time Layna has heard him raise his voice to Lady Anora. She looks at the woman in anticipation of a heated retort, but Lady Anora remains silent and steady. She keeps her eyes leveled at Des until he stops pacing and resumes his seat next to her, hanging his head in penitence.

"Sorry," he mumbles.

Lady Anora addresses all three of them in a susurrating voice that betrays her own frustration. "I, as a member of the Consulate, have taken an oath. An oath to not pursue any avenue of offense or other activity as it relates to the Order, without the advice and decision of all Consulate members. So I cannot begin looking through that book for any answers before we come to a unanimous decision."

Des makes a defeated noise and drops his head in his hands.

But Lady Anora continues in an even softer tone, "However, I cannot be in this house at all times, and I have no control over what the members of my household may or may not do in my absence."

Des pops his head back up to look at her, his eyes softening as one corner of his mouth ticks up roguishly. Layna exchanges a determined look with Blake. *Finally, we can do something useful.*

"Now, getting to the second matter at hand. Layna, do you think the gravity of the Consulate's decisions today sufficiently explains your telesthetic impulse?" Lady Anora asks.

Layna closes her eyes, trying to piece together anything sensible from her episode, but she is only grasping at the frayed threads of a dream. She shifts her focus away from her muddled memory and into her gut, which has always been more reliable. She is not comforted by what she feels. "I...I think it's just out of my reach, but..."

"You think we're missing something," Lady Anora muses, as she studies Layna. "Given the strength of your ability, we should presume that your instinct is right. We must listen to it."

"But how can we, if I can't get any details from the impulse?"

Lady Anora considers this a moment and then addresses Blake, "Have you had any prophetic dreams lately that may corroborate what Layna might have seen?"

Blake shakes his head. "I'm sorry. I haven't had any flashes since we've been here. Especially with those bomb teas you've been making for us."

Lady Anora's eyes light up as she nods. "Well, not to worry, you've just given me another idea. I believe I have a formula that would work for this." She looks at Layna and explains, "It would induce a kind of hypnosis that would get you to essentially...relive the impulse."

"Oh..." Layna murmurs, having no desire to ever relive that experience. But what choice does she have? She was spineless not to let the impulse take her before, and now she's being offered a chance to redeem that mistake. She has to take it. "Okay. But what if I can't grasp it again or remember it afterwards?"

"You won't need to remember it afterwards, so long as we can get you to visualize it and relay to us what you're sensing," Lady Anora replies. "Desmond, I know you haven't reached training on the third

263

Tripartite Power. Would you kindly give a quick primer so Layna can decide whether or not she is truly comfortable doing this? I will go prepare the tea."

Des nods, and he grabs a sandwich and shoves it in his mouth as he mulls this over. Layna doesn't understand how he can think about eating after just having learned that the world might be ending. "Alright, as you may have gathered by now," he begins after swallowing his food, "the third Tripartite Power is our power of divination. Layna, your telesthetic impulses are the manifestation of the third power. Just like Blake's flashes, my readings, and Lady Anora's sight. Though divination is considered an official Naut power, it's not really a power at all. It's more of a fluke—a side effect of giving humanity the power of oneironautics."

"What do you mean, it's like a mutation or something?" Blake asks.

"Aye, I reckon it is. I'm no scientist, but I think it has something to do with the way our genes have interacted with our cross-dimensional nature over time. It's the only power that's coded to our human DNA, and it's that which determines how or if your gift will manifest. It's evolved over time from the first manifestation of the divination power—oneiromancy. The types and strengths of divination powers are completely unique to each Naut. And then there's about a third of Nauts who are *dyads* and don't have any form of divination whatsoev—Oops..." Des looks over his shoulder and leans in closer to Layna and Blake to whisper, "Don't tell Lady Anora I called them that because it's not exactly PC."

Blake gives him a disconsolate smile and asks, "What was the original power you mentioned? Oneiromancy?"

"Actually, oneiromancy is your ability, Blake. Prophetic dreams. It's actually fairly rare now for Nauts to have that purest form of divination since it's become all muddled and mixed over time. It's one of only two types that can see into the future, though typically those with oneiromancy can only see their own future in their dreams. So, yours is particularly intriguing."

"What's your power called, Des? And Lady Anora's?" Layna asks.

"Lady Anora's is claircognizance, a type of clairvoyance that gives her intrinsic knowledge on people. Mine is called psychometry. Lucky for Nauts, it's one of the newer manifestations. I've personally only met one other Naut with it. Poor bloke, he's gone a bit mental, actually. The divination abilities can be more of a curse than a gift unless you learn to control them and eventually achieve augury, which isn't in the cards for all Nauts. Augury is the third and final phase for a Naut after activation and ascendance, and it takes the longest to achieve—sometimes a lifetime, sometimes never at all. But it means you've mastered all the Tripartite Powers and you become a candidate to join the Consulate."

"So we can control these divination abilities? Like, make it not happen if we don't want it to?" Layna asks.

"Well, yes, you would have the ability to turn it on and off, and use it to its maximum potential, whatever that may turn out to be. So, Layna, during a telesthetic impulse, your mind is essentially being yanked from your body to attend to something outside yourself. But

265

since you haven't been trained in your ability, your mind resists. Naturally, it doesn't want to leave your body. So, it fractures. One piece of your mind remains with you and one goes where it's beckoned. And that's why you can't remember. Your brain can't reconcile the two experiences, so they cancel each other out. I believe what Lady Anora intends to do is basically shut down the part of your mind that remained here with us, and put the other part in a suggestive state in which we can prompt it to relay what it experienced when it was pulled away."

As he is speaking, Lady Anora reappears carrying two small mugs of steaming liquid and sets one down on the coffee table in front of Layna. "Layna, as Desmond was just explaining, this is the tea that will help put a part of your consciousness to sleep."

Layna gets a whiff of the tea—if you can even call it something so innocuous—and the smell turns her stomach. She was hoping for something similar to the delicious, calming tea that Lady Anora has given them at night. But drinking this is definitely not going to be a pleasant experience.

"Are you sure that stuff isn't going to make her have an attack like the one she had upstairs?" Blake asks, warily regarding the contents of the mug.

Lady Anora hesitates in responding as she sets the second mug down on the coffee table. "No...I'm afraid I can't say for sure. It depends on Layna, really. As I assume Desmond has explained, each form of divination is completely unique to its Naut. And as we have not started training the two of you on yours, we don't yet know their particulars and parameters."

"Who's the second mug for?" Layna asks, as she tries to steady her nerves.

"Also for you. The first is to put part of your consciousness to sleep. The second is for the part of your consciousness that receives the telesthetic impulses, which will hopefully get you to visualize the last one," Lady Anora explains. "Now, given my uncertainty over what may happen, I leave it up to you to make the decision of whether you feel comfortable doing this, Layna. If you are not, I will bring what we know to the Consulate at once and they will investigate."

"Which one is more likely to get answers?" Layna asks.

Lady Anora quietly assesses her, her eyes unreadable. "The tea," she answers definitively.

"Then the tea it is," Layna concludes. Before she can lose her nerve, she grabs the first mug filled with a dark, crimson liquid that smells of rust and rotting meat, and she downs it in three gulps. It burns her throat going down, and not just because of the heat. It feels like she just swallowed gasoline. She gags on the aftertaste and prays it doesn't come back up. She can only handle a one-way trip of that sludge.

Lady Anora gestures for her to lie down on the cushions and places a pillow under her head. "Are you comfortable?" she asks.

"Sure," Layna croaks.

"Try to relax."

"Okay."

Layna takes deep breaths and tries not to regret her decision. She knows whatever revelation awaits her will likely be terrifying and possibly painful, but she's also starting to feel that time is running short. If she doesn't soon figure out what her telesthesia was trying to tell her, it could be too late.

She looks around at Lady Anora, Des, and Blake, who all stare down at her intently, waiting for something to happen.

"You guys seriously aren't helping. Just chill," she murmurs.

Des smirks and shuffles back to sit against the pillows. Lady Anora rises and stands nearby, hands clasped in front of her. But Blake stays where he is. Layna meets his eyes. She pictures how they look when they are in the Ouroboros—mesmerizing, little, blue fires. It calms her to picture them, and she keeps her eyes on his, until there is nothing.

Layna is outside, and in a dead run. Utterly bewildered, she stops short, her momentum causing her to stumble forward on the dirt road. She hears yelling and turns to see Blake sprinting toward her with Des not far behind. Blake's nose appears to be gushing blood, and he is trying to staunch it with a hand as he runs. She looks behind them at Lady Anora's house in the distance. She must have run at least half a mile from the house, but she has no recollection of it whatsoever. Or perhaps she ported? She raises her hands to her throbbing head and yells, "What happened?"

Blake slows down as he gets close and realizes she's lucid, and Des ports to his side. They get all blurry at the edges, and as Blake tilts his head back, the world tilts with it. Stars pop up across Layna's vision as Blake pinches the bridge of his nose and shouts, "You just—"

Layna is on her back screaming something inaudible to her own ears, and she can feel hands holding her down. She begins panting, unable to catch a breath. She is back in the Delaware police station, terrified and confused.

"I'm not crazy...I'm not crazy..." She hears herself murmuring it like a chant and abruptly comes to her senses.

No, I am not crazy. I'm a Naut.

She looks up to see Lady Anora's house towering above her, and closer, the frantic faces of Des, Blake, and Lady Anora. Blake's nose is still dripping blood, but more slowly now. He has her legs pinned down, and Des has her arms. Lady Anora is holding her body steady with her own and she holds a half-empty mug in her hand. Layna can feel hot liquid on her face and neck. She realizes Lady Anora and Des are trying to speak to her.

"Layna! Focus on my voice, my darlin'," Lady Anora urges.

"I—I'm sorry. I'm sorry," Layna stammers.

"Good! Good girl." Lady Anora breathes with relief as she moves off Layna, and Des moves forward to lift Layna's head onto his knees.

"What was I yelling?" Layna asks, her voice and body shaking uncontrollably.

Des responds without meeting her eyes, "You were screaming 'we have to save them', over and over." He looks frightened, and it sends a prickling of fear down Layna's spine. *Who? Save who?*

"Come, darlin', drink the rest of the tea so you can tell us what you saw," Lady Anora encourages, her eyes pained as she raises the mug to Layna's mouth. Layna parts her lips and drinks down the liquid. It tastes significantly better than the last concoction, but it still goes down harshly, as though her body knows its intention and struggles to remain ignorant.

Almost immediately, the world clouds over and Layna gets a series of dark visions and sensations flashing across her mind in such rapid succession that she has a hard time keeping up. But as their meaning becomes clearer, it fills her with an escalating terror. She becomes vaguely aware that she is speaking, relating what she senses to the others in a sort of stream of consciousness.

"—can sense it out there, it's alert and it's coming. It's been waiting so long but it's done waiting, done hiding. It's found…it knows something about our world. A weakness here…a way in. It knows, but…it hesitates…it waits for something. The umbrae are gathering, it's directing them…who to target, so that it can come. I can see them…*us*. It's us, we're the target—the young Nauts, the new Activates. It wants to draw us out. It's setting a trap—no, it's set, already in motion. It's…it's going after our families! They're all in danger! Mom! No, please, we have to save them!"

Layna is screaming again, but she can't stop herself. The umbrae are coming, and they have her mom and Jim in their hollow and unfeeling sights. Fear grips her heart as her vision returns to normal and she can see Lady Anora, Des, and Blake again. For a moment, time stands still, and they all remain motionless in shock.

Then Lady Anora jumps to her feet and looks at Des. "Desmond—"

"Go," he says, nodding. And Lady Anora vanishes. Layna cries out at Lady Anora's abandonment. *Not now. Please don't leave now when my mom needs us.*

"She'll be right back. Stand up, love," Des gently commands.

Layna stands on quaking legs as Des and Blake support her. She looks at Blake and expects to see the fear that she feels inside. Instead, she sees a sort of calm rage. He is steady, and his fearlessness helps steady her.

"We are going to save your families," Des assures them.

"*Please*, we have to," Layna stammers. "But we'll be knowingly walking into a trap."

"It won't be a trap now that we know," Des replies. "Lady Anora is handling it."

Lady Anora reappears then with two others. One of them is a short, stocky man who looks slightly younger than Lady Anora with a full head of salt-and-pepper hair. With his rosy cheeks and light eyes, Layna would regard him as your average, jovial grandpa if not for the currently gritty expression on his face. The other newcomer is an immensely tall and broad middle-aged man with ebony skin and intense eyes.

As soon as they materialize, Lady Anora says to Des, "The others are all in motion." Then she shouts out instructions, "Nuru, with Desmond and Layna. Thaddeus, with me and Blake."

The tall man steps to Layna's side in one giant stride as the grandpa walks to Blake's side opposite Lady Anora. Layna feels Desmond and Nuru place their hands on her shoulders as Lady Anora and Thaddeus do the same to Blake. For a brief moment, she catches Blake's eye, and all at once she feels terrified for him. She starts to tell him to be safe, but he is gone. And then so is she.

CHAPTER

B efore she sees anything, Layna hears the deep hum of a massive engine coming to life. It takes longer than she's used to for the world to come into focus, a sort of mental whiplash from traveling farther than usual through the Ouroboros. When things become clear around her, she realizes she's standing on the top deck of a cruise ship, and through the grey shimmer of the Ouroboros, she can see palm trees and towering mountains beyond it. She feels a surge of panic as she realizes she never told anyone her mom's ship information. What are they doing? Blindly porting her around to all the cruise ships currently docked at sea until they find her family? They'll never find them in time.

She sees Des' golden light shining over her left shoulder and Nuru's dark light over her right—another Nyx, like Blake.

Des takes her by her shoulders and turns her to face him. Before she can protest their idiotic plan, he says, "Layna, your mom and Jim are somewhere on this ship, but we need you to pinpoint their location now."

"What?" she cries. She's surprised at the sound of her own voice coming through strong and clear in the Ouroboros. "Wait, how did you—"

"There's no time to explain, I just need you to focus and listen..."

But Layna's frantic mind can't focus, and she begins scanning the grey figures on the crowded deck, trying to distinguish her family. If Des could find them this easily, what's to stop the umbrae from doing the same? They could already be here. She could already be too late.

She shrugs out of Des' grasp and tries to force her way through the nearly motionless crowd, noticing at once that there is no give to the bodies in the other dimension. They might as well be walls, because of course, she can't touch anyone or anything in an entirely different dimension. The only thing they can affect here is the umbrae who share the dimension by latching to human minds in the homeplane. She considers projecting back into the homeplane to get through the crowd easier, but she will save time if she stays in the Ouroboros. And right now, every second is precious. She doesn't get three feet before Des grabs the back of her t-shirt and yanks her back toward him.

"Hold it," he commands. "We're not going to find your family in time that way. Listen to me, *please*. You're going to have to use your telesthesia to—"

"Des, I can't!" Layna yells. "You saw what happened. I don't know how to control it yet. What if I have another attack like before and I can't help you protect them? I just need to look for them!" She tries to break free of him again, but he holds tight.

"Layna, just breathe. I need you to focus. Remember the alley. Remember what happened right after I found you…"

Layna shakes her head to dispel the legion of fear storming her senses. She can feel the umbrae coming, they're so close, and she is just standing here throwing a tantrum. Her mom needs her now more than ever. She takes a deep breath and returns to that day in the alley. Des showed up and expelled the umbra before it could attack her. And then…

"Blake! I knew where to find him!"

"Exactly. You did it then, and you can do it now. Think of your family, concentrate, try to remember what it felt like when you found Blake."

Layna doesn't have to think of her mom and Jim, they are already the only things on her mind, just like Blake was in the alley. And all she did then was…ask herself a question.

Which way?

Just like in the alley, the answer is already there in her mind. She sees it like an invisible arrow guiding her heart. "This way!"

She races across the deck with Des and Nuru flanking her, with the weight of the Ouroboros slowing her only a little now. She scans the people in the distance to see if she can identify Jim or her mom. Then she gets a vision, clear as day, of the two of them walking up the steps to the sky deck at the back of the ship.

Without halting, she shouts, "Sky deck!" to her companions and immediately ports there.

As she reappears on the landing at the top of the staircase to the sky deck, she comes face to face with the black, empty sockets of an eclipsed man walking toward the stairs. Before she can even take a breath, she ports to the bottom of the staircase, and walking up toward her is another eclipsed. The woman appears to be carrying a broken wine glass, gripping it like a weapon. At the middle of the staircase is Jim and her mom, shrouded through the grey of the Ouroboros.

They're trapped.

Jim has an arm draped over her mom's shoulder and a bottle of champagne and two glasses in the other hand. They move in slow-motion up the stairs, completely unaware of their daughter's presence and the otherworldly threat she is trying to protect them from.

Nuru and Des appear on either side of Layna and her family, and they waste no time firing off simultaneous light and dark lucetelum at the eclipsed at the top and bottom of the staircase. It takes only a few respective shots before the umbrae are expelled and the humans return to their normal faint, white glow beneath the grey shroud. They both stop advancing toward the stairs.

"Des, you take the top, I'll stay down here," Nuru bellows in a heavy accent.

Des shouts down to Layna, "There will be more coming. Stay close to your mom and Jim."

"Can't we just port them to safety?" Layna pleads, though she already knows what the answer must be.

"We can't port any living beings with us aside from other Nauts, I'm afraid," Des says, a pained expression on his face.

"I want to help," Layna insists.

"You are. You're the last line of defense for them if there's a breach," he replies, stepping onto the top deck and taking up a defensive stance in anticipation of the ambush.

Layna walks around her mom and Jim so that she's facing them. They've moved up only two more steps since she appeared. Even though she can't see their faces clearly through the grey shimmer, she can tell her mom is laughing at something Jim has probably just said. She hears her mother's laugh in her mind and feels a deep ache welling up in her throat. She instinctively throws her arms around them both, but instead of the warmth of their bodies, all she feels is the cold, impenetrable barrier of the Ouroboros. A sob escapes from her lips, and she tries to imagine her mother's arms closing around her, keeping her safe and warm and loved as she has done Layna's whole life. If it comes to it, she will project back to the homeplane and fight these people with her bare hands. Screw the consequences.

"Oy!" Des yells from above. "Here we go, Nuru!"

"Got it, brother!" Nuru yells back.

Layna turns away from her family and runs up a few more steps so she can see what Des sees. She watches as three grey figures on the sky deck begin to turn—tendrils of darkness snaking out from their temples, down their necks, and across their torsos. And then they each take a slow, simultaneous steps toward the stairs.

Des begins firing off lucetelum, and as Layna turns and stumbles back toward her family, she sees Nuru firing with each hand in opposite directions at the bottom of the stairs. The ambush has arrived.

She positions herself next to her mom and Jim, with one hand aimed toward the top of the stairs and one toward the bottom. Palms forward and ready to fire, she feels the energy itching just beneath the surface of her skin. Her breath becomes shallow with apprehension as she swings her head side to side, trying to gauge whether the breach will come from below or above. The crackling of the lucetelum fills her ears, and she realizes that if the breach comes from above, it means that Des has lost. That Des could die. She takes a single, frantic step toward her imperiled Guide, but she can go no further. She can't leave her family's side. Through gritted teeth, she yells in agonized frustration, as she continues moving in time with their unbearably slow ascent to the sky deck.

After several excruciating minutes, the deck finally becomes visible. But the sight is far from comforting. Des is battling a semi-circle of eclipsed—*six* of them—as they move in uniform toward the stairs to box in her family. There are at least another dozen humans milling about behind them who either have not yet turned or whose umbrae have already been expelled.

It's clear that Des is exhausted, but Layna has never seen him more intensely focused. His movements like a choreographed dance of storm and starlight, he deftly fires one lucetelum after another while evading the onslaught of shadowspears. But there are so many that he can't focus his lucetelum long enough on any one eclipsed to expel the umbrae. *There's no way he can survive this much longer.*

Layna permits herself to move up two steps away from her family so that her hand is cleared of the stairs and she can fire her own lucetelum. She attempts firing from one hand as she keeps the other aimed at the bottom of the staircase where she can no longer see Nuru or hear his respective battle. But, single-handed, her lucetelum aren't strong enough to do much damage, and she reluctantly turns her back on the threat below to bring her hands together. She fires three consecutive times at one of the eclipsed, who goes grey on the third shot.

Des gives her a brief look of gratitude over his shoulder as Layna works on taking out a second one. But this one is more prepared for her, and before she can expel the umbra, a vortex forms around its abdomen. She ducks as a shadowspear flies over her head and then pops right back up to continue her rapid-fire as the vortex begins swirling again. This time, it's the umbra that's too slow, and it is expelled before it can launch a second shadowspear. Despite the circumstances, Layna begins to feel a thrill working its way through her body. It's the thrill of filling the role she was born to play. She finally feels the *destiny* of it. This was always going to be her future.

Her mom and Jim are nearly at the top of the stairs where they pause in the face of the group of now four people coming toward them, blocking their path. They're running out of time, the umbrae now mere feet from Layna's family, with Layna and Des the only things standing between them. She doesn't know what they'll do when they are in reaching distance. Push them down the stairs? Beat them to death? She can't think about it. She just has to stop it.

Layna's ears buzz with her own cries of fury as she continues firing, hitting as many of the eclipsed in front of her as possible as she barely dodges another shadowspear. She feels it breeze by her cheek, passing an inch from her skull. Des shouts something inaudible, his eyes wild as he looks back at her.

Focus, Des. Save my family.

279

He turns back to the fight and Layna watches in dismay as he inexplicably bends and takes a knee before them, as though he means to surrender. *No, no, no. It can't be over. You can't be giving up.*

She frantically widens the range of her lucetelum as several eclipsed prepare to launch simultaneous shadowspears at Des' bowed figure. But then she sees him begin to glow rapidly brighter. In a blinding flash, he leaps to his feet as a ring of light explodes outward from his body like a shockwave. It tears through the entire group of eclipsed with a thunderous roar, instantly blasting the umbrae back to their netherworld and releasing their hold on the humans.

It also hits Layna.

Well, that was efficient, she thinks, as the biting pain rips through her stomach and she goes flying backward toward the staircase. She is going to be tossed back into the homeplane and unceremoniously exposed to her mom and Jim. In the same second, she feels the whooshing sensation race across her body, she focuses on projecting right back into the Ouroboros. And before she even lands on the stairs, she is out and back in, faster than the literal blink of an eye.

She lands hard. The wind is knocked from her lungs as she holds her hands out, barely managing to keep from tumbling down the rest of the stairs. She's now face-down, looking toward the bottom of the staircase. And what she sees there nearly makes her heart stop. Slowly turning the corner at the bottom of the staircase is a detached umbra. A nine-foot, human-shaped, black shadow split from its human counterpart like the ones in the alley. It moves at normal speed up the stairs, now unhindered by the body of its human in the homeplane.

She jumps to her feet and pours every ounce of her energy into the lucetelum she fires at it. Barely deterred, its arms begin to elongate, forming blades nearly the length of its massive body. The edges are so sharp that Layna can't see where they end and where the air begins.

Without warning, it speeds up the stairs so quickly that it almost moves in a blur and is towering over Layna before she can even react.

She screams out in shock and stumbles backward, falling against the stairs. She and the umbra raise their arms simultaneously, but neither strike before the thing is hit from the front and behind by a multitude of dark and light lucetelum. It spins wildly as it tries to determine which direction the light is coming from and who to strike first. Layna adds her own lucetelum to the onslaught and it is just enough to overpower it. She swears she can sense a silent scream of rage escape from the shadowy figure as it spins in on itself and is gone.

Without the crackling of the lucetelum, the air rings in deafening silence. Layna becomes aware of her own rapid breathing and that of her two companions. She is still facing the bottom of the stairs where Nuru now stands. He leans against the railing for support, a fresh dark mark stretching down the side of his arm where his blue light no longer emanates. It is much larger than the markings Layna noticed on Des and must have come from the detached umbra's blades rather than a shadowspear.

"I've never…I didn't realize…" Nuru stutters, as his eyes linger on the spot where the detached umbra just stood. He comes to his senses and looks toward the top of the stairs. "Des, there's another ambush in Region Three. I must go to them," he rasps, his voice barely audible.

Layna turns to look at Des, who is nervously eyeing the dark mark on Nuru's arm. "You'll make sure that doesn't spread, mate."

Nuru winces and nods in reply.

Des taps a fist to his stomach before raising his hand in front of him, palm forward in a kind of salute. "Be safe, brother. Go light 'em up."

Nuru returns the salute and vanishes before Layna can thank him for risking his life for her family. She stands and heads back up toward Des. The group of formerly eclipsed humans now innocently files down the stairs as Jim and her mom make their way to the railing of the deck. Layna and Des remain on defense, scanning the remaining humans for signs that they may still go dark. There must be only a few left up here who were not already expelled. A minute of calm passes, and then another. Layna's heart begins to steady.

"I'm sorry about the lucy-bomb," Des says beside her, as he wipes the beads of sweat from his brow. "It was the right moment. I had to go for it. But bloody well done popping right back in. I've seen veteran Nauts have more trouble focusing enough to do that than you did."

"Lucy-bomb, huh?" Layna says with a weary smile. "Don't apologize, that was totally awesome. You...*exploded*. You have to teach me how to do that."

Des returns the smile. "You did brilliantly, Layna. Saved my neck back there."

"Well, I thought it was time I returned the favor."

"And I think it's about time we go back to check on the others. We'll have the Consulate send a pair of local Nauts to keep watch over them until we—oh, bloody *hell!*" he yells, looking over Layna's shoulder.

She spins around to see two men behind her being eclipsed, and they slowly begin to turn away from the railing.

Des pushes Layna behind him and commands, "Go stand with your family in case there are more coming."

But Layna doesn't even have time to move before she sees the shadows around both humans pooling around their feet. The umbrae are detaching—two of them at once.

Des curses under his breath. "Layna, listen, a detached umbra has fully entered the Ouroboros with us, meaning it can no longer affect humans in the homeplane through its counterpart," he explains in a frenzied whisper. "They aren't here for your family anymore. They're here for you. You need to port off the ship now. I'll be right behind you."

"Are you kidding?" Layna whispers, as she watches the heads and arms of the two umbrae finishing their formation. "I'm not leaving you here to fight two of these things by yourself, you'll be *killed*. If they're not after my family anymore, just come with me."

Des turns to protest, but before he can say anything else, the umbrae suddenly speed toward them.

"Duck!" Layna yells.

They both duck at once as an umbra swings an arm-blade over their heads. Des shoves Layna roughly out of the way of the other approaching umbra and she uses the momentum to tuck and roll as she has seen Des do. She pops up next to the railing and aims her shot directly toward where she just stood, hitting the umbra that has already pivoted and is racing toward her.

The umbra slows nearly to a halt, and she can feel her lucetelum getting stronger as she fires at it relentlessly. It leaps left and several feet closer to her in a blur of movement. She ports to a spot on the other side of the deck away from her family. Despite Des' assurance it's not after her mom and Jim, she doesn't want to take the chance that he might be wrong. She fires at it from her new position, but it is already on top of her again. Beyond it, she sees Des porting out of the way as the other umbra barrels toward him. *These things are too fast.*

Des reappears between the two umbrae, and he aims one hand toward each of them and fires. The umbra closest to Layna grows fainter with both Layna and Des' lucetelum trained on it. It shifts to the right to escape the barrage, but they both anticipate its attempted escape and continue to light the thing up. At the same time, the umbra that Des is firing at with his other hand moves to the left. Des is facing Layna and does not see as it spins wildly toward him.

"Des!" Layna screams, moving her aim from the umbra in front of her to the one launching itself at Des. He looks up at the approaching blur of darkness just as it swings its arm-blade down on him.

Des ducks forward, but not fast enough. The blade swings over him and slices through the top of his back.

Layna hears a scream as Des falls forward to the ground, and she realizes it's coming from her own mouth. Des doesn't make a sound. He doesn't move.

The other umbra looms over Layna now, arms raised and ready to strike. But it doesn't. Instead, she can sense it reaching inside her mind, invisible black tentacles seeking out her fear and hopelessness and pulling them toward the surface. The umbra standing over Des raises its arm to bring the blade down a second time and end it. She feels the rage and determination boiling up inside of her, a river of heat and energy that she concentrates on channeling through her hands and into her lucetelum. She feels something click deep inside her, and the light discharges from her hands in blinding bursts. She hits both the umbra standing over Des and the one closer to her, and they writhe wildly to escape the attack.

Although the two umbrae grow fainter, they still remain, as if they are just waiting for her to expend all of her energy. And Layna realizes that she is going to fail. She is using everything she has, and it won't be enough to expel them on her own.

As she feels her energy waning, her thoughts return to her mom and Jim, so close by. She steals a glance in their direction. Jim is down on one knee, and Layna's heart breaks in two. While it's a comfort that their love will be one of the last things she witnesses in this world, she is agonized at the idea that she won't be there to share it—that she is going to die and ruin all their joy. She has an overwhelming urge to project back to the homeplane and run to their arms and away from this nightmare. She almost does it, even begins to feel the tugging in her gut. And that's exactly what the umbrae are here for.

Stop. If there was ever a time to be stubborn, it's now. Be stronger than the monsters. Be stronger than your fear. You are a Naut. Time to be one.

Layna refocuses on the umbrae and wills her lucetelum to grow stronger. She will not run from this battle. She will not risk putting her mom and Jim and who knows how many others in danger by allowing them to take her. And she won't port away and leave her family—both the one in the homeplane and the one lying motionless feet from her. The umbrae would surely kill Des, and they could very well reattach to their human counterparts again if they are not expelled and attack her mom and Jim. So instead, she will simply fight and die here in the Ouroboros and hope that once she is gone, they will leave her family alone. What use could they be then?

She feels her knees begin to buckle. The two umbrae are weakened too, but they seem to sense her withdrawal and both spin simultaneously out of the path of her lucetelum. She falters as they move toward her, but then she sees movement behind them as Des rolls onto his side to face her. He brings his arms in front of him and fires. It's all the help she needs, and as she takes aim once again, both umbrae finally spin in on themselves and disappear.

Layna drops to her hands and knees in exhaustion and looks across the deck at Des, who grimaces as he tries to prop himself up on his elbow. "Are you alright?" he yells weakly.

"I'm okay. You're hurt," Layna responds, as she rises shakily to her feet and walks over to drop down next to him.

"I'll be alright," he assures her. But he looks so tired. She rolls him sideways and inspects his back. The dark mark stretches down the length of his spine. She needs to get him back to Lady Anora. She'll know what to do.

Layna looks toward the railing and sees her mom and Jim embracing each other in the glow of the late afternoon sun, oblivious to the battle that just took place behind them. She inspects the other people on the sky deck and focuses inward, trying to tap into her telesthesia. She can sense the retreat of the umbrae. They have given up this fight, and her family is safe for now. She blows her mom a kiss. It will have to do for now, until Layna can safely get back to her. Maybe she will feel it somehow.

"The umbrae are done here. I can feel it. We should go back."

Des nods feebly and moves his hand toward her shoulder so he can port them both back together. But as he does, Layna gets another telesthetic vision. It's just one image this time, and it comes through clear and chilling.

Kat and Suzanne. Climbing into a flashy, neon-green Camaro. Hunter sits in the driver's seat, empty sockets where his eyes should be and his body swirling in black shadow.

Layna only now remembers the phone call she got from Kat asking her to come to see the show on Monday night. Hunter's friend's band. So much had happened that she completely lost track of time and never called them back. And now they are getting into a car with an eclipsed behind the wheel. Erebus isn't done with her yet.

In a moment, Hunter will speed away, and they will be a moving target. Another minute and it will be nearly impossible to port to them. And Des is in absolutely no shape to help her fight. He needs to get back to Lady Anora. She convinces herself it's only Hunter's umbra she has to deal with, and she will be able to expel it on her own. She tries not to think about the fact that she knows this is a trap.

As Des places his hand on her shoulder, she focuses on Hunter's car with every last ounce of concentration she can muster. She prays that she will be able to use North Carolina as a rebound point to get to her friends.

Just before they disappear from existence, she pulls her shoulder out from under Des' hand. She can sense his alarm as she travels away from him.

It's working, she thinks, as the world comes into focus and she begins to visualize the inside of a car. But before it can become fully clear, she hears the muffled sound of screeching tires.

She lands on her hands and knees on the pavement as she watches the car and her only chance to save her friends peel away from her.

CHAPTER

No, no, no. You can't have them.

Layna concentrates on the car and tries to port inside, only to land on the road again as it continues to move away from her. Twice more, she tries with the same result. It's already moving too fast. She stands and runs after the car, a desperate cry escaping from her as she comes to a halt and realizes she's wasting valuable energy. *Pull yourself together. Think.*

To get into the city, they need to cross the bridge over the canal out of Caledon. That's where she needs to be, the only place she knows for sure they will pass through. She conjures up every memory of the bridge she can recall, and within seconds, she has ported to the center of it. If they get past it, they will be able to go on any number of freeways and she won't have another opportunity to stop them.

The small bridge is eerily quiet. Several cars pass her by, but not the one she is waiting for. But she doesn't have to wait long before she sees Hunter's Camaro coming around the bend. She takes aim and begins firing long before it's possible that she would hit anything. She isn't even sure if lucetelum can travel through solid mass. But lucetelum is light, and light can travel through windows.

Layna aims for the driver's side windshield as the car reaches the bridge, but she feels a biting pain rip through her ear as a blur of dark whizzes past her head. She spins around to find two eclipsed approaching from the opposite side of the bridge. From their tattered clothing, she realizes it's the two homeless men she and her friends refer to as Bicycle Bob and Shopping Cart Larry who sleep beneath the bridge on warmer nights. She bought them McDonalds once last year.

That was too close. You're no good to them if you're dead.

She cries out in frustration as she begins lighting Bob and Larry up. The pain in her ear dissipates but is followed by a numbing cold that seems to echo across her skull.

Layna returns half her focus toward the car, which is approaching fast even in the Ouroboros. She can see Hunter now and he is smiling, or rather the umbra who has control of him has turned the corners of his mouth up in a menacing smirk. She has seconds only until the car gets past her.

Over her other shoulder, Bob and Larry are about to deliver two more shadowspears in her direction, and she shoots toward them at the same time. Light and shadow meet in the air and explode between them. It's now or never.

She aims at Hunter and channels everything—her love for her friends, her fear for their lives, her hope she can save them, her despair that she can't—and fires a single, powerful lucetelum right at Hunter's head. It goes straight through the windshield, a direct hit.

His umbra is expelled. But it's too late.

At the moment she delivered the blast, the umbra made Hunter turn the wheel ever so slightly right, in her direction. She dives out of the way as she sees an uneclipsed Hunter trying to regain control of his car. It veers off the road and smashes sideways through the guardrail, plummeting toward the water below.

Layna screams and runs toward the gaping hole in the side of the bridge. Two more shadowspears fly past her, one skimming her arm and again producing that icy, ripping emptiness. She ignores the pain and the threat to her right as she concentrates on porting to the car, which has just hit the water. She reappears in the backseat, now in the homeplane.

The shocking chill of the water takes her breath away. The whole passenger side of the car is smashed, and the water is already pouring in. Layna looks to her right and sees Kat unconscious next to her, the window cracked where her head must have hit it as they went through the guardrail. In the front, Hunter slumps against the wheel, and Suzanne is screaming Kat's name and struggling to unfasten her own seatbelt, which is already underwater. Layna unbuckles Kat, then reaches forward through the water to find Suzanne's hands around the buckle of her belt.

Suzanne stops yelling and goes rigid. Layna looks up to see Suzanne staring at her in wide-eyed shock. Layna fumbles clumsily with the buckle to try to get it loose, but something is catching. She holds her breath and submerges her head in the water to see if she can get a better look at it. The latch is smashed, making the release button useless. She yanks at the strap as hard as she can, but it won't budge.

She emerges from the waist-high water and yells, "Suzanne, your buckle is busted! You need to try to slide out of it!"

Suzanne still sits motionless in shock.

"Suzanne, just do it!"

Suzanne gives her an empty nod as she twists in the seat to try to free herself. Layna crosses her arm over the driver's seat and unfastens Hunter's seatbelt.

She turns back to Kat, who has flopped forward as the front of the car sinks further into the canal, with the water now engulfing her face. "No, Kat!"

Layna lurches, pushes Kat back out of the water, and wraps her arms around her. She concentrates on porting to the bank of the canal. It takes her a few extra seconds of precious time, but soon she feels dry land beneath her.

She opens her eyes to find herself alone on the bank. In her haste, she already forgot what Des just told her on the ship. She can't port her friends to safety. She lets out an agonized cry as she pounds the ground with her fists and ports back into the car. She has to do this the traditional way.

The car has now pitched backward and is up to Kat's shoulders. Suzanne is screaming for Layna.

"I'm here, Suze!" she shouts, as she reaches forward toward Suzanne's hands.

"Layna," she cries, "I can't get out. I'm stuck!"

"I'll get you out, I promise!"

"Layna, please get Kat out," she says with a heaving sob.

"I'm not leaving you," Layna argues, as she continues tugging on Suzanne's buckle. But panic is bubbling ferociously inside her. She doesn't know how she is going to save them all. Suzanne is stuck and Kat and Hunter are unconscious. There has to be a way out of this.

"It's my fault she's here, I made her come! Please get her out!" Suzanne cries breathlessly. She looks so pale.

"Let's pull together!" Layna shouts over Suzanne's frenzied cries. "On three." Suzanne grabs the buckle as Layna counts down and they both pull at once, screaming with the effort. But it does no good.

Then a random memory pops into Layna's head. She takes a breath and goes under as she pictures Hunter flicking his pocketknife open and closed. The knife attached to his car keys. She searches with her hands in the dark water, and her fingers curl around the metal dangling from the ignition. She yanks as hard as she can, and the key breaks in the ignition as the rest of it comes away in her hand.

She emerges into the pocket of air left as the water continues pouring into the cabin, and she begins sawing at Suzanne's belt with the knife. She feels it tearing through the fibers as Suzanne makes a feeble sound of elation as she realizes what Layna is doing.

"I got this!" she sputters, as the water reaches her mouth, and she grabs the knife. "Get Kat."

Layna turns to Kat, who is now fully submerged. She looks back at Suzanne and chokes out, "Get that off and follow *right* behind me, okay? Back right window! I'll come back for Hunter!"

Suzanne nods as she tries to keep her nose and mouth above the water. She keeps her eyes on Layna as she continues sawing at the strap around her waist.

Layna takes a deep breath as she goes under again and positions herself on her back against the seat, holding the seatbelt for leverage. She knows this next move will quickly flood the rest of the car and she needs to move fast, praying that Suzanne does the same. She kicks hard at the already cracked window. It only takes two tries before she feels it give way, sucked out as the water pours in.

The weight of the water pushes her down and she fights against it. She grabs Kat and pushes her out the window against the torrent of water. Then she kicks hard off the back of the seat and follows Kat out the window. She loses her bearings immediately in the darkening water. But she reaches out for her friend, grabbing whatever material she finds and heading toward the only light she can see.

Kat is dead weight in her arms, and she tries not to think about the fact that it may already be too late for her. Layna's lungs burn as she kicks frantically upwards. Her head breaks the surface, and she sucks in deep breaths of air as she continues toward the nearby shore, trying her best to keep Kat's head above the surface.

As she finds her footing on the floor of the bank, she links her arms under Kat's and drags her up to the edge of the water where she collapses beside her. She hears her name shouted from above and looks up to see Des leaning over the guardrail on the bridge, along with several onlookers who have pulled over at the site of the crash. More bodies for the umbrae to control. As she thinks it, two of the onlookers narrow their sights at Des and begin moving toward him. He crouches behind a car and disappears back into the Ouroboros.

Somehow, he was able to follow her here despite his injury, and now he's fighting the umbrae by himself to keep them from going after Layna. If any umbrae detach now, she's a sitting duck. Her concern for Des' life triggers the panic to finally boil over, and she struggles to keep breathing and moving and thinking.

She scans the surface of the water in search for Suzanne's head bobbing above the waves. There is nothing.

She looks down at Kat, and the skin around her lips and eyes is turning a terrifying shade of blue.

She threads her hands in her hair as her mind races. *How do I do CPR? Where is Suzanne? The belt was almost off, why isn't she up yet? How many eclipsed are up there with Des? Go back in now or try to help Kat? Do one and the other dies. My friends are dying…What do I do? What can I do?*

She gets an answer as Des appears by her side. "Des! You were an EMT, right? I don't think she's breathing!"

She doesn't wait for his response but holds her breath and ports back into the fully submerged car. It's Des, he can do it. He will bring Kat back to her.

She hopes with every fiber of her heart that Suzanne will not be in the car. That she is already making her way to the surface and that Layna can focus on getting Hunter out. But as she opens her eyes in the deepening darkness, she sees that both front seats are still occupied. The pocketknife floats in front of Suzanne's unclenched fist and her eyes stare forward, unblinking.

Anguish rips through Layna as she screams into the water, squandering all of her air. She grabs the pocketknife but realizes the belt is already cut and off Suzanne. She tries to lift Suzanne from the seat, but she still doesn't budge. That's when Layna notices a steady stream of blood seeping out of Suzanne's right side. The damaged car has pierced through the flesh of her hip, pinning her in place. She was never going to get out.

Layna's lungs threaten to burst open, and she wants to let them. She tugs helplessly on Suzanne's lifeless figure as spots bloom across her vision and pain splits her chest open. She feels a disturbance in the water next to her as a pair of strong arms encircle her. She gives a feeble shake of her head, knowing she is about to be ported away.

Oxygen replaces the crushing weight of the water, and her traitorous lungs suck it in gratefully as Des releases her. He flops onto his back and lies there looking shattered. They're on the stone floor of the athenaeum at Lady Anora's house.

No. I can't be here.

She still feels as though she's underwater, can't catch her breath. She is so far from her friends. She needs to get Suzanne out, she needs to make sure Kat is alive, she needs to go back. She struggles to her feet and tries to think of the car again, but Des tackles her.

"Layna, stop! I'm sorry, I'm *so* sorry, but they're gone. You have to let them go," Des pleads, as he holds her from behind and pins her arms to her sides. As if that could even stop her from porting.

She struggles against his hold and convinces herself that he is lying. It isn't true. "No, I can save them. Let me go, Des!" she screams, as she tries desperately to picture the car and focus her rattled mind on her friends.

Des spins her around so that she is facing him, and he holds her to him. "Layna, there is nothing more you can do," he whispers. The ache in his voice is what convinces her. He couldn't bring Kat back. She couldn't get Suzanne out. It doesn't matter if she is here or if she's there, or nowhere at all. Her friends—the foundation of her heart—are gone from this world while she is somehow still in it.

"*No!*" she sobs in desperation, shoving away from Des and falling to the floor.

"I'm so sorry…I tried to…" Des says weakly.

Layna looks up at him and notices the color has entirely drained from his face. "Des?" she whimpers.

He blinks at her and tries to say something that comes out as air. His eyes roll back, and he collapses to the floor.

"Des!" she cries. She scrambles over to him and shakes him, yelling his name over and over as she feels herself unraveling. She looks around frantically for the others. "Lady Anora! Blake! Someone, help!"

There is no answer. They didn't come back.

She doesn't know how to help him. She takes his shoulder and projects them into the Ouroboros. Turning him to his side, she lifts up the back of his shirt, and her breath hitches. Little tendrils of darkness branch out from the wound along his spine. *It's spreading.*

Layna returns them to the homeplane, her mind blank. She grabs his hand and sits there watching him, listening to his shallow breathing. All she can do is be here with him. He will wake up, and he will be fine. He has to be. He's the strongest person she's ever known. He's covered in battle scars. This is just one more story. She will wait, and he will wake up.

No. You don't get to sit here. Move.

She shoves the pocketknife she realizes she's still holding into her pocket and grabs a cushion and blanket for Des from the sitting area. Then she is once again in the Ouroboros, standing in front of the Dream Book. She stares at the glowing book intently as she fights to slow her erratic breathing and pounding heart. "Show me," she urges. "Show me like you did before. Tell me what to do. How do I save him?"

She concentrates, waiting for some vision or instruction to appear in her mind. Something. *Anything.* But the book is silent. "Come on, you've been talking to me for a year and *now* you decide to shut up?"

Nothing. Layna feels something shattering inside her. Everyone is gone, and she is alone.

"Show me, damn you!" she screams at the top of her lungs, as she falls to the floor. Through the sound of the blood rushing in her ears, she hears muffled noises on the other side of the wall. Then someone calls her name.

She returns to the athenaeum. Lady Anora bends over Des, and Blake stands in the doorway staring down at them in dismay. He looks up to see Layna and takes a limping step toward her, but as he looks into her eyes, something he sees there makes him stop.

Layna wants to feel relief at seeing them both alive, but there is only a vibrating numbness. "Can you save him?" she asks Lady Anora.

Her voice is steadier than she thought it would be. Too steady. Deadened.

"I will do everything in my power," Lady Anora whispers, and, holding Des close, she ports them both away.

Layna can't stay in this room a minute more. The numbness is suffocating her. She needs air—she needs to escape. She walks stiffly toward the door. Blake reaches for her as she passes, but she can't stop. Faster now, she breaks into a run down the curved hallway, through the kitchen, bursting out the porch door toward the beach. She runs across the sand and collapses before the surf. She can't outrun it. She can't catch a breath. She sucks at the salty ocean air in heaving gasps as the numbness crumbles and a tsunami of grief devours her.

CHAPTER

L ayna isn't aware of how long it has been since she collapsed onto the beach, but the sun has long since set and she has moved little. Time seems irrelevant and her mind is barren. She watches the crescent moon as it moves in and out of the clouds. There are few stars tonight.

There came a point a few hours or maybe a few minutes ago when she became aware of Lady Anora's presence as she draped a blanket around her shoulders. Layna jumped at her touch, and before she could ask, Lady Anora told her that Des survived the critical window. She did what she could to stop the spread of darkness, and all they could do now was wait. She handed Layna a cup of tea, and she sat silently beside her in the sand until Layna finished it. Then she took the cup back and planted a kiss on Layna's forehead before porting back inside.

Layna didn't bother to ask what the tea was for. She was hoping it would put her into some kind of deep sleep so she could forget everything, even for just a little while. But instead, it simply left a hollow absence of emotion. It was far from pleasant, but it was an improvement. Now, as the night deepens, she feels its effects wearing off as she slowly becomes aware of the stiffening ache in her joints.

She pulls out Hunter's pocketknife. It's engraved with his initials—H.N. It glints in the dim moonlight as she turns it over in her hands, unsure whether it brings her pain or comfort. She pockets it again. Her feet are barefoot, and she vaguely realizes she lost her purple Keds at some point in the water. The fact is so inconsequential that she nearly breaks down again. If only for a distraction, she stretches her legs out in front of her, wincing as they scream in protest. Then she moves onto the muscles in her arms, legs, neck, hands, and toes, and relishes the pain shooting through her sore body.

She feels a particularly sharp pain in her ribs and lifts her shirt to see a sizeable grey-green bruise forming down her left side. Where she landed on the stairs after Des' lucy-bomb. Then she registers a different sort of pain in her arm and remembers that at some point she had been grazed with a shadowspear there. She examines her arm and can see nothing—no evidence of her injury while she's here in the homeplane. But the skin there feels cold to the touch, and there is a deep, unfamiliar kind of ache. She touches her ear where the first shadowspear made contact and feels the same sensation.

Layna hears footfalls in the sand and turns to see Blake heading toward her, his head bent low and his hands in his pockets. He's no longer wearing his glasses. He collapses down next to her, and she realizes that she has no idea what happened with his family.

"Blake, I'm so sorry for not asking before," she says, her voice hoarse from crying. "Are your parents alright?"

"They're going to be okay," Blake murmurs. "They met up for lunch at the strip-mall near our house and were heading back to their cars. The umbrae took control of this gang that hangs around there. We were able to expel most of their umbrae before they got to my parents, but my dad had to fight two guys off my mom. He's in the hospital, some broken ribs and a concussion. Mom's okay, mostly just shook up."

He pauses, and Layna can see him reliving the fight in his mind.

"Even after the gang was done, it seemed like they just kept coming out of the stores…random people. I thought it was never going to end," he says, his voice far away. "I don't know what I would have done if they had…you know. And I swear, if Des doesn't make it…"

Behind his placid demeanor, Layna can sense his rage vibrating just beneath the surface. She looks at his hands clenched in his lap and notices that his knuckles are bruised and torn. That injury would not have come from the fight with the umbrae. No doubt he took his anger out on some wall inside the house. His anger is contagious, and Layna begins to feel the seeds of fury and seething vengeance taking root inside of her.

"Layna…I'm so sorry. I wish I could have been there to help you."

"Your family needed you," she responds, shaking her head. "My friends were my responsibility, and I couldn't save them. I promised

303

Suzanne…I promised I'd get her out. And I didn't. Even with these stupid powers, I was useless. It's my fault they're dead."

"Don't say that," Blake says firmly as he turns to face her. "You fought for them. You did everything you could to save them. This was Erebus, *not* you."

"But it was me, Blake," she whispers as she examines her hands. "Erebus went after them to get to me. It went after them because…" Her voice breaks as she tries to hold back the sorrow and guilt threatening to engulf her again. "Because I loved them."

Blake watches her silently for a moment, and then responds, "We're not going to give up, Layna. And we're not going to just take a back seat while the Consulate sits around and argues about what they want to do. We'll search the Dream Book. We'll use our divination powers and do whatever we can to find answers. This is our fight now, and I don't care if it's some all-powerful cosmic entity, Erebus is going to pay for today, even if we have to make the weapons ourselves. Okay?"

Layna lifts her eyes to his, and the look they share is of such intensity that she once again feels that sourceless charge of electricity in the air. It's so palpable that she swears she can see it spark in the darkness between them. It's a wordless pact—a renewed and shared purpose. So instead of responding, she keeps her eyes locked on his and indulges herself in this moment. This fleeting sensation of taking her future back into her own hands.

As the moment passes and the electric tingle subsides, she whispers, "You lost your glasses."

Blake reaches into his pocket and pulls them out. One lens is missing and the other is cracked. He puts them on and looks at her. "How do they look?"

She gives him a weak smile. "They've seen better days."

He nods and puts them back in his pocket. "I don't really need them anyway. They're not even mine."

Layna gives him an inquisitive look, but then she hears the screen door shut behind them. They turn to see Des, wrapped in a blanket, alive and conscious and hobbling gingerly down the back steps.

"Des!" she and Blake shout in delighted surprise, as they jump up from the sand.

"You're alright! How are you feeling?" Blake yells with relief, as they make their way toward him.

"Like a million bucks, give or take a million," Des groans. "Can barely even bloody port." He's holding a nearly empty IV bag with an iridescent, amber liquid being fed into a vein in his arm. But as they get closer, he yanks the needle out and drops the bag into the sand. He's clearly not supposed to be up and about yet, but Layna can sense his agitation, whether from pain or worry, she can't immediately tell.

"Layna," he says breathlessly, as they all reach each other, "Kathleen is still alive."

Layna nearly ports right out of her skin. "Des," she gasps. "She really is? You're sure?"

"Aye, positive. I traveled while I was unconscious, and I was called back to the bridge. The umbrae were there, but when I got there, they disappeared without a fight. Very unusual but so is everything

305

these days. Place was swarming with emergency crew. I overheard one of the EMT guys say her name. Said she had a decent GCS and good pupillary reactions and that they'd had her transported to the hospital. That means she's unconscious but alive. When you pulled her out of the water, I was only able to do CPR on her for about a minute because you were under for too long and I got worried, but I guess it worked and—"

Layna interrupts Des by throwing her arms around him, eliciting a grunt in pain. She hastily removes herself as she lets the news sink deeper into her heart. He saved her. Kat is not gone from her life forever. "I don't know how to thank you, Des."

"Hey, don't thank me," Des replies, as he places a hand on her shoulder. "You're the one who pulled her out of that car and got her to shore. She wouldn't have had a chance if it weren't for you."

She wouldn't have been in danger if it wasn't for me.

"Did you overhear anything about Suzanne? And Hunter?" Layna asks hopefully.

Des glances at his feet and nods. She doesn't need any further explanation. The pain of losing Suzanne hits her all over again. She feels Blake slip his hand in hers and she grips it tightly.

"I need to go see Kat," she croaks.

"Layna, she's still not conscious" Des murmurs. "And, well, we can't be sure when…or if she'll wake up."

"She'll wake up," Layna says, shaking her head. "She will."

Des and Blake exchange a fleeting look of uncertainty, but she ignores them. They don't know Kat. They don't know how tough she is.

As Layna thinks of her, she gets a vision, just as she did with Blake and earlier with her family on the ship. An arrow in her mind. She knows exactly where to find Kat.

"Layna, I really need you to stay here," Des urges. "We have to—"

"I'm sorry, Des, but Kat needs me too," Layna says, as the world falls away and she ports without another word.

Kat is lying in the hospital bed, tubes everywhere, her chest rising and falling with life as the monitors beep in recognition of her beating heart. As painful as it is to see her in such a state, it's also the most beautiful sight Layna could have imagined.

She thinks of Kat sitting cross-legged on her bed, holding her favorite stuffed animal, smiling and laughing and sometimes crying as they talked late into the night. She aches for the chance to talk with her now. To tell her how much she loves her. How she needs her. And then she has a thought. If dreams are a window into the Ouroboros, then maybe...

She projects into the Ouroboros, her heart leaping to see the white glow of Kat's Aether. "You're still in there," she whispers. "You're still you. Kat, if you can hear me, please wake up," she murmurs, leaning in close and stroking her friend's bandaged head even though she can't feel anything but the barrier of the Ouroboros.

"I'm so sorry for getting you into this. I'm sorry for kicking you and Suzanne out of my kitchen when you were only trying to apologize, and I'm sorry for avoiding you at school last week, and for not returning your calls, and for being a terrible, awful friend this year. And I'm so...so sorry that...I couldn't save Suze," she chokes. "Oh my god, Kat, she's *gone*. Please wake up. I need you. *Please.*"

Her throat clenches as a sob explodes from deep in her chest. She pulls away to catch her breath and turns to find the comfort of Blake's warm, blue glow next to her. She stumbles toward him as he opens his arms and wraps them tightly around her. She buries her face in his shoulder as if she can hide from the burning pain inside her.

"I was so mean to them, Blake," she cries. "The last time we talked, I yelled at them for something so stupid."

"Don't think about that," he whispers. "People who love each other fight. That was one moment in a whole lifetime of friendship. Think about all the good times instead. Bet there were way more of those, right? Whatever happens, they both knew you loved them."

Layna grips him tighter as she murmurs, "So did Erebus...somehow."

"Lady Anora explained it to me earlier," Blake says softly into her hair. "Apparently when you love someone, it forges this ethereal connection with them. She said it's like a thread of light that's only visible in the deepest darkness. That's how it found them. And for Nauts, the thread can sort of...tug at us, when the people we love are in danger. It knew we would come for them."

Layna hears a soft pop and lifts her head to see Des leaning on the chair across the room. His face is twisted with discomfort and exhaustion, and he has now abandoned his blanket as well as the IV fluids.

"I'm sorry, Des," she says, sniffling as she reluctantly withdraws from Blake's arms. "I just had to see her for myself. I didn't mean to make you follow me. You should be resting."

Des looks at them and runs a hand over his face. "Listen, I know you two are hurting, and I wish I could fix that, believe me, I do. And I know this is not what you need to hear right now, but we need to get back. I need to know you're both safe at Lady Anora's while I—we—search the Dream Book. We're running out of time. Erebus is coming. I don't know how you did it, Layna, but you saw that yourself. You...you saw into its...Anyway, Lady Anora is meeting with the Consulate as we speak. After this, they're bound to vote to find a way to make weapons that will be effective against the umbrae. And then the Dream Book will be turned over to them and all we'll be able to do is wait."

"What do you mean weapons that will be effective?" Blake asks. "We have the lucetelum. Isn't that a weapon?"

"It's only a defense," Des explains. "It can only be used to expel the umbrae back to their netherworld. We have no way of fighting them—killing them."

"But..." Layna shakes her head and tries to comprehend what Des is saying. "I thought you said that one couldn't exist without the other. That humans can't exist without their umbra counterparts."

"Aye, I did say that," Des says darkly. "And it's true."

"So, if we find a way to kill the umbrae, we'd also be killing their human counterparts?" Blake asks in surprise.

"Why do you think the Consulate has avoided doing it until now?" Des replies with a heavy sigh.

"We can't *murder* people," Layna protests. "We're supposed to protect our world, not kill everyone in it. There has to be another way. The Prophecy said something about closing the gateway to stop Erebus. Shouldn't they be figuring out how to go about doing that instead?"

Des looks at her, confused. "Which prophecy?"

"Oh, right, we never told you. We read the Prophecy already," Layna says dismissively. It hardly seems important now.

"The *Phantom's* Prophecy?" Des presses.

"What other prophecy would we be talking about?" Blake replies blankly.

"No, no, you read a different prophecy. The Phantom's Prophecy doesn't say anything about a gateway. Besides, you wouldn't have been able to find and read it this soon. The mysteries are extremely difficult to navigate. You must have stumbled upon a different one."

"No, Des, it was the Phantom's Prophecy, we're sure of it," Blake argues, glancing at Layna for confirmation. "Layna's telesthesia led her right to the page, and I saw the same page in one of my flashes. Like it wanted us to find it. It talks about the gateway at the end of the third part."

"There are only two stanzas in the Phantom's Prophecy," Des says impatiently. "Though it may read slightly differently for each Naut based on differences in language, it's always only two, with the same meaning. The Standard English interpretation is, 'Bound as one, twin fates are sealed—'"

"'Neither light nor dark may yield,'" Layna and Blake continue, reciting it with him until he stops and gapes at them in disbelief. When they reach the third stanza, his face goes ashen.

"Bloody hell," he whispers when they finish. "Lady Anora needs to know about this immediately."

"What does it mean?" Blake asks.

"I'm not entirely sure, but I think she may know. Let's get back," Des urges.

"You guys go. I'll be right behind you," Layna says. "I *promise*. I just need a second," she adds in response to Des' hesitant expression.

Des nods once as Blake takes his shoulder to help him port back. Layna glances toward the hall to be sure no one is watching, and she projects back into the homeplane. She bends down and kisses Kat on the forehead. "Get better for me, okay, weirdo? I'll be back soon. I just need to try and help...save the, um, universe. Or something. You'd be so much better at this," she sighs. "I love you, Kat."

She hears footsteps echoing down the hallway, and she gives Kat's hand a final squeeze before returning to North Carolina.

Layna watches Blake pace across the tiled floor of Lady Anora's kitchen. It's been over an hour since Des left to get Lady Anora. And that's *real* time. How many hours have passed in the Ouroboros, and what's taking so long?

Layna looks into the cold bowl of soup on the table in front of her. Blake heated it up for her, but she absorbed most of the heat into her hands as they waited. The warmth of it conjured a memory—not so long ago but also lifetimes ago—of lying in her bed holding the warm bowl of clam chowder in her hands, Moxie purring at her feet and her mom sitting on the edge of the mattress. She aches to return to that moment in time. To erase all that's happened since. She can't comprehend how just yesterday she felt optimistic about this new life of hers. Happy, even. It seems so naïve and careless now. She didn't know what she was dealing with. She didn't realize the stakes. She was charmed only by the power she felt inside of her—powers that were useless when it really mattered.

Maybe this is all a nightmare. Maybe she is still in her bed, and she will soon wake up with the covers pulled over her head and her whole average teenage life ahead of her. How could she ever have wished for any different?

She flinches as a hand closes over her shoulder. Blake is standing beside her, his brow knitted with concern. "Are you alright? Did you hear what I was saying?"

Layna shakes her head. "I'm sorry, what was it?"

Blake takes a seat across from her. "I was wondering if you think it's possible Erebus could have attacked the Consulate and that's why they haven't come back."

"I'm sure the Consulate can handle themselves," Layna says, as she stares at the clock and watches the second-hand move around and around. The thought had occurred to her too, and it got her thinking. "I don't think Erebus can go after them anyway."

"What makes you say that?"

"I keep remembering bits of my telesthetic impulse. How Erebus targeted the Activates. It seems like it would make more sense for it to go after the Consulate. You know, cut off the head of the snake or whatever. The Order would probably fall apart without them. Maybe because we haven't completed ascendance, we are easier to control."

"So you think it was trying to control us?"

"I do. I think it wanted to take control of us and turn us against the Consulate. Why else would they want to target Activates when we don't matter at all? We don't even know how to fight yet. The Consulate's theory is that detached umbrae can take control of us only while in the homeplane. I think Erebus was counting on us newbies getting scared and projecting back to the homeplane. Because we don't know any better. I almost did, too."

"Me too," Blake murmurs. "But we can't fight, so turning us against the Consulate wouldn't have gone very far, I wouldn't think."

"Maybe we weren't meant to attack them…maybe we were meant to spy on them. Erebus is waiting for something, I felt that. There is a piece to the puzzle it hasn't figured out yet. I mean, it could theoretically end humanity right now by having all the umbrae across the world take control of their human counterparts like the ones today did…but it hasn't."

"Because it *can't* yet, you're saying. It's not strong enough. But it's definitely getting stronger. We fought two more detached umbrae today."

"And we had three," Layna adds.

"At least the umbrae clearly weren't prepared for Consulate members being there. Lady Anora and Thaddeus fought hard for, you know, the elderly. Legit have never seen anything like it."

"We were really lucky to have them with us," Layna agrees. "Unless…it wasn't luck. Before he left us, Nuru said something about an ambush in Region Three. I think that was his region. So why was he here with us in Region Six? And didn't Lady Anora tell us before that Thaddeus is from Region Two?"

Before Blake can respond, Lady Anora and Des materialize in front of them. They look tired but unscathed, and Layna relaxes for a fleeting moment until she notices the look on Des' face. He looks even more distressed than he did before he left them, and he refuses to meet her eyes. Even Lady Anora seems off—guarded. The hairs on Layna's neck stand on end. Whatever news they carry with them is not going to be pleasant.

"What's going on?" she asks warily.

"I apologize for keeping y'all waiting," Lady Anora says to them both. "Each of us needed to report on the damage to our region and make some decisions in light of this turn of events."

"How bad is it?" Blake asks.

Lady Anora hesitates before responding. "Not as bad as it could have been. We've never seen Erebus stage an organized attack like that, take *control* like that…and it has fundamentally changed the way we must think of our enemy. We were wrong. About so many things. But thanks to you, Layna, we were able to spread word fast enough to Nauts in each region that many were saved."

Many. Not all. Not most. Lady Anora's commendations only add salt to Layna's gaping, bloody wound. If Layna just had the courage to deal with her impulse to begin with, maybe she could have prevented this entirely. Maybe Suzanne wouldn't be gone. Maybe Kat wouldn't be fighting for her life. Maybe the others wouldn't have died.

"There's something else you should know," Lady Anora adds. "I am proud to tell you that you have both completed ascendance and are now official Nauts, ready to be accepted into the Order. Typically, we hold a ceremony, but given the circumstances, I will just offer my utmost congratulations to you both."

"How does that work?" Blake asks. "How did we complete ascendance?"

"It typically occurs when a Naut successfully uses the Tripartite Powers during physical projection to expel an umbra back to its netherworld," she replies. "It's essentially the full opening of the mechanism in our brains that allows us to channel Aether. You both will have felt it as a sudden surge of power as you were fighting the umbrae today. Blake, I know you did—I saw it in your lucetelum when it occurred."

Layna recalls the moment on the sky deck when she felt that peculiar click in her brain. It did feel like something had opened up inside her. But she is crestfallen at the realization that she failed even as a full-fledged Naut.

"Congrats to both of you," Des offers halfheartedly, refusing still to meet their eyes. "Now, Anora, I think you need to hear firsthand what Blake and Layna told me."

"Yes, of course," Lady Anora replies. "Desmond told me you both believe you read the Phantom's Prophecy and that it was…different?" She casts an uncertain glance toward Des.

"We did read the Prophecy," Blake affirms. "Layna found it with her telesthesia. Des said it was different for us than it is for other Nauts."

Layna and Blake recite it together, and when they finish, Lady Anora drops unsteadily onto the bench beside Layna. "I didn't see this. Why couldn't I see this?" she murmurs to herself. "The Consulate is going to need a direct report from you two."

She rises again and begins pacing as she continues, "In light of today's events, the Consulate has voted to weaponize. I am to bring Oneironautica to Athens so that we can begin working around the clock to scour the mysteries for an answer." She pauses and looks at them, hesitating before adding, "We have also decided to bring all Activates and newly ascended Nauts to Athens to train. We must prepare you all for what is to come as best we can in the time we have left. And though I instructed him to take some time off to heal, Desmond has volunteered to be one of the Guides who will conduct the training. We will all be leaving shortly. Desmond is not strong enough yet to travel that far through the Ouroboros, so I have arranged for a private jet for the three of you that will be leaving from New York at midnight."

Layna looks at the clock on the wall, which reads ten past eleven. "You expect us to leave for Athens in less than an hour? Like for the foreseeable future?" she exclaims. "I can't just vanish to Greece. I need to be here for Kat when she wakes up, and my mom and Jim when they get back in a couple days."

"Yeah, and my dad is in the hospital," Blake remarks. "I have to get back to help him and my mom after what happened. They need me. What am I supposed to tell them?"

Lady Anora and Des exchange an uneasy glance.

Des finally looks up at them, a tortured expression on his face. "We need you both to understand the gravity of what we are dealing with," he says quietly. "The Consulate doesn't make these decisions lightly, and believe me, Lady Anora and I both tried to think of any other way to do this. But desperate times…" He trails off as he meets Blake's eyes, unable to complete the thought. He shakes his head and looks to Lady Anora for help.

She steps forward and continues for him, "We simply can't ask Lucien to continue using his oneirokinesis to manipulate the memories of all the families of the young Nauts who will be coming to Athens. We have no idea how long we will be there, and, to be frank, we don't know if we will be returning. The world as we know it may not exist in a month's time. It would be too much for him to carry on an elaborate false memory pattern for everyone, and we need all the members of the Consulate to focus their time on finding a way to weaponize our ranks. So, the Consulate decided that he must implant just a single memory for each young Naut. One that will continue to explain your absence…into perpetuity."

"*No*," Layna urges, as she jumps up from her seat. She is not going to allow them to do this to her mom and Jim. Blake looks at her, and she watches as his expression melts from apprehension into cold recognition.

His eyes snap toward Des, and then Lady Anora. "No way. That is *not* happening! You are not going to make our parents believe we're dead."

"It's already done," Des mumbles, as he lowers his head in remorse.

Layna feels like someone has just knocked the wind out of her. "Take it back," she whispers, her voice quivering with fury. "Make him undo what he did."

Des looks back at her sadly. "I'm sorry, Layna. I can't."

Lady Anora steps toward Layna and takes her gently by the shoulders. "I am so sorry, but it is the only way. We don't know that we will succeed in this fight, but if we don't all come together now then all is surely lost. If you want to fight for them, this is what must be done. We must hurt them for the chance to save them."

Layna shrugs out of her grasp and turns her back on them. She walks in a daze toward the windows and stares out at the ocean. She imagines her mom's ship out there. *It's already done.* They were probably celebrating their engagement when this Lucien brutally invaded their minds and stole their future from them.

"Des…" she hears Blake plead behind her. "You *know* what this will do to my parents. You saw…they can't…this will destroy them," he sputters helplessly. "How can the Consulate do this? We don't even matter. Can't they just let us stay with our families for now? We don't even really know how to use these powers yet. What difference could it make?"

"Each one of us matters, darlin'," Lady Anora replies softly. "The Consulate is asking only that we each fulfill our destiny and our duty. To fight to save the world—fight or die."

A silence falls over the room. In the glass of the window, Layna sees the image of her mom's face. Her worried expression as she hugged Layna before she and Jim left for their trip. Her last, loving glance at Layna out the window as the car pulled away. Covered in blue and yellow paint, eating Chinese food on a tarp in the living room on that perfect day. Layna squeezes her eyes shut. She expects the tears to come again, but her eyes remain dry. She has nothing left.

"We deserve to know what our parents were told," Blake finally demands, his voice sedated.

"If you wish, Blake," Lady Anora murmurs. "Your parents will remember you being at lunch with them during the attack in the parking lot. You...were killed in the struggle."

Blake sits there a moment more before he stands and speeds for the doorway toward the foyer. They listen in silence as he runs up the stairs and slams the door to his room.

Des makes a move to follow him, but Lady Anora puts her hand out and gently shakes her head. "Layna, do you also wish to know?" she asks.

Layna hesitates, and then nods. She's sure she will regret it, but she needs to know what they've been led to believe.

"One of your sneakers was found with the wreckage at the canal," Lady Anora explains. "A driver gave a statement to the police that he saw a blonde-haired girl pull another girl from the water. Lucien guided the police to conclude that you drowned trying to free your friends, and your body was carried away by the current. The evidence was already there. It was the easiest way."

Layna tries to let this sink in. "There...won't be a burial then?"

"No. There will likely be a search, but Lucien will not implant any more memories, and allow them to reach their own conclusion," Lady Anora explains.

Layna shakes her head and sputters, "My mom will never stop hoping. She'll never have closure."

"Well...perhaps we will succeed," Lady Anora suggests, "and you can return to her when this is all over."

Layna holds onto that hope as she leaves them to head upstairs and pack her few belongings for Greece. Her mind a complete blank, she showers quickly and throws on her black leggings and a hoodie. She slips on her running sneakers in place of her lost Keds, and she grabs her phone from the vanity before she realizes it's pointless to take it with her. She's supposed to be dead—she won't even be permitted to use it. The battery is already dead, probably has been for hours. Her mom would have disapproved. She gently places the phone into a drawer and shuts it. It's the closest she will get to a burial.

Blake sits on the steps of the foyer trying to get his bag to close, and he doesn't look up as Layna appears in front of him. But she can see his blue eyes are red and raw, and she yearns to see his smile again. Or to be enveloped again in the comfort of his arms. Des arrives moments later and looks mournfully from Layna to the top of Blake's head. He opens his mouth to say something a couple times but is unsuccessful in getting anything out. When they're ready, Des wordlessly places his hands on their shoulders to ports them to the airport.

They disappear into nothingness and reappear in some quiet, unoccupied waiting area at the airport in New York. As she and Blake follow Des toward the small jet that awaits them, Layna can sense the call of their new life from across the world. She tries to cling to anything familiar from her old life, but there is no solace in her past. It's as though she actually did die in that car with her friends.

Until today, death was something removed, something abstract. Something she need not yet be concerned about because she was young and healthy and naïve. But now death has reached out and stolen her heart, and she must acknowledge that it may soon be coming for the rest of her. For all of them. It is out there, waiting. She has felt death's intentions herself. It is coming for Earth, and it brings with it the end of everything.

As the door to the plane closes behind them, she knows she will never be coming back. She lives now for one purpose only. To fight. Fight to avenge her friends, fight to protect her family, and fight to save the world and the universe from being ripped apart by darkness. She is just a single soldier in a galactic army. She realizes that now, and she's ready for whatever awaits her on the other side.

Acknowledgements

My most heartfelt thanks to the 'Dream Team': Mom, Lara, and Meg. Without the unwavering support of this incredible trio, these dreams and words and worlds would never have come to life. I thank them for their insightful feedback and constant encouragement, particularly during the periods when I was filled with doubt. An especially big thank you to Lara for patiently reading through each draft over every year of this endeavor. Love you, always.

Thank you to my editor, Ceri Savage, for taking such good care of Layna, Blake & Company and for making this book the best it could be. Thank you for being a source of wisdom in helping me to navigate the publishing process.

Thank you to Lauren T., my 'twin flame', for reading my manuscript and cheering me on in the pursuit of my dreams. Thank you to Dad and Aunt Carole for instilling a love of fantastical stories in me at an early age, my sisters for all the adventures that ignited my imagination, and Jimmy for inspiring me to put my stories on paper.

K.A. Vanderhoef

Thanks to all the beta readers I've enlisted over the years of work on this series, and finally, thank you to *all* my family and friends for your infallible love and guidance throughout my life.

About the Author

K.A. Vanderhoef grew up in Rockland County, New York and spent a good portion of her childhood exploring imaginary worlds co-created with her triplet sisters or otherwise found between the pages of a book. She holds a Bachelor of Arts in Psychology from Quinnipiac University and a law degree from Seton Hall University School of Law. She started writing speculative fiction and poetry while in law school, and her ardor for the hobby has only increased during her years working as an attorney, as one must always maintain the balance of light and dark in life. She currently lives in a peaceful lake community in New Jersey with her cat, Moxie.

Made in the USA
Middletown, DE
27 February 2021